TOGETHER IS ALL WE NEED

**Center Point
Large Print**

**This Large Print Book carries the
Seal of Approval of N.A.V.H.**

TOGETHER IS ALL WE NEED

MICHAEL PHILLIPS

CENTER POINT PUBLISHING
THORNDIKE, MAINE

This Center Point Large Print edition
is published in the year 2005 by arrangement with
Bethany House Publishers.

The text of this Large Print edition is unabridged. In other
aspects, this book may vary from the original edition. Printed in
Thailand. Set in 16-point Times New Roman type.

ISBN 1-58547-668-4

Library of Congress Cataloging-in-Publication Data

Phillips, Michael R., 1946-
   Together is all we need / Michael Phillips.--Center Point large print ed.
      p. cm.
   ISBN 1-58547-668-4 (lib. bdg. : alk. paper)
      1. Female friendship--Fiction. 2. Plantation life--Fiction. 3. Race relations--Fiction.
   4. North Carolina--Fiction. 5. Reconstruction (U.S. history, 1865-1877)--Fiction.
   6. Teenage girls--Fiction. 7. Orphans--Fiction. 8. Large type books. I. Title.

PS3566.H492T64 2005
813'.54--dc22

                                                                    2005014047

CONTENTS

Another Uncle Comes to Call

1

E ven if Katie had known about the visitor to Greens Crossing ahead of time, it probably wouldn't have changed anything. What could she have done about it anyway?

As it was, our friend Henry was the first to know. But he was busy in the livery, and his son Jeremiah, who was working for Mr. Watson at the mill, was off making a delivery out of town. There was no way for Henry to get word to us.

The man rode into the livery and dismounted.

"Hey, boy!" he called to Henry, who was probably five or ten years older than he was. "Get over here and give my horses some water and feed."

"Yes'uh," said Henry, ambling over and taking the reins from him.

"The name's Clairborne," said the man, "—Burchard Clairborne. I've got some business at the bank, then I'll be heading out to my brother's place."

Thinking about Katie and me and wishing he could do something, Henry watched the man walk down the street toward the bank, then tended to his horse. Every now and then he glanced toward Watson's Mill in hopes that Jeremiah might get back soon enough to ride out to Rosewood and be there when Katie's uncle arrived.

Meanwhile, at the bank, Burchard Clairborne and Mr.

Taylor were continuing a conversation that had begun a couple months earlier at a social gathering in Charlotte, North Carolina.

"I got to thinking mighty hard about what you said in Charlotte," Clairborne said after he was seated and they had exchanged greetings. "So I did me some nosing around. I looked into the army records and what do you suppose I found?"

"I couldn't say, Mr. Clairborne," said Mr. Taylor.

"That my brother and his two sons—the one was killed, but the other two made it through the war—that they were discharged the week after Appomattox."

The banker took in the information with obvious interest.

"That is peculiar," he said. "As I told you, no one has seen him in what must be three years. Though since we spoke in Charlotte, certain other facts have come to light."

"Facts . . . what kind of facts?"

"Well, for one thing, the girl, who is the only one I've seen for a year, now says her father *did* return home and is presently up north somewhere working to help support the plantation."

"Hmm . . . I see. And the sons?"

"She made no mention of them," replied Taylor.

"And you still have seen nothing of his wife?"

"Nothing . . . only the daughter—Kathleen. As I told you, Mrs. Clairborne sends the girl into town to conduct all their business. And that is another interesting thing," the banker went on. "As I told you, there has been considerable indebtedness to the bank, which has accounted for my own involvement in the affair. We have nearly had to foreclose . . . twice. But then two months ago suddenly the girl appeared again—without mother or father or anyone. She walked in with an even more smug expression than usual and plopped down three hundred and fifty dollars on my desk . . . in cash."

"Cash! Where could they have come up with that kind of money?"

"I haven't an idea . . . although there had been some gold involved earlier."

"Gold—this thing gets more and more interesting all the time," said Clairborne, clearly intrigued by this new information.

"There have admittedly been certain peculiarities to the case. In any event, the three hundred and fifty dollars paid off the loan in full. In fact, the Clairborne account, though obviously I cannot divulge specifics, is in a very healthy condition at present. I will simply tell you it is over two hundred dollars."

"Not much to run a plantation with."

"But considering that a year ago they were five hundred dollars in debt with foreclosure inevitable, there has certainly been a remarkable turnaround."

"And what do you think can account for it?"

"I have no idea. They do hire a few of the local coloreds and managed to get in a decent cotton crop last year, as I understand it. At least it was enough to put their account in the black, as I say, and finance a new planting this spring. But they maintain the most peculiar attitude, shall we say, toward all the changes since the war, taking them a little too far if you ask me."

"What do you mean?"

"There is talk that they allow coloreds into the house . . ."

Clairborne raised one eyebrow.

"—and the daughter, young Kathleen, wanted me to open a bank account for one of her darkie girls."

"Whatever for? They know nothing about money."

"I can't imagine her motive."

"What did you do?"

"I opened it, of course. What else could I do? But I only mention it as an example of the kind of thing I am talking about."

"Well, something about it don't smell altogether right to me," said Clairborne. "I got my suspicions, and one of them's that maybe my brother never made it home after the war, whatever the girl says now."

"What are you saying?"

"I ain't rightly sure. But something either waylaid him or happened to him. He might have found another woman, got involved with some kind of criminal activity—you can never tell."

"That wouldn't account for the sons."

"Exactly my thought, which makes me think it's more serious, that he's either laid up bad . . . or something worse. Lots a men come back crippled and in bad shape. Maybe they're trying to hide his condition to keep creditors at bay."

"What about the girl's claim that he is working in the North?"

"I don't know. Don't that sound a mite convenient to you? Anyway, that's what I come to find out. After all, I've got to look after my interests. I can't have that sister-in-law of mine thinking that whatever may have belonged to my parents and my brother automatically belongs to her if something did happen."

"What do you plan to do, Mr. Clairborne?"

"First off, I'm going to find out if my brother's there once and for all and what kind of condition he's in if he is. If he ain't dead, then I'm figuring they know where he is. If he's up north, then I intend to go find him and lay my own eyes on him for myself. And if he is dead . . . well, then, you and I both know what that means . . . by rights that plantation belongs to me. That's why I come to see you—I figure I better know where I stand legally."

"I'm no lawyer, Mr. Clairborne."

"You're likely the closest thing this town has to one."

"Don't you have a lawyer in Charlotte who handles your affairs?"

"Yeah, but I want someone here that's close by. No telling what this thing might lead to, and I don't want no old pinstripe paper pusher sitting behind some fancy city desk twenty miles away."

"I've an acquaintance in Oakwood you might speak with."

"A lawyer?"

"That's right."

11

"Any good?"

"I've heard no complaints from any of the plantation owners he represents."

"What's his name?"

"Sneed . . . Leroy Sneed. He's already had a few dealings with Rosewood."

"All right, good . . . maybe I'll look him up."

Burchard Clairborne rose. "But first," he added, "I'm going to pay a visit to my brother's wife and find out for sure if she *is* his wife . . . or his widow."

FATHERS AND UNCLES

2

What made it awkward for this man to visit his brother's plantation, where I lived with my cousin Kathleen Clairborne, who they'd been talking about, was that right then Katie's *other* uncle was gone.

This other uncle I'm talking about also happened to be my father. His name was Templeton Daniels. That's how Katie and I got to be cousins, though we didn't know it when we first met. How we happened to be at Rosewood Plantation together like we were, well, that's a long story I'll have to tell you another time!

My name's Mary Ann, or Mayme for short.

It was awkward, like I said a minute ago, because Katie's uncle Templeton, who was my father, was from the other side of the family from the uncle who'd been talking to the banker.

Burchard Clairborne was Katie's *father's* brother.

Templeton Daniels was Katie's *mother's* brother, and so he wasn't really related to Richard Clairborne, Katie's father, at all.

I reckon it sounds a mite confusing. I had trouble keeping it all straight myself at first too!

But even though my father, Mr. Daniels, wasn't related to the Clairborne side of the family, he had been living at Rosewood with us for the better part of a year helping us get the plantation on a firm footing again. He'd been learning all about crops and weather and ploughing and animals and cotton and wheat. He'd helped with our second harvest of cotton, which wasn't such a big one because we hadn't been able to plant as much cotton by ourselves as Katie's mama had. He'd gotten blisters on his fingers, and his face and arms had grown tan. I'd even shown him how to milk our cows! And he'd been taking care of us like about the best father and uncle any two girls like Katie and me could have had.

But just last week he'd left on a trip. He'd been with us close to a year and finally had to take care of some things, he said. The new cotton crop was in and starting to come up, and he figured it was a good time to be gone. It was spring of the year 1867.

"But you set your minds at ease," he said to Katie and me, both of us wearing long faces as he got ready to go. "This is the new Templeton Daniels. I'll be back as soon as I can. You will hardly know I'm gone!"

"Do you *have* to go, Uncle Templeton?" asked Katie for about the eleventh time.

He laughed and kissed her on the forehead.

"You four girls will have a great time without me," he said. "Don't you remember how much fun you had with your scheme before I got here? You fooled the whole town. They still don't know! It will be just like old times!"

"But it was scary too, Uncle Templeton."

"Well, then, why don't you go pay Mrs. Hammond a visit? That will take your mind off the fact that you're alone again."

"I don't know if we could stand her suspicious looks!"

He paused and became serious again.

"I *do* need to go, Kathleen," he said after a moment. "I am sorry. I may have been a wanderer before, but there are still places where I set down a few roots. There are some things I've got to pick up, a chest of clothes near Baltimore, a saddle I left with your aunt in Philadelphia, odds and ends like that. And I left a few debts behind me too that I need to clear up. No more running, remember? It's time I faced up to those things too. I need to clear off my obligations so that my slate is clean."

"What kind of obligations?" I asked.

A look came into his eyes and I couldn't quite tell what it meant.

"There are a couple people I owe money to that I

skipped out on," he said with a sigh after a moment, "and a thing or two a little more serious than that. But I'm going to straighten them all out. It's time my past was clean. And I need to have a talk with Nelda too," he added, "though she probably won't be all that happy to see me. But she deserves to know what happened to Rosalind. They were never very close, but she was her sister."

"When will you be back, Papa?" I asked.

"Two weeks . . . three . . . four at the most. I promise to hurry."

He saw the look of sadness in both my eyes and Katie's.

"Don't worry," he said. "This is my home now. This is the last time I'll leave. You are my family. Like I told you before, now that I've found you, I don't intend to leave you. In the meantime, I've spoken with Henry. He and Jeremiah will be there if you need something, just like always."

Neither of us wanted to see him go. But we trusted him. He was different now.

And that's how it was that we were alone again, without any grown-ups or men at Rosewood, when Katie's father's brother came to call.

3

Aleta was the first to spot the rider coming toward Rosewood in the distance.

He wasn't riding fast, so we had plenty of time to get things ready. With my papa—Katie's uncle Templeton—gone, we had decided to go back to what we used to do to make people think there were more people around than there really were. By the time the rider came past the outbuildings and into sight of the back door of the house, we had smoke rising from a preset fire I'd just lit in one of the slave cabins, along with the smoke from the kitchen fire that was already going. Ten-year-old Aleta had run outside and quickly got to pounding on the anvil in the blacksmith's shop. And Emma and her nearly two-year-old little boy, William, hurried upstairs out of sight.

Katie had begun busying herself with supper preparations, and so she kept working in the kitchen.

As the man rode up, I was walking back from the slave cabins trying to look like a "hired darkie"—which some folks called us coloreds who had been set free after the war between the North and the South. That wasn't the worse thing they called us either.

We were a little family, the five of us living at the plantation called Rosewood. We were two white girls— Katie and Aleta—and three of us who were black—

Emma and William and me. Actually, William and I were half black and half white, though that still makes a person colored in most folks' eyes. There were only three others who knew that the five of us had been living there for nearly two years, running the plantation ourselves without any grown-ups—Henry and Jeremiah in town, and Katie's uncle Templeton—my papa—who I told you about. Jeremiah and Henry had been a big help to us, both before Mr. Daniels came and afterwards too. They hadn't told anyone about our secret scheme to keep the plantation going as if Katie's family was still there. And Henry and my papa were gradually becoming good friends, which made us all happy.

After Katie's and my family were all killed by Bilsby's Marauders right after the war, Katie and I found ourselves together at Rosewood doing our best to survive. We became good friends long before we had any idea we were related. Turns out my mama used to live at Rosewood and Katie's uncle fell in love with her during his visits there. But Katie's father had sold my mama to another plantation without telling Templeton where she'd gone—or that she was expecting his child. Anyway, once we knew that we were cousins—though it plumb caps the climax of anything we'd ever expected!—it's made us closer than ever. It's made us all the more a *family* at Rosewood, and made my papa's leaving again all the harder.

As the man rode up, he glanced over at me from up on his horse with a look of disdain, like I was a dog or something. He continued straight on toward the house, dismounted, threw his reins over the rail as he paused to glance around at the house and barn and grounds, then slowly climbed the steps to the porch and knocked on the door.

As I usually did when Katie had to talk to someone, I tried to stay as close as I could without arousing too much suspicion, so that I could hear what was going on. Katie often said, "Stay close to me, Mayme—I might need you." She always talked like I was the brains of the partnership, but *she* was the mistress of Rosewood now, even though she was only sixteen, and all the rest of us knew it.

Katie came to the door, opened it, and looked out to see a man standing there she recognized. Even from where I stood I saw her eyes widen and her face go white.

"I see you recognize me," he said gruffly.

"Uh . . . yes, sir . . . hello, Uncle Burchard."

"You're Kathleen, I take it."

"Yes, sir."

"You've grown some since I saw you."

"Yes, sir."

"I came to see your daddy."

"He's not back from the war yet."

"Not back—the war's been over almost two years."

"Yes, sir."

"I heard that your father came back and then left again to work in the North."

"Oh . . . yes—uh, that's what I meant . . . that he

wasn't back to stay. He just came for a few days before he left again."

"What about your brothers?"

"They're not back yet either."

"Where in blazes are they?"

"We don't know, sir."

"All right, then," he said in a frustrated tone, though it seemed like what he had expected to hear all along, "go fetch your ma. I need to talk to her."

"She's not here either, Uncle Burchard."

"What!"

"She's visiting a sick neighbor, sir."

"I see," the man said, then paused and looked about, rubbing his chin for a moment. "Well, tell her I called and that I'll be back."

"Do you, uh . . . want to come in, Uncle Burchard?" said Katie. "Would you like something to eat or drink?"

"No, don't bother. Just tell your ma I'll be back to see her."

"Yes, sir. When, Uncle Burchard?"

"I don't know, maybe tomorrow." He turned to leave.

"Are you going home now?" asked Katie.

"No, of course not—it's too far."

"Do you want . . . uh, to stay here, Uncle Burchard?"

He paused, seemingly surprised at Katie's offer of hospitality. Not half so surprised as I was! What if he said yes!

"No, that's all right," he said after a few seconds. "Thanks anyway, but I'll make my own arrangements."

He continued on down the steps to his horse, threw

me another unfriendly look, and a minute later was riding away out of sight.

A TALK WITH HENRY

4

The instant he was out of sight, Katie came running toward me.

"Mayme . . . that was my uncle Burchard from Charlotte! He's the one I've been telling you about all this time!"

"I overheard a little," I said.

"What are we going to do? Did you hear him . . . he's coming back. He's not like the others. He's going to expect to see my mother."

"What do you think he wants?"

"I don't know," said Katie.

"I reckon we'll have to think about this a spell."

"I wish Uncle Templeton was here!"

We did think about it the rest of the day, without much success in coming up with any ideas. About the only thing we thought to do was try to hide Katie's family's graves as best we could. Katie's uncle hadn't noticed them, but he would eventually. The result was that when he arrived at Rosewood again about midmorning on the next day, there were a bunch of straw bales piled around the stones. Katie had been nervous the whole time and didn't know what else to do but what she always did—say that her mother was gone again.

She did. But it was clear enough her uncle didn't like it.

"Didn't you tell her I was coming?"

"Yes, sir. But you didn't say when, Uncle Burchard."

"Well, then, this time you can tell her I will be back this afternoon."

"I'm sorry, sir," said Katie, "but she won't be back."

An exasperated curse came from her uncle's lips.

"Why in blazes not!" he half shouted.

"She needs to stay until Mrs. Thurston is better."

"Who made her nursemaid over the whole county! I'd think she'd have better things to do with Richard gone. And I suppose you have nothing more to tell me about your father's whereabouts?"

"No, sir."

He drew in a breath, irritated but not knowing what to do, and glanced around.

"The place looks run-down," he said. "Who's doing all the work, who's planting the crops and bringing them in? Who's tending the livestock?"

"We all do, Uncle Burchard. And we get people to help with the crops when we need them."

"Hired darkies, you mean?"

"Yes, sir." Something told Katie he wouldn't be pleased to hear that the ne'er-do-well brother of his sister-in-law had been around slowly taking charge of the place.

"All right, then," he said with another sigh. "I'll give your mother two days to get your sick friend back on her feet. You tell her I'll be back morning after next, and I want to talk to her. I don't care if your neighbor is *dying*—you tell her to be here! You got that, Kathleen?"

"Yes, sir," said Katie. Her uncle turned again and left. Katie was still standing on the porch.

We went into the kitchen and sat down. I pumped Katie a glass of water and she drank it down in three swallows. It seemed to bring her back to herself.

"I would like you to ride into town, Mayme," she said at length. "Take an extra horse and ask Henry if he could come out. We need to talk to him. I don't know what to do. I'd almost forgotten what it was like before Uncle Templeton came."

Henry came out that same evening on the horse Katie had sent for him. I'd only told him briefly about the situation earlier, but he'd been involved with us long enough to know Katie's fear that her uncle might try to take Rosewood from her. So as Katie told Henry about her uncle's visit, he just sat and nodded as he took everything in.

"I lied to him, Henry," said Katie finally, slowly getting tearful. "We've been trying so hard all this time to do the right thing, but look what it's led to. I thought with Uncle Templeton here, the lying was all over. But suddenly there I was not telling the truth again. Yet at the same time, I'm afraid to tell him the truth."

Henry sat thinking a minute or two.

"Ah reckon dat's a trial ter bear, all right," he said. "Tryin' ter do da right thing's mighty hard sumtimes. Ain't easy ter walk an upright life. Lot easier not ter worry 'bout truf an' right. But w'en a body wants ter live by truf, sum er life's questions git a mite mo com-plercated. Yer facin' one er dose now."

"What am I going to do, Henry?" asked Katie in almost a pleading tone.

Again Henry was thoughtful.

"You got ter listen ter yo heart—what does yo heart tell you is da right thing? Wha'chu think *God* wants yer ter do?"

"I don't know!"

"But you think lyin' ter yer uncle's wrong. Ain't dat what I'm doin' here? Ain't dat why you ax'ed fo' Henry's advice?"

"I don't know . . . yes, it must be wrong, mustn't it?"

"Ah reckon mos' ob da time lyin's wrong, all right. Ah always figger what makes a lie a lie is tryin' ter deceive sum one fer a selfish reason. Ah reckon effen a man was tryin' ter hurt Jeremiah, I'd lie all day long ter keep him from findin' him. But I don't figger dat'd be selfish ob me—I'd be tryin' ter protect my son, an effen dat was wrong, well, ah reckon I'd have ter talk ter God 'bout it later. So you gotter ax—is you bein' selfish, Miz Kathleen?"

"I don't know. I suppose a little. I'm just trying to think what's best for everyone. But I'm trying to find what's best for me too."

"But ain't nobody's life in danger."

"Except Emma's."

"Yep, dere is dat, all right. You's right dere."

"Were you thinking about those things when you shot that man Bilsby?" Katie asked, thinking back on

23

Henry's loathing of guns, yet of how he shot a man to protect Katie and me—as it turns out, the very man who killed our families.

A faraway look came into Henry's eye.

"No, Miz Kathleen," he said at length, "ah can't rightly say I wuz. Sumtimes things happen so fas' you gots ter trust yer instincts 'bout right an' wrong. Dat's why you gots ter practice so hard doin' right da res' ob da time, so dat w'en da time er crisis comes, ye'll do it wiffout thinkin' 'bout hit. I'll go t' my grave wonderin' ef I did da right thing. But at dat moment w'en I wuz lookin' out dat winder wiff dat gun in my han's, ah wuzn't 'bout ter see Miz Mayme, an' maybe you too, killed in front ob my own eyes when I cud stop it."

Henry paused and sighed at the memory.

"Yep, Miz Kathleen," he said, "right an' wrong's a mighty difficult thing ter see wiff clear eyes sumtimes, an' dat's da truf."

"Then you think I should tell my uncle . . . tell him everything?"

"Only you can say dat fo' sho', Miz Kathleen. A body's gotter listen t' God fer hisse'f. Dat's why I can't tell you what you oughter do, 'cuz I ain't wearin' yo shoes."

Again it was silent a long time and finally Henry rose to go.

I don't know what Katie was thinking about what to do. We didn't talk about it again that evening or the next day. But she was unusually quiet and thoughtful the whole time.

5

W hen her uncle came two mornings later, she went to meet him again at the door. I still wasn't sure what she was going to do. I couldn't help wondering if this was the day we'd get found out and everything would change. When Katie had told her uncle Templeton, that is, my father—it still sounds mighty strange hearing that word out of my own lips and writing it down and looking at it with my own eyes—he was kind as he could be to Katie and me and the others. He is different for a white man, which makes me proud that he is my father.

But this uncle Burchard of hers—one look at him was enough to tell that he *wouldn't* be so considerate, especially to me and Emma. The way he looked at me reminded me of Master McSimmons, and I knew that once Katie told him, it would be the end of everything for us, and yet I didn't know if Papa could do anything to help. I know Katie was wrestling with her conscience, and that's a mighty powerful thing sometimes when truth is silently shouting at you from inside. Sometimes you gotta obey what it says no matter what the consequences.

Katie opened the door and stood staring at her uncle. I think she was planning to tell him but couldn't bring herself to it, or else just didn't know what to say. One look at her face, and Katie's uncle seemed to realize he was not going to see Mrs. Clairborne that day.

"Your ma's not here, is she?" he said brusquely.

"No, sir," replied Katie softly, looking down at the floor.

He shook his head in exasperation.

"All right, then, if that's the way you want it, I'll deal with this legally. I have tried to be civil and give you every chance to explain yourself, but if you won't, then you leave me no choice."

I didn't know what he meant. He turned around and went back to his horse and rode away without another word, leaving Katie standing there, having planned to tell him but now watching him disappear without her saying a word. Whether she felt relieved or more guilty yet, I don't know.

We would find out soon enough exactly what Katie's uncle had meant by his parting words. This time he didn't even return to the boardinghouse in Greens Crossing where he was staying but rode straight to Oakwood to see the lawyer Mr. Taylor had told him about. Within the hour he was sitting across the desk talking to the attorney Leroy Sneed.

Of course, we didn't have any way of knowing about their meeting at the time, or knowing what they said to each other. We didn't find out those details till quite a bit later. All we found out then was the effect their conversation would have on our lives.

Anyway, their conversation went something like this.

"I can't prove nothing, Mr. Sneed," said Katie's uncle

Burchard after explaining the situation. "But I'm convinced my brother is dead. Can't nothing else account for it. He ain't the kind of fellow that'd just leave wife and kid and house without a word. They know the plantation ought to have been mine all along. They're trying to keep me from finding out. So what can I do?"

Sneed had, of course, long harbored his own suspicions and annoyances about what we were up to. But he kept them to himself for the present.

"Without proof of your brother's death, of course," Sneed began, "and absent a will, the legalities are somewhat murky. I suppose you could file a claim for temporary guardianship as an intermediate measure, pending resolution of your brother's, shall we say, condition."

"Guardianship . . . you mean over that wool-brained kid of his? I couldn't care less about her and ain't too fond of the idea of being her guardian. Besides, there's my brother's wife."

"I mean guardianship over the estate, the land—giving you temporary power over decisions made, effectively giving you the power of an owner without actual ownership."

Katie's uncle nodded. He liked the sound of what he had just heard.

"And what would happen after that?" he asked.

"It would depend."

"On what?"

"On whether your brother turned out to be dead or alive. If he is dead, as you suspect, then of course you could file a claim for full ownership, although it would be sure to be contested by the man's widow."

Burchard Clairborne thought a minute. "All right, then," he said, "file the papers. I'll worry about the rest of it later."

When Mr. Sneed arrived at Rosewood to deliver the papers two days later, Katie couldn't believe she was seeing *him* again. Her heart sank at the thought! He rode up in an expensive buckboard, dressed in suit and tie almost as nice looking as my father used to look when he wore ruffled shirts. He walked to the door. I was hanging wash out on the line and strained to listen.

"I have some papers here for Mrs. Clairborne," he said when Katie answered the door. After several previous interviews with Katie, he didn't even bother to ask if her mother was at home.

"Give her these," he said, handing Katie the short stack of official documents.

"What is it, uh . . . Mr. Sneed?" she asked.

"It is a filing by one Burchard Clairborne—would he be your uncle?"

"Yes, sir."

"I see. Well, this is a filing for guardianship of the Rosewood estate in the absence of your father's appearance to claim his legal rights of ownership."

"Uh . . . what does that mean, sir?" asked Katie.

"It means that Burchard Clairborne will be given guardianship over the plantation known as Rosewood in his brother's stead."

"But what about my mother, sir?"

"She has ninety days to contest the action. That is why I must see her. If she does not contest it, the court will grant Mr. Clairborne's request and award him guardianship."

A bewildered Katie stood blankly trying to absorb his words. The lawyer turned and walked down the stairs and back toward his buckboard.

"Uh . . . Mr. Sneed," called Katie after him.

He paused and glanced back.

"Could I, uh . . . could I contest it for my mother?"

A confused expression passed over the man's face. Then slowly he began to laugh.

"You?" he said.

"Yes, sir."

"Don't be ridiculous," he replied, still chuckling. "How old are you?"

"Sixteen, sir. But I'll be seventeen in a month and a half."

"Then you are not even of age, or anywhere close to it. The court wouldn't recognize anything you did. I need your mother's signature and no one else's in order to stop this injunction from taking effect. So tell her it is imperative that I speak to her."

He got into his buckboard and rode away.

6

I ran up to Katie, who was holding the papers with tears in her eyes.

"I think it's over, Mayme," she said in a sad and defeated, though strangely relieved, tone. "Uncle Burchard isn't going to give up. Did you hear what that Mr. Sneed said? Uncle Burchard's filed some kind of legal thing to take control of Rosewood."

"What's a guardianship?" I asked. "I heard him use that word."

"I'm not sure," replied Katie. "All I know is that without my mama's signature, the man said Rosewood will become Uncle Burchard's."

"What about Papa?" I asked.

"He's not here," said Katie. "But I don't think he could do anything anyway, since he's not blood kin to my daddy like Uncle Burchard is."

"Maybe you should look at the papers and read what they say," I suggested.

Katie nodded. We went inside and sat down.

But after a few minutes looking at the papers, Katie just shook her head. "I can't make heads or tails of it, Mayme," she said.

"Is it written in another language or something?" I asked. "Didn't I hear someplace that lawyers use a different language for saying things?"

"No, everything's written in English. I just can't make anything of what it means. It sounds like nonsense."

"Should we show it to Henry?"

"Henry can't read as well as you, Mayme. If I can't understand it, he couldn't. I wish Uncle Templeton would hurry. I'm sure he would know what to do."

I didn't say anything. What could I say? She wasn't just talking about her uncle. She was talking about my father. I wished he was there too.

It was pretty somber around Rosewood for the next several days. We'd had a lot of close calls and a lot of visitors who were suspicious about what they saw. We'd even had to cope with Mrs. Hammond's hawk eyes looking us over like we were up to something . . . which we were. But she had never found out. No one had ever found out.

But Katie was right. There didn't seem any way around the fact that our scheme was about over now. Her uncle Burchard *was* going to find out. If we didn't get separated, at the very least we'd both be working for him before long, and it seemed likely that he'd run off Mr. Daniels just like Katie's own father had years before. The idea of all that didn't seem altogether agreeable to either of us. I started thinking about paying jobs again, wondering if a sixteen-year-old white girl and a seventeen-year-old black girl could live on their own if they didn't have a house like we'd had for the last two years.

And what about Aleta, Emma, and William!

The days went slowly by, and Papa didn't come back. He'd now been gone about two weeks, and even though he said he might be gone four, we couldn't help starting to look down the road, hoping he'd ride in and solve everything for us. But he didn't come.

Katie's uncle Burchard came around again, and then a few more times. After the lawyer's visit he didn't even bother trying to talk to Katie. The first time we saw him riding out in the fields, just riding about looking at things, and then after a while he was gone. One morning we got up and saw his horse tied outside. When I went out to gather the morning's eggs and start the milking, there he was in the barn. He was writing things down on a paper, looking about, inspecting everything, looking the equipment over. Then he went out to the stables and spent a good while looking over the horses. He took no notice of me, and we both went about what we were doing, paying no attention to the other. It was a mighty peculiar feeling.

After another hour he got on his horse and rode away.

"What was he doing, Mayme?" asked Katie, who had stayed in the house all the time he was there.

"I don't know," I said. "Just looking at everything. He was writing something down on a piece of paper."

But there was no doubt that things were different already. Katie's uncle felt comfortable coming and going like Rosewood was already his. And it seemed pretty likely that before long it would be!

Gradually he took more and more liberties. He even came into the house a time or two, mostly just to get something to eat or get a drink of water. But he was always looking around. And it was obvious he didn't like what he saw, especially if he saw Emma or me inside. He looked at us all, even Katie, with an expression that was anything but nice. Aleta, especially, cowered whenever he was around. I wondered to myself if he was thinking that he couldn't wait to get rid of us all. He seemed to despise Katie just as much for being nice to us as he despised Emma and me for being colored.

One afternoon Katie and I saw him out by the graves, just standing there. He kicked at one of the bales we'd put there and rolled it back, then just kept standing looking down. I glanced over at Katie. Her face went white.

A few minutes later, as we were lugging the cheese press off the porch to let it drain, we heard footsteps behind us. Katie turned. There was her uncle staring at her with a serious expression. We set down the press and just stood there. It was quiet a long time as he looked back and forth between us. Somehow as he did, I had the feeling that he was putting everything together in his mind.

"You been lying to me all along, ain't you, Kathleen?" he finally said. "Your pa ain't never coming back, is he? He ain't up north. He's dead, ain't he?"

Katie's eyes filled with tears. I could see from the expression on her uncle's face that he knew he was right whether she answered him or not. He began to nod and the hint of a knowing grin came to his lips.

"I figured it all along," he said, then paused. He got real thoughtful again.

"And your ma's dead too, ain't she?" he said after a bit. "That fourth grave out there ain't Jason's, is it? He died in the fighting. There was only three of 'em that came back from the war . . . but there's four stones over there. Something happened, didn't it—something bad that you ain't told nobody? That fourth grave's your ma's, ain't it?"

Katie couldn't take it anymore. She burst into tears, then turned and fell sobbing into my arms where I stood next to her.

Her uncle just stood there. He didn't show any tenderness like my father did when Katie told him. He just kept standing there with a look of impatience waiting for her to stop crying. When she finally managed to take a few breaths and release herself from my embrace and turn to face him, he spoke again.

"That's what this is all about," he said, "these coloreds and that kid . . . that baby the talkative fool's carrying around—ain't nobody here, is there? That's why the place is a mess and it don't look like no work's being done—because there ain't. You just been play-acting all this time."

Katie struggled to keep from crying again. "They were all killed, Uncle Burchard, all but me. Men came, after the war. Men with guns . . ."

"Was it that Bilsby's gang I've heard tell about?"

"Yes, sir."

"Well, your little charade's over, missy," her uncle

said, and I was shocked at how unfeeling the man was. "You should have come to your kin first, right when it happened. Maybe then I could have helped you. But lying to me, pretending your folks was still here . . . ain't much I can do for you now. 'Course I'll take care of you. Kin's kin. I ain't going to throw you out. All I'm saying is you should have come to me first. Meantime, these darkies'll have to go. And I want you getting rid of that girl too. I'll have no kids or darkies around the house. I'll be bringing my own people in now."

Still Katie stood speechless.

"Well, speak up, girl. You're standing there like an idiot. Don't you have nothing to say for yourself?"

"No, sir," Katie whimpered.

"I'll warrant you'll find your tongue soon enough once the work starts. Your kind always does." He glanced over at me, then back at Katie. "Just get rid of the rest of them, you hear?"

He walked back to his horse and rode away, leaving Katie and me in stunned silence.

Burchard Clairborne went straight to Oakwood and to the office of Leroy Sneed.

"You might as well cancel those other papers," he said. "I've just learned that they're dead—the whole lot of them . . . my brother, his wife, his sons, all but the dimwitted daughter. They're all buried there, all but the son who died in the war."

Sneed nodded as he listened. Things immediately began to make sense.

"I don't know how she escaped," Clairborne went on, "but she's alone. That makes the place legally mine. We don't need to bother with guardianship—I want you to file papers claiming full ownership on my behalf."

"Do you know if there is a will?" asked Sneed.

"How should I know? If there is, it's sure that fool girl of his knows nothing about it. You're the only lawyer for miles—you know anything about one?"

"No, but he could have filed in Charlotte."

"What difference would a will make anyway? She's not of age."

"Yes, right . . . I see what you mean."

"The place is finally mine and I don't want to fool around with niceties any longer than necessary."

"It would just make matters simpler with a will," added the lawyer.

"In any case, Richard would have left it to his wife. And she's dead. The sons are all dead. The girl can't make a legal claim, can she?"

"Not until she's twenty-one. Even then, it's possible your claim would take precedence."

"Good, then file the claim. I don't want to wait five years. I want that place now."

On his way back to the boardinghouse in Greens Crossing, Burchard Clairborne stopped at the general store to pick up a few things. In the exuberance of his discovery of that morning, he was a little freer with his tongue in the presence of the shopkeeper than was his normal custom.

The result was that within two days everyone for miles around knew of the Clairborne massacre and what Katie and I had been doing. Mrs. Hammond confessed herself scandalized at the thought of a black girl and white girl living alone together all that time. Mostly, though she did not admit this openly, she was irritated at herself for having been duped along with everyone else. There were others, however, who professed a grudging admiration for the Rosewood girls and their scheme.

Mrs. Hammond, of course, made it clear that she had suspected the truth all along.

RUMORS SPREAD

7

We saw no more of Burchard Clairborne after that—for a while at least. And during those first few days we didn't know that Mrs. Hammond was busy spreading news about "little Kathleen Clairborne and that darkie girl of hers" all over town. We didn't know it in fact until Jeremiah's next visit.

"The two of you's 'bout the mos' famous people in all Greens Crossing!" he said with a big grin as he walked up to where I was working.

"What do you mean?" I asked.

"What you mean what do I mean? Jus' dat everyone's talkin' 'bout you, dat's all."

"They're talking about us!" exclaimed Katie, walking

over from the washtub. "*Who's* talking about us?"

"Everybody . . . mostly dat grouchy storekeeper lady. She been spreadin' news all roun'bout ob you two bein' all alone wiff a couple strays. I kep' yer secret fer more'n a year, but dat busybody's spreadin' it every-where!"

"Oh no!" exclaimed Katie.

"But how did she find out?" I said.

Katie and I looked at each other. We always seemed to think alike and both realized the answer at the same time.

"Uncle Burchard!" said Katie.

Immediately we knew that the biggest danger wasn't to us.

"What are they saying, Jeremiah," began Katie in a lower voice, "about the others? Do they know about Aleta and Emma? I've got to know."

"Dat dey do, Miz Kathleen," replied Jeremiah. "Not by name dat I heard. But dey's sayin' you got a white kid an' a dimwitted colored girl an' her baby wiff you."

"Oh no!" said Katie a second time.

I wish Emma hadn't heard. But she had ears too big for her own good sometimes. She'd been so used to being called names—I reckon all black folks are used to that, but that doesn't mean it sometimes doesn't hurt—that she didn't even seem to notice what he'd said about a dimwitted colored girl. But she had heard well enough that folks were talking about us . . . all of us.

"Dey know 'bout me an' William!" she shrieked, running toward where we were talking. "Dey know my baby's here! He's gwine fin' out! It'll be da death ob me fo' sho'!"

And we had to admit that whatever Katie's troubles and mine, they weren't so bad as Emma's. What were we going to do to keep her safe? We had Henry and Jeremiah to help us, and maybe, if it came to that, Katie's uncle Burchard too, for that matter. Not that he'd lift a finger for Emma. But knowing another white man was around might make William McSimmons think twice before he tried to do something bad. He couldn't just come and kill us all without *someone* finding out.

Although maybe he could, for all I knew. Killing blacks wasn't regarded as much of a crime. There were blacks being killed all over the South as a result of the resentment and hatred that sprung up after the war. No one around Greens Crossing would likely raise a ruckus if one little black baby was dropped in the river in a sack full of rocks . . . or if Emma and I disappeared one day and were never heard from again.

Now more than ever Katie and I began desperately watching the road in hopes of seeing Mr. Daniels riding back to Rosewood.

By now it was getting close to three weeks since he'd left. But still there was no sign of him.

8

Luckily for all of us, by the time the news from Mrs. Hammond's wagging tongue widened to encompass the McSimmons plantation, the rumors had changed enough to make them hardly recognizable. And Mistress McSimmons did her business at Oakwood and rarely went into Greens Crossing where she might have heard more.

As it was, when William McSimmons' wife caught wind of what was being said, she heard nothing about the Clairborne estate, only rumors of a fatherless colored baby being hid somewhere with a houseful of urchins, mostly black, who had managed to keep from being detected, some said, since the war.

Thinking that her troubles from her husband's promiscuity were behind her, and probably made worse by the fact that she had yet been unable to give him a child herself, Mrs. McSimmons went into a rage at the news. She took it out on the nearest and most convenient person she could, whom she still suspected of knowing more about the affair than she let on, and whom too she never once suspected of having the gumption to resist her.

The tirade so caught Josepha off guard at first that she hardly knew its cause. She had heard the rumors too and of course *did* know more than she was telling. But why Mistress McSimmons would direct such venom toward her, she didn't understand.

"No need ter git riled at me," Josepha said in an irritable voice. "I don' know nuthin'. Why wud I know what you's talkin' 'bout?"

"You fat old sow!" the lady shrieked. "I'll teach you to talk back to your betters! Maybe the sting of the whip will put some respect into you, and loosen that lying tongue of yours!"

Three quick strides took her to the wall where her husband's riding whip hung. She grabbed it and turned on Josepha.

Josepha had had her fair share of whippings during her forty years or more as a slave. But she had not felt the lash since learning that she was a free woman. As a result it stung all the more keenly.

Three or four sharp blows to her arms, shoulders, and back were sufficient to rouse all the proud indignation of her race against its oppressors.

She put up her hand, trying to ward off the blows and grab at the whip.

"How dare you raise your hand against me!" cried Mrs. McSimmons, preparing to begin a new volley more violent than the first. But suddenly Josepha stepped toward her, fire in her eyes, and latched on to the lady's wrist with fingers as strong as a vise. Her hand stopped the whip in midair and shocked her mistress into a fuming silence.

"I don' hab ter take dis no mo!" huffed Josepha. "You may be white an' I may be black, you may be thin an' I may be fat like you say. But I's a person ob God's makin' jes' like you, an' you ain't got no right ter—"

"How *dare* you talk to me in such a tone!" cried Mrs. McSimmons in a white wrath, struggling with all her might to free her arm from Josepha's hold.

"An' how dare you whip me like I wuz one ob yer barn dogs!" retorted Josepha, continuing to hold her fast, for she was easily the stronger of the two by at least double. "I's a free woman, I ain't yo slave. I can come an' go when I like an' I ain't gotter put up wiff no whippin' jes' 'cuz you married a low-down man what can't keep his trousers on. Miz Mayme'll gib me work too, so I think I'll jes' be movin' on. Effen she can' pay me, she ain't likely ter let me starve neither an' it'll be a sight better'n puttin' up wiff da evil mischief ob a lady like you. So I'll thank you ter gib me da week's pay I gots comin' ter me an'—"

"You swine!" seethed the woman through clenched teeth. "You'll get not a cent if you desert me without notice!"

"Well, den . . . no matter. I's leavin' anyway," said Josepha.

Still holding the lady's wrist with one hand, she now reached up with her other and twisted the whip away from her, then released her and walked to the door and threw it out into the dirt. She then turned, went to her room trembling but with head high, and packed her few belongings and put them in a pillow slip. Three minutes later she was walking out the same door for good, leaving Mistress McSimmons in stunned silence behind her.

Josepha had no more idea where Katie and I lived than did her now former mistress. But she was familiar with Henry from an occasional delivery he had made through the years to the McSimmons plantation. She knew that he worked at the livery at Greens Crossing and was more likely than anyone she could think of to have caught wind of where a black girl calling herself *Mayme* might have got to.

Three hours after Josepha's unceremonious departure from the only home she had ever really known, Henry looked up from his work and saw the large black woman ambling wearily in his direction. He set down his pitchfork and waited.

"You be Henry, effen I'm not mistaken," she said, puffing from her long walk.

"Dat I is," said Henry.

"I'm Josepha," said Josepha, "from da McSimmons place."

"I knows who you is," chuckled Henry. "I seen you dere many er time. But wha'chu doin' so far from home, an' on what looks ter be sech tired feet?"

"Ain't my home no mo," said Josepha. "I's a free woman, so I dun lef'. I ain't gotter take dat kin' er treatment no mo from nobody. An' now I'm lookin' fer Miz Mayme, an' I'm hopin' you might be familiar 'nuff wiff her ter be able ter direc' me ter where I kin fin' her."

Henry chuckled again. "I reckon I kin do dat all right," he said. "Why I might jes' take you dere myse'f, effen you ain't in too much a hurry. Hit's a longer walk den I think you wants ter make, an' effen you kin wait till I'm dun here, I'll fetch you dere in dat nice buck-board ober dere dat I's repairin' fer Mr. Thurston. I reckon hit's 'bout ready fer me ter take ter him, an' Rosewood's right on da way. I don' think he'll min' a passenger ridin' 'long wiff me."

Just as the sun was going down that evening, we heard the sound of a horse and wagon approaching. Now that everyone knew about us, it didn't seem to matter making preparations to fool people anymore. It didn't matter anyway because we saw soon enough that it was Henry. But never could anything have surprised me as much as to see Josepha's plump frame sitting there beside him!

Henry reined in as I ran toward the buckboard. It took a little while for Josepha to get down to the ground, even with Henry's help. One look at her face told me she was exhausted.

"Mayme, chil'!" she said, taking me in her arms. When I stepped back a minute later I saw that she was crying.

"What is it, Josepha?" I said.

"I lef', Mayme," she said. "I dun lef' Mistress McSimmons. She's a bad woman an' I finally jes' lef'. I didn't know where ter go 'cept ter you."

"Oh, Josepha . . . I'm sorry." I embraced her again, feeling how strange it was for me, just a girl—though I guess I was almost eighteen by now—to give comfort to someone so much older, especially this lady who had given comfort to me as a child and who I always saw as such a tower of strength among the slaves.

"Does you think yer mistress'll hab room fer an' ol' black woman sumwheres?"

Just then Katie ran out of the house.

"We've always got room," I said, "—especially for you! Don't we, Katie?" I added, turning to Katie as she ran up.

"Of course!" exclaimed Katie. "You are welcome here. I'll hurry back in and start preparing one of the rooms immediately."

"What dat she say?" said Josepha in surprise as she watched Katie go. "She can't be fixin' no room fer me! She's da mistress!"

"Things are different here, Josepha," I laughed. "There's no black or white, no mistress or slaves. We're not even hired coloreds because there's no money either. I'm sorry, but Katie won't be able to pay you any more than she does me. But we're a family and we've got enough to eat. We've learned that being together is all we need, and being a family is the most important thing of all. I reckon that's a sight better than money. We're happy to have you."

"Den let's go an' help Miz Katie wif dat gettin' ready. I still don' like the idea ob her white han's waitin' on me nohow."

Henry and I got Josepha inside and sitting down in a chair with a glass of cold water. I could tell Henry wanted to say something to me. He and I stepped back outside for a minute.

"Any word yet from Mr. Daniels?" he asked in a quiet voice.

"No, Henry," I said, shaking my head. "We haven't heard a thing."

SEARCH FOR THE DEED

9

After a good night's sleep, Josepha was almost back to herself, though her feet and legs were sore for several more days. She'd walked a long way for a woman her size! The morning after her arrival with Henry, she was bustling about in the kitchen, singing and waiting on everybody like she'd been at Rosewood for years. Having a family to be mammy to made her happier than just about anything. Even Aleta took to her cheerful spirit almost immediately, and by that afternoon was following her around like a puppy dog asking ten questions a minute.

But Josepha's appearance had put Emma in a state of panic.

"If she's here, dey'll foller her an' fin' me shure!" she said to Katie, half wailing in despair.

"Dey ain't nobody gwine hurt you, Emma, chil'," said Josepha. "Dat mistress, she don' know where I's gone, an' ol' Uncle Henry, he ain't gwine tell."

And after a day or two of reassuring talk from Katie and me, Emma gradually calmed down, like she usually did. But as confident as were Josepha's assurances,

Katie and I knew how unlikely it was that a black man everyone knew and a huge black woman they didn't, riding through town in a white man's buckboard, would have escaped notice. We knew one person especially who was bound to have noticed! How long it would take for Mrs. McSimmons to initiate inquiries, we didn't know, but once she did, it wouldn't take long for her to put two and two together, especially if she got curious about Josepha's blurting of my name and put it together with Emma's disappearance and all the rest of what happened.

I mentioned all this to Henry next time I saw him.

He nodded as he listened, but then began to chuckle. "You's right to be a mite cautious, Miz Mayme," he said. "But hit ain't likely folks'll be talkin' anytime soon. I went out from da livery in da opposite direction from Rosewood jes' in case, an' speshully so's we wouldn't go past da store. Effen we could jes' keep dat ol' Hammond woman from layin' her eyes on us, I figger we'd be safe enuff."

Even with Henry's precautions, however, we knew that if Katie's uncle caught sight of Josepha, news would spread just like it had before. Neither Katie or I wanted to spoil Josepha's happiness at being away from Mrs. McSimmons, but we had to tell her how things stood with Katie's uncle, and that it wouldn't be much longer before we were all going to have to leave. And for the present, we knew that if he came back, we had to keep him from seeing Josepha for Emma's sake.

And indeed, Katie's uncle did begin coming around

again, though I think he might have gone back home in the meantime to Charlotte where he lived. But when he did come back, he acted more familiar than ever, as I said before, like Rosewood was already his.

We had no warning of his coming until he was riding into the yard and dismounting from his horse.

"Uncle Burchard!" yelled Katie into the house. "Uncle Burchard's here!"

There was no time to scurry Josepha upstairs, and as it turned out it was a good thing because that's right where Katie's uncle went when he came in. And we certainly had no intention of trying to hide her in the cellar like we had Emma do before. Josepha would never fit through the cellar door!

We were in the kitchen, and without even thinking about it, Katie motioned quickly to Josepha and stuffed her into the larder and closed the door just about the same second her uncle walked into the opposite side of the kitchen from outside—as always, without knocking.

"Oh . . . hello, Uncle Burchard," said Katie, hurrying away from the larder door.

"Never mind your hellos," he said, glancing toward me. "I see you haven't gotten rid of her yet."

"She's got no place else to go, Uncle Burchard."

"What's that to me? She'll have to go soon enough. Are the others still here too?"

"Yes, sir."

He shook his head in annoyance, then headed into the house and toward the stairs. We watched him go, wondering what he would say when he saw Emma and William in one of the upstairs rooms. He paused in the parlor and looked back.

"Well, come on," he said to Katie. "I want you to show me where your father kept his papers. Did he have a study or secretary or something?"

"Yes, sir," replied Katie, going with him. When they were out of sight, I slowly followed.

I reached the upstairs landing and heard their voices coming from the room that had been Katie's Mama's office.

". . . deed to the place?" her uncle had asked.

". . . don't know, sir . . . what does it look like?"

"Never mind . . . must be here."

It was quiet a long time and I heard nothing but papers shuffling as he rummaged through the desk and all its drawers.

"What about a safe . . . did your father have a safe?"

"Yes, sir."

"Well . . . where is it? Are you a simpleton?"

"Over there on the wall," said Katie, "behind the picture."

"Why didn't you say so in the first place?" said her uncle. I heard the clomp of his boots walking across the floor. "It's locked," he said a few seconds later.

"Yes, sir."

"And I suppose you have no idea of the combination?"

"No, sir."

"You're a big help! Well, I'll have to find the combination. The deed's got to be inside. All right, leave me alone now. I'll look for it myself. There's always a hidden record of the combination somewhere nearby."

Katie left the room and saw me standing there on the landing. We didn't say anything. I tiptoed down the stairs beside her.

"What's a deed?" I whispered when we were back in the kitchen.

"I don't know," replied Katie. "I think it's something about who owns things, or a piece of paper that says you own something. He said he was looking for the deed to Rosewood."

"Is that what would make him own it?"

"I don't know . . . maybe."

"What if you had the deed? Maybe that would make *you* the owner."

"I don't think it works that way," said Katie. "I'm not old enough to have a deed. And I'm a girl. I don't know if girls can own things like houses, can they?"

"I don't know. Coloreds probably can't either. I reckon that puts us in a fix."

"No worse than the one we've been in all along."

Our conversation was interrupted a few minutes later by the sound of Katie's uncle's footsteps coming down the stairs. When he walked back into the kitchen there was nothing in his hands.

"Did you find it, Uncle Burchard?" asked Katie.

"No, if that combination's there, they hid it good. Doesn't matter. I don't need the deed. It'd just make it easier, that's all. And I'll get into that safe one way or another."

"Are you . . . are you going to take Rosewood away from me, Uncle Burchard?" asked Katie timidly, but being pretty blunt at the same time.

He turned and looked at her as if the question was ridiculous.

"I'm not going to take it *away* from anyone," he said. "It *belongs* to me because of what happened to your pa and ma. You're underage and I'm the nearest kin. Ain't you got it through your head yet—Rosewood is mine. Or at least it will be in sixty days. That's why I'm telling you to get rid of all these coloreds."

"Why do you want to find that deed?"

"Because I want to make sure everything's done legal so the likes of you don't grow up and marry some Northern lawyer who thinks he can file some claim against me ten years from now, that's why!"

Her uncle's harsh tone finally broke down Katie's defenses and she started to cry.

"But . . . but *why* do you have to take Rosewood, Uncle Burchard?" she asked. "You have a place of your own . . . why can't you just let us all stay here? We're not bothering anyone."

"Why?" he laughed, again as if what Katie had asked was the most ridiculous thing he'd ever heard. "Because it's mine. What other reason do I need than that! Do you actually expect me to let a houseful of brats stay rent free in a plantation that will add thousands of dollars to my income? If you keep on with notions like that, I might not even let you stay."

He turned and walked out the door and was gone. We didn't see him for another week.

At about this same time, though we didn't know anything about it, someone in Charlotte had heard about the scheme of the two Shenandoah County girls. I don't know how. I doubt Mrs. Hammond's influence extended quite that far. But however they found out, they did, and a small article about it appeared in the newspaper. Maybe Jeremiah had been right, and we *were* the most famous people in Greens Crossing!

And after that, one at a time a few newspapers in the North picked up the story about us too. Of course, we didn't find out about this until much later.

All we were thinking about was why Papa hadn't come back yet. We needed him now more than ever. We were in trouble!

THE LUMP IN ALETA'S HEART

10

One day I came upon Aleta sitting by herself out behind the barn. She was unusually quiet and was just sitting there staring down at the ground. One of the dogs, Rusty, lay sleeping next to her, but Aleta hardly seemed to notice him and wasn't petting him like she usually did. As I looked at her face, I had the idea she'd been crying.

I went over and sat down beside her. She didn't even look up.

"What are you thinking about?" I asked after a bit.

"My mama and daddy," she said softly.

"What about them?"

"I was wondering if my daddy knows about Mama."

"No way he could, is there?" I said.

"I suppose not."

Again it was quiet for a minute or two.

"I miss my mama," said Aleta.

"I miss mine too," I said.

"You're lucky . . . you've got a nice papa."

"I'm sure your papa has nice things about him too."

"I don't know what. He was mean."

"No man is perfect. No father is perfect."

"But your daddy's nice."

"He's done some bad things, though," I said.

"Like what?" she said, glancing up at me with a puzzled expression on her face.

"I don't know," I answered. "But that's what he's doing now, trying to take care of some of those things he did that he regrets now."

"Take care of them—what do you mean?"

"Making them right, however he has to. I think he's going to pay some money back to some people. Maybe he's going to apologize . . . I don't know, he didn't tell me. But everybody's got things in their life they've got to make right one day or another."

I half expected Aleta to get up and walk away. She was a pretty smart girl and I figured she knew what I was getting at and wouldn't want to listen, like when Katie had tried to talk to her after Reverend Hall's visit. But this time she didn't take offense but just sat there. I had the feeling things were starting to get inside her in a new way. Maybe she was finally ready to listen to some things she needed to hear.

It was quiet a moment and then I got up my gumption to press a little harder and see how ready she really was. "You remember when the minister came out visiting a while back?" I asked.

Aleta nodded.

"You remember what he said about your papa?"

"Yes."

"You reckon maybe he's doing what my daddy's doing—trying to make some things right that he's done wrong in the past?"

"Maybe," she said.

"What if he wants to make it right with you too?"

"He can't make it right with Mama. She's dead."

"No, maybe not. I don't reckon we can make everything right. But don't you think you ought to give him the chance to make right what he can?"

"But he yelled at my mama and beat her sometimes."

"Yeah, those are terrible things. I can't say how a man makes them right. I reckon that's between him and God. But it ain't too late for him to make it right with *you* . . . or for you to make it right with him."

"Why should I have to make it right? I didn't do anything wrong to him."

I heard a sound behind us and looked up. There was Henry ambling toward us from the direction of the barn. From the look on his face, I had the feeling he'd been listening.

"Miz Mayme's right, Miz Aleta," he said, leaning against the wooden fence of the horse corral. "Makin' things right's a two-way street. Mos' ob da time it ain't sumfin' a body kin do all by demselves. Hit may be dat yo papa needs yo help ter make his life right agin."

"What could I do, Henry?" asked Aleta.

"I reckon you's gotter do yer half ob da makin' right."

"But what's that? I didn't do anything wrong."

"You may hab dun mo wrong den you know."

"Me . . . like what?"

"You got sum unkindness in dat heart er yers tards yo papa, an' dat's jus' as bad a sin as whateber he dun hisse'f."

"But I didn't hurt anybody."

"Ah, Aleta, chil', din't you, now? You don' think hatred an' unkind thoughts kin hurt folks?"

"I don't know," she said softly.

"I reckon dey's jus' 'bout as hurtful as anything yo papa's dun. Da way I see it, you's got a heap er makin' right ter tend to jus' like he has—jus' like we all hab ter ten' to in our own lives sooner er later."

"I don't know what you mean, Henry," said Aleta.

"Jus' dat everbody's gotter ten' ter makin' things right in dere own hearts, not jus' wait fer udder folks ter do da makin' right. Miz Mayme's gotter make things right in her heart, an' I gotter make things right in my heart, an' Miz Kathleen's gotter make things right in her heart."

"Miss Katie! She could never do anything wrong."

"Everbody does wrong, Miz Aleta. Dere's wrong an' dere's wrong. Dere's da kind er wrong yo daddy's dun, but dere's wrong dat happens inside dat nobody else kin see, wrong ways of thinkin,' selfishness, hatred, and the like. An' dey kin be jus' as wrong in God's eyes as da udder kin'. So you see, everbody's got things in dere heart dey gotter make right, wiff God an' wiff folks dat hab hurt dem and wiff folks dat dey've hurt demselves. Miz Kathleen an' me an' everbody."

It got quiet again.

"And me too?" said Aleta finally.

"Dat's right, Miz Aleta," said Henry. "You too. You got sum makin' right ter do wiff yo papa. It ain't yo business how he makes right da wrong dat he's dun. Dat's atween him an' God. It's yo business dat you make right da wrong you've dun tard him. Dat's da only way things can git right atween you."

"What do you want me to do, Henry?" she asked.

"Ain't me dat wants you ter do anything, Miz Aleta. I'm jus' tryin ter hep you figger out what you wants ter do yersel'."

Henry paused a few seconds. "Ain't you feelin' a lump er wrongness in yo heart?" he said. "Ain't you feelin' sumfin' inside you dat don' feel good when you think 'bout yo papa?"

Aleta nodded.

"Does you want ter git rid ob it?"

"Yes."

"You can't git rid ob it unless you want to yerse'f. I can't do it fo' you. An' you can't git rid ob it jus' 'cuz I say so, but only effen you wants ter make it right yerse'f."

"What do I have to do to get rid of it, Henry?" asked Aleta.

"Hit's a mighty hard thing, Miz Aleta," answered Henry. "Ain't too many folks got da courage ter do it. Hit's one ob da hardest things in da whole world."

"But I want to do it, Henry. I want to get rid of the lump inside me. It doesn't feel good."

"Well, den, I reckon dere's two things you gotter do ter git rid ob it."

"What?"

"First, you's gotter ax God ter forgive you fo' da hateful feelin's and da unkindness dat's caused dat lump er sin ter grow in yer heart. You see, Miz Aleta, what yo papa did wuz wrong all right, but you let dat lump er hatred grow in yo heart. Yo papa din't do dat, you did. Dat's da wrong in *you*. Dat's what you gotter ax forgiveness fo'."

I couldn't believe how hard Henry was being on Aleta. I glanced up and looked in his face. It was full of love, but it was almost a stern kind of love like I'd never seen him have before, like he knew it was time Aleta faced herself. Even though she was young, he seemed to know now was the time, and it might not come again.

"What's the second thing, Henry?" she asked softly.

"After you ax God ter forgive you," he said, "den you's gotter forgive yo papa."

This time Aleta sat a long time staring down at the ground. None of us made a sound. I couldn't imagine what kinds of things she was thinking. It had been different when I'd had to forgive my papa. He'd never done the kind of things Aleta's daddy had. But maybe it doesn't matter how bad the sin is—people still have to be forgiven anyway.

"What should I do, Henry?" she said finally.

"Does you want ter ax God ter fergive you?"

Aleta nodded.

"Den jus' ax Him," said Henry. "Jus' say, God, I know dis lump er bad feelin's in my heart's my fault, not my daddy's. Hit's wrong er me ter hate him no matter what he's dun. I ax you ter forgive me for dat wrong in me, an' den I ax you ter take care er my daddy in yo own way. Dat's all you gotter say, sumfin' like dat."

"Should I say it now?"

"Effen you want."

"Out loud . . . with you and Mayme listening?"

"We kin leave effen you want."

"No . . . I guess it's all right if you listen."

Aleta closed her eyes. "God," she began, "I want to ask you, like Henry said, to forgive me for hating my daddy. I know it was wrong of me. I'm sorry, God."

Aleta began to cry. I reached over and put my hand on her shoulder. At the touch, she began to shake and sob. She cried for several minutes. I sat with her but said nothing. When I next looked up, Henry was gone.

A CHANGE COMES TO ROSEWOOD'S FAMILY

11

Henry had been at Rosewood most of that day working on a broken wagon wheel. After the talk with Aleta, he kept to himself in the barn. I think he knew he'd said what he had to and now was content to just wait and see what came of it.

It didn't take long either.

Henry was still out in the barn when supper came, but he didn't come in. The rest of us sat down at the table and started eating. Emma was her usual talkative self, and Josepha was carrying on about the food and how she was going to make bread the next morning. I'd told Katie about my conversation with Aleta and what had happened when Henry'd come. I could tell Katie was watching Aleta out of the corner of her eye as we ate.

When we were nearly done, Emma had turned to William and was tending to him, and Josepha had a mouthful of food. So it got quiet for a moment around the table.

When Aleta spoke, her voice was so soft I could hardly make out what she'd said. Katie's eyes opened wide and she turned toward her.

"What was that, Aleta?" she said.

"I want to go home to my daddy," Aleta repeated.

Katie and I looked at each other. I knew both of our

hearts were pounding with joy, but we didn't want to seem too excited all at once.

"All right," said Katie. "Do you want to go now . . . tonight . . . or tomorrow?"

"Maybe tomorrow," answered Aleta.

As soon as supper was over, while Aleta was busying herself with Josepha cleaning up the kitchen, Katie went out to the barn. She told Henry what Aleta had said.

"Praise be ter Jesus!" he said softly. "Dat's good . . . dat be mighty good! Da Lord'll work healin' atween dem now fo' sho'. Dat's real good!"

"When are you going back into town, Henry?" asked Katie.

"Wheneber you like, Miz Kathleen. I kin stay or I kin go."

"Would you like something to eat first?"

"Dat be nice."

"Then when you leave, would you please stop by the church and ask Reverend Hall to come out tomorrow?"

"I's do dat, Miz Kathleen."

"Tell him it's about the girl he has been looking for. But don't tell him anything more," Katie added. "I want to do that myself."

Reverend Hall's buggy drove up to Rosewood a little after ten o'clock the next morning. For once Katie and I were looking forward to seeing him.

I think he noticed a difference in Katie immediately the moment she greeted him. She walked straight up to him like she was a grown woman and in charge of the place.

"Hello, Reverend Hall," she said as he stepped down. "Thank you for coming. Mayme and I—this is Mayme," she added, nodding toward me.

I smiled and offered my hand. He shook it and nodded.

"Hello, Mayme," he said. "I saw you here when I came out once before."

"Yes, sir," I said.

"Mayme and I have to talk to you," said Katie. "Would you come inside?"

"Of course, Kathleen."

Katie led us into the house and we sat down in the parlor. We'd asked the others to stay outside when we talked so that we could be alone in the house, although Aleta was up in her room with the door closed.

"I'm afraid I have an apology to make, Reverend Hall," said Katie once we were seated. "I'm sure you've heard all about us, and my family and everything now that it's all around town."

"Yes, Kathleen. I am very sorry."

"Thank you."

"I was planning to come out to see you. I only heard a few days ago."

"And so you know what we've been doing here?" Katie said.

He nodded.

Katie went on to tell him about Emma and Uncle Templeton and about finding out that she and I were cousins. Reverend Hall took everything in with interest, nodding and commenting occasionally but mostly just listening as Katie told our story.

"I'm afraid I wasn't honest with you," Katie said at last. "We do know about the girl you've been looking for. She's . . . she's here with us."

A strange smile came over the minister's face.

"I halfway suspected as much," he said.

"You did?"

"I had the feeling something more was going on than met the eye."

"Why didn't you say anything?" asked Katie.

"I assumed you had good reason for keeping it from me," Reverend Hall replied. "I knew the truth would come out eventually, and I also knew that it had to come from you. I'm not a man who believes in pushing. Truth, I have always found, is powerful enough on its own to find its way where it needs to go."

"We weren't trying to do wrong, Reverend Hall," said Katie. "Sometimes everything was . . . just very confusing."

"It must have been extremely difficult for the two of you."

"We didn't mean not to tell the truth. But sometimes it just happened and I always felt terrible afterward. Sometimes I got so afraid of what would happen if people found out. And from what Aleta told us about her father, I was afraid for her too. I just didn't know what was best to do."

"I understand, Kathleen. I'm sure God understands too."

"I've asked Him to forgive me."

"Then I know He understands."

"We told Aleta what you said after your last visit. We tried to get her to go home. But she said she would run away if we made her go back to her father. We didn't know what to do."

"Why are you telling me now?" asked the minister.

"Because she is finally ready. She wants to see her father again."

"Oh, that is wonderful news!"

"Tell him what you and Henry said to her, Mayme," said Katie.

I briefly recounted the conversation of the previous day.

The minister smiled.

"That Henry is quite a man," he said. "If the people of Greens Crossing had any idea what kind of spiritual wisdom is in his heart, they would . . ." He began to chuckle. "Well, I don't know what they would do!" he added. The smile gradually faded from his face. "Actually, they would probably resent it," he said. "They would call it uppity. No one wants blacks acting *too* intelligent.—So have you spoken with the girl about actually going home?"

"Yes," replied Katie. "She says she is ready. She says she'll go with you if you'll take her."

"Wonderful. Nothing could make me happier. Hank will be overjoyed."

Again a serious expression came over his face. "What about her mother?" he asked. "What exactly happened? I assume you've not seen her?"

"She's dead, Reverend Hall," replied Katie.

"I feared as much."

"They were riding away, trying to get away from home, and she was thrown from the horse. When Aleta couldn't rouse her, she began wandering and that's how she ended up here. She just appeared one day at the door."

"And you . . ."

"She took me to her mama and told me what had happened. She was dead when I got there."

"And . . ."

"I buried her. I can show you where. It's about three miles from here."

"I see. This will be a terrible grief to the girl's father. But I have to say, having heard nothing from them in so long, it is what I expected. I am just glad to find that Aleta is safe."

He drew in a breath and exhaled.

"Well . . . this is a dreadful tragedy," he said, "though no more than what the two of you have had to endure. These can be terrible times. We must just pray that the Lord will bring healing between father and daughter that will allow them to forgive one another . . . and to forgive themselves."

"Yes, sir," said Katie.

"I would like to talk to her before we go."

"She's upstairs getting ready," I said. "I'll go get her."

I left the parlor and returned a minute or two later with Aleta.

"Aleta," said Katie, "this is Reverend Hall. He knows your papa."

"Hello, Aleta," said the minister with a smile as Aleta sat down beside Katie. "Kathleen and Mayme tell me you would like to go home to your daddy."

"Yes, sir," said Aleta softly.

"Kathleen told me what happened to your mother," he said. "I am very sorry. That must have been terrible for you."

Aleta stared down at the floor.

"It will be very painful for your father too," Reverend Hall went on. "He feels bad for the way he used to be. He will need your help, Aleta."

"My help?" she asked, looking up for the first time.

"That's right."

"How could I . . . help him?"

"By loving him, Aleta. He needs your love to help him overcome his guilt and grief for how he treated you and your mama. Guilt is a terrible burden for a man to bear, Aleta. Only love and forgiveness can give a man the strength to bear up under it. Do you think you can help your daddy? Can you love him?"

"I'll try, sir."

"Good. That is all any of us can do. He loves you very much and has missed you. But we will have to tell him about your mother, and he will need as much of our love as we can give him."

Aleta nodded.

"Are you ready to go home?"

"Yes, sir."

"Good. Why don't you go get your things while I have a few last words with Kathleen and Mayme."

Aleta bounded out of the room and up the stairs.

"As soon as it is practical," Reverend Hall said when she was gone, glancing toward Katie and then toward me, "I would like to bring Hank and Aleta out for a visit, perhaps a meal together."

"Of course," said Katie.

"I want him to meet you and to know what friends you've been to Aleta. And she will need you to continue being her friends. It will be hard for them for a while. She is a growing girl who will need the two of you as much as ever. And, too, I think it will be important for Hank eventually to see his wife's grave. These things have to be completed in our minds. For full healing to take place in his soul, he will need to see where it happened and make his peace with God about it."

Aleta's steps sounded again on the stairs.

"Thank you both," said Reverend Hall. "I know you struggled with what to do, but I think everything will work out for the best in the end. You have been true friends to Aleta. I know her father will be grateful."

He rose as Aleta came into the room holding the few things that had come to be hers.

We all walked outside. Now that the decision had been made, Aleta seemed eager to go. Emma and Josepha were nearby and walked over to Reverend Hall's buggy. We all said good-bye with many hugs.

Aleta stooped down and picked up William, although

he was just about more than she could lift by herself.

"Good-bye, William," she said, giving him a kiss. "You be a good boy."

"Goom-bye, Leeter," he said.

Aleta set him down, climbed up into the carriage beside Reverend Hall, and then they were off.

She kept waving with a smile on her face until they were out of sight. It felt different as we all walked back toward the house. Our family had changed. As glad as we all were that Aleta had decided to go home, her absence made us all quiet and thoughtful for the rest of the day.

BROKEN BUT HEALED FAMILY

12

Two weeks passed before we saw or heard anything from Aleta again. Even with our trouble with Katie's uncle Burchard, we could not help thinking about her all the time and wondering how it was with her father.

Then one Sunday afternoon a buggy came into sight. As soon as it neared the house we heard shouts that we instantly recognized. Before it even came to a stop, Aleta was on the ground and running into our arms with happy hugs and exclamations and tears of greeting. Emma came running out of the house, followed by William toddling along behind calling out, "Leeter . . . Leeter!"

Reverend Hall and another man stepped to the ground and walked toward the scene of the reunion.

"Hello, Kathleen . . . Mayme," said Reverend Hall. "I would like to introduce you to Aleta's father, Hank Butler."

He wasn't anything like what I had expected. He was clean-shaven and well groomed, and a smaller man than Reverend Hall. He had almost a timid expression on his face, like he was embarrassed for what we might think of him after what we'd heard. I think I had expected a mean-looking ogre or something, but he was just a normal and decent-looking man. Yet you could see the grief in his eyes.

Katie went forward and shook his hand. "Hello, Mr. Butler," she said. "I am Kathleen Clairborne."

"I am happy to meet you, Miss Clairborne," said Aleta's father, shuffling back and forth on his feet. "Aleta has told me all you did for her. I want you to know how appreciative I am."

"Thank you," said Katie. "This is my cousin, Mary Ann Daniels," she added, turning toward me.

"That's my friend *Mayme,* Papa," said Aleta. "We all call her Mayme."

"Hello," I said.

"It is good to meet you also, Miss Daniels," said Aleta's father, offering me his hand.

I don't know what I expected, but as he shook my hand he tried to smile. After all Aleta had told us in the beginning about his hatred of blacks, he must have changed. As Katie introduced him to Emma and

Josepha, I wondered what he thought—that his daughter had been living in a colored village for almost two years! But if he did think that, he didn't say anything. Seeing how much Aleta loved all the rest of us, and how much we loved her, couldn't help but have some effect on him I suppose. Maybe he had changed in more ways than just what Reverend Hall had told us about. He seemed to treat Emma, Josepha, and me like we were just regular people.

"Would you like to come inside for some iced tea?" asked Katie.

"That would be very nice, Kathleen," said the minister. "I do apologize for the impromptu visit. Hank and Aleta were at church this morning, and as we were talking afterward, Aleta kept mentioning all of you here and how she missed you. So Hank suggested we ride out to see you . . . and here we are."

"We are so glad you did," said Katie.

"Miz Katie," said Josepha, who had been walking behind but listening to every word, "I cud make us a nice pot er tatters an' fry up a coupla chickens an' make a right nice dinner, maybe wiff sum biscuits fo' everbody."

"Oh no," said Reverend Hall, "we didn't mean to impose on your—"

"Please, Reverend Hall," interrupted Katie, "it would be no imposition whatever. If I know Josepha, there is nothing she would enjoy more than preparing a meal for you."

"Dat's right, Miz Katie!" chimed in Josepha. "An'

maybe Miz Aleta'd jus' like ter hep me like she used ter do."

"Yes, yes . . . please, Papa—can we please stay!"

Reverend Hall laughed. Mr. Butler looked at him with a questioning expression, then smiled and nodded. "I suppose if the reverend ain't in no hurry to get back to town."

"Not at all," replied Reverend Hall.

"Dat's good," said Josepha. "Den I'll jus' git out ter dat hen house an' kill us a coupla fat ol' hens an' get ter pluckin' dem."

She waddled off, happy as could be, as the rest of us walked into the house.

"Papa, Papa!" cried Aleta. "I want to show you my room!"

She grabbed his hand and tugged him toward the stairs.

"This is good," said Reverend Hall when they were gone. "Aleta needed to come here again, and I think Hank did too."

"How has it been?" asked Katie as she offered him a seat at the table while she and I started fixing some tea and put on a pot of water to boil for Josepha.

"Very good," he replied. "Obviously Hank has a great burden of guilt to bear. But Aleta has been wonderfully tender toward him. Somehow the time was right. And I have no doubt that the seeds you and Henry planted in her mind, Mayme," he added, turning toward me, "have helped too. Great healing is taking place, though they still have a long way to go.

They are having to get to know one another all over again. But I am so grateful to God for what He is doing between them."

"We are so glad to hear it!" said Katie. "That is wonderful news. Does he . . . will he want me to show him where the accident happened," she went on, "and where I buried his wife?"

"I don't know," answered the minister. "It may be a little soon for that. I will mention it to him if I get the opportunity."

Our conversation was interrupted by the sound of Aleta's feet running back down the stairway, again followed, though more slowly, by her father.

"Come on, Papa!" cried Aleta, running through the kitchen heedless of the rest of us. "I want to show you the blacksmith's shop where I pounded the hammer to make people think there were grown-ups here!"

Before Mr. Butler even appeared, Aleta was running out the opposite door and outside. Laughing, he hurried after her.

A minute or two later we heard the familiar *clang, clang, clang* from Aleta's hammer.

"So that was what I heard when I came out here!" said Reverend Hall.

Now it was Katie and I who burst out laughing.

"We had all kinds of schemes to make it seem like we weren't alone," said Katie. "We built fires in the slave cabins and sometimes I even dressed up and pretended to be my mama. It wasn't honest, but I was so afraid of what would happen if people found out. I was afraid they would make Mayme leave and worried what my uncle would do."

Katie paused and sighed. "I suppose all that didn't do any good anyway," she said. "He found out anyway and now he's going to own Rosewood before long."

"Yes, I have heard," said Reverend Hall. "But what about your other uncle, the one who was here for a while?"

"He's gone," said Katie. "We haven't heard from him in a long time. And he couldn't help anyway, since he is from my mama's side of the family."

"Ah yes . . . I see. Well, if there is anything I can do, please let me know."

While we were drinking our tea a little while later, and Emma and I were cutting up potatoes, and Aleta was chattering away telling her father everything she could think of about her time at Rosewood, Josepha came in with two headless, plucked chickens and put them in the pot to boil. Then she and Aleta set about mixing up the biscuits, and before long the kitchen began to smell like good things were coming.

"There is certainly a difference in a woman's kitchen, isn't there, Reverend?" said Mr. Butler.

"It is a wonderful thing to behold indeed!" laughed Reverend Hall. "I can see why you call this a family, Kathleen," he added, glancing about at all the activity, "and why Aleta was so fond of you all. There is truly life here!"

"There wasn't at first," said Katie. "I'll never forget that day when I first saw Mayme. My family was all dead. There was blood everywhere, not all of it even completely dry. Mayme's family had just been killed too. There were no more of our people left to die, and it seemed that death was all we knew."

The kitchen fell silent in the midst of Katie's reflections.

"Then Emma came," Katie continued, "because they were trying to kill her, and Aleta was alone after her mother—"

She paused and glanced across the table.

"I'm sorry, Mr. Butler."

"That's quite all right, Miss Clairborne. Go ahead. I want to hear what you were going to say."

"I was just going to say that death is what brought Aleta to us too. It was almost like death was the only thing we had in common right at first. With everyone except for Josepha."

"Dat mistress ob mine, she'd a killed me effen she cud!" piped up Josepha from the other side of the room.

We all laughed. But Katie continued, still in a serious tone.

"There were times back then when I didn't know if I could stand it another day," she said. "It was so horrible, so sad, and I was afraid of what would become of us. Even though my uncle's going to take Rosewood away, we were all so happy together. You're right, Reverend Hall . . . we are a family."

"God has been good to you—that is obvious," he replied. "He has brought life out of death, as He always does. That is what our faith in Christ is all about, and you are living examples of it."

He turned to Mr. Butler. "And He is bringing life back to your home, is He not, Hank?"

Mr. Butler nodded, but again I saw the look of pain in his eyes. "It is nice to have Aleta home," he said. "And you all must have taught her well. Sometimes she is as busy in our kitchen as you are here—aren't you, Aleta?"

"Yes, Papa.—I fix all Papa's meals, Katie!"

"How old are you now, Aleta?" asked Reverend Hall.

"Eleven, sir."

"Eleven already! You will be a lady soon."

"She just had a birthday last week," added her father. "Although she had to bake her own cake!"

"What kin' you make, chil'?" asked Josepha.

"Chocolate."

"Dat soun' mighty good, all right!"

Aleta went over and stood behind her father.

"Dese yere hens an' biscuits be nearly dun," said Josepha. "How 'bout dem taters, Emma?"

"Dey's ready too, Josepha."

"Den I reckon hit's time dat y'all git washed up 'cuz we's nearly ready wiff dis dinner."

As we sat down around the table a few minutes later, steam rising from several platters of hot food in front of us, I realized that this was the first big meal like this we'd had, with guests and everything, since we'd been together. Was this how life used to be all the time on big plantations for white folks? And here we were sitting down together, four whites and four blacks, like there was nothing unusual about it at all. Mrs. Hammond would probably have been scandalized!

It got quiet and everyone unconsciously looked toward Reverend Hall. He bowed his head and closed his eyes and we all did the same.

"Our Father," he began to pray, "in the midst of the grief that these, your precious children, have endured, and the pain of death that has touched them so closely, we are thankful to you this day for your great love, which touches us even in the midst of life's anguish. We thank you that you always bring life out of death, good out of failure, healing out of heartache. Though it is sometimes hard to see, you are a good Father, whose goodness to your children will always find a way to get into our lives if only we will look for it. So we thank you for the goodness you have brought to every life represented at this table. Death has touched us, but your goodness is always greater, and will always triumph. We give you thanks for the healing that is taking place between Aleta and Hank in the midst of their loss, and even guilt, for you will reunite them one day again with their beloved Sarah. Make their lives whole again in you. We give you thanks for the new life represented by little William, and pray for a bright future for him and his mama Emma. We thank you for what you have accomplished here at Rosewood between these dear ones to make them a family, and we now pray for your guidance and your will to be done with Rosewood, and in Kathleen's life and Josepha's and Mayme's as this change in circumstance comes to them. May your will be done for us all, heavenly Father, and may we always give you thanks in our hearts for the goodness of that will. Amen."

As we opened our eyes, I could see on Emma's and Josepha's face the same thing I felt in my heart—a quiet joy to have had a minister pray for us like that. It felt good knowing that people cared about me, like I knew everyone around this table did.

And that God cared about us all too.

DEVASTATING NEWS

13

The last person we'd have expected, and certainly the last person we'd have wanted to change our future was Mrs. Elfrida Hammond. But unfortunately she was the one who brought the terrible news to us.

One day she rode up to Rosewood in her buggy. I think she was just looking for an excuse to come out to see the place ever since learning that Katie's family was dead. The whole time she was there, which wasn't long, she kept looking around like she was trying to see something strange that she might gossip about when she went back to town.

Katie walked out to meet her.

"Hello, Mrs. Hammond," said Katie, trying to sound friendly. Judging from the look on the woman's face, Katie's smile was lost on her. I walked over toward the buggy and she glanced my way with her hawk eyes. I had the feeling that she wanted to talk to Katie without me listening, but I didn't want Katie to be in an awkward position and so I went right over and stood a few feet away. It was obvious that Mrs. Hammond was annoyed.

"I brought out a letter that came, Kathleen," she said. "It arrived a while back, and since it was addressed to your mama, I thought I should wait and give it to her. But, of course, now . . ."

Katie waited. For a few seconds Mrs. Hammond just kept sitting there in her buggy.

"It's from that Daniels fellow that was here," she said after a bit.

"Uncle Templeton!" shrieked Katie. "Where is it . . . where's the letter?"

"I told you, I have it right here."

"Give it to me, then . . . please, Mrs. Hammond."

"But I told you—it's addressed to your mother. So I—"

"Mrs. Hammond," interrupted Katie with as insistent a voice as I'd ever heard come out of her mouth. "You had no right to keep that letter, whoever it's addressed to! It might be important. Now give it to me . . . please!"

Taken aback by Katie's raised voice and flaming eyes, Mrs. Hammond fumbled a minute with the bag sitting beside her on the seat, then took out a white envelope and handed it down to Katie.

Katie stepped forward and grabbed it without even saying *Thank you*.

"It *is* from Uncle Templeton, Mayme!" she said,

turning toward me as she hurriedly scanned the enve- lope. "But it's addressed to *Rosalind Clairborne,* just like she said. Come on, let's go inside and read it."

"But, Kathleen . . ." came Mrs. Hammond's flustered voice behind us.

Katie didn't even slow down and I followed her inside the kitchen. Katie ripped open the envelope and sat down at the table, just about the same time as we heard the buggy turn around and leave.

"Maybe he wrote it before he knew about your ma," I said, sitting down beside her.

"I don't think so, Mayme," said Katie. "It's addressed to you and me."

"Read it out loud," I said.

"Dear Kathleen and Mary Ann," Katie began,

"I wrote Rosalind's name on the envelope, because I didn't want that nosey lady at the general store who distributes the mail to get too curious. I know that's a little bit of a gamble, but I didn't want her asking too many questions and I thought a letter from me to you, Kathleen, might do that and I wanted to make sure your secret was safe. I sure hope she doesn't get too nosey and open this up— she'd know everything then! I just hope you get this letter, because I'm in a little bit of trouble and I didn't want either of you to think I'd deserted you again. Truth is, I think about you both every day and I'd have been back with you a long time ago if I could have been.

"I told you that I had some old things to take care of. I haven't always been the most upright man in the world, which I'm ashamed to admit to you two more than I would be to anyone. It's not that I've ever stolen money or anything like that, but I've done enough to make a few people hate me, and I suppose they had a right to. One of those is a pretty powerful and important man in these parts. I was intending to go see him and try to work something out to pay him back the money he thinks I swindled out of him a few years back. But before I could do anything, some of his men spotted me even before I got to town. They grabbed me and took me to the sheriff, and before I knew it I was sitting in jail.

"Well, the long and the short of it is, that's where I am now. I been trying to tell them that I came back to make things right. But they don't believe me, and as I've got no money to show I'm telling the truth, the sheriff's determined to keep me here. It doesn't help that the sheriff was in a poker game with me once and didn't come out so good.

"I'll get it worked out and be back as soon as I can. But I've got to find some way to convince them that I've changed and that I mean what I say that I'll pay back every dime, even if it takes me the rest of my life. Until then, I want to tell you how sorry I am that I didn't come back soon like I said I would. But you two've been running the place all this time without me, so I imagine you're

doing just fine. I love you both more than I can tell you.

"I'll be back just as soon as I can get out of here.
"Your uncle and papa,
"Templeton Daniels"

To hear him say he loved us like that, and to hear the word *papa,* couldn't help but bring tears to my eyes. But Katie wasn't thinking quite such sentimental thoughts. For once she was the practical one.

"Oh no!" she moaned, setting the letter down on the table. "What are we going to do, Mayme? I was so sure he would come back in time to save Rosewood from Uncle Burchard. But now what are we going to do!"

"Why don't we write back to him," I said, "or maybe go see him ourselves!" I added, suddenly excited about the idea that had just come to me. "Why couldn't we tell the sheriff that what he says is true?"

"Yes . . . yes, that's a great idea, Mayme!" exclaimed Katie, grabbing the letter again and scanning it from top to bottom. But gradually a worried look replaced her expression of excitement. She turned the sheet over, then picked up the envelope from the table and looked at it again.

"There's just one problem, Mayme," she said. "There's nothing that says where he mailed it from. There's nothing on the envelope but *Templeton Daniels.* There's no place or town or return address or anything."

"Maybe Mrs. Hammond would know," I suggested.

"She couldn't know either," said Kate. "Mail comes from all over and she just gets a bag full that might be from anywhere. Unless something's written on the envelope, she's got no more way of knowing than we do."

I picked up the envelope and looked at it. Everything was just like Katie'd said.

"What's that little mark over the stamp?" I said. "It looks like some kind of writing."

I handed it to Katie and she squinted as she looked at it.

"I don't know," she said. "I can't tell if it says anything. It's too faint. It doesn't look like anything."

We sat a few minutes thinking.

"And you don't remember your mama ever saying anything, or hearing your uncle say anything himself about where he was or had been or where he lived or anything?" I asked after a while.

Katie shook her head. "No," she said. "I don't remember hearing anything except that he and Uncle Ward had gone to California and that then he had come back, just like he told us."

"I don't know what to do, then," I said.

"What else can we do but wait," said Katie, "and hope he comes back?"

"But what if we're gone before he does?" I said. "Your other uncle isn't going to wait—that's for sure."

14

T he letter from my papa changed everything. Now there was no hope left, it seemed. When Katie's seventeenth birthday came in May, she was too sad even to let us have a party for her, though Josepha baked a cake.

As the time got closer to when Katie's uncle Burchard said he was going to take over Rosewood, he came around almost every day and acted like the place already belonged to him. He never spoke to any of the rest of us, only Katie sometimes. When he happened to look at me or Emma or Josepha, though he ignored us, you couldn't help thinking that he hated us at the same time. I still can't figure what it is inside a person that could make them hate someone else. I've spent a life-time trying to figure it out, but never have.

Sometimes the man named Mr. Sneed came with him too. He carried a leather briefcase and papers and things and didn't pay any more attention to any of the rest of us than Mr. Clairborne did. The two men walked around the place keeping to themselves, talking and writing things down and making lists. I heard the word *inventory* once, at least I think that was the word, though I didn't know what it meant.

But most of the time when Mr. Clairborne came he went upstairs to Katie's mama's office, sometimes with tools, and we'd hear banging and clanking and hammering and other noises coming from inside. Once he came with a man in a buggy that said "Locksmith" on the side of it. Katie and I watched through the crack in the door as the man tried spinning the dial back and forth and muttering various numbers to himself. "*Right* thirty-seven, *left* twenty-eight, *right* twenty-nine . . ." and even tried opening the safe with some sort of drill, but as far as Katie and I could tell, nothing he did seemed to work, and more often than not Katie's uncle would come back down the stairs angry and swearing and muttering to himself.

One day Katie decided to try to open the safe herself. She was desperate, and it was all she could think to try. Katie told me she remembered enough bits of her parents' conversations over the years to know they feared Burchard might try to take the plantation from them, but Katie said she didn't know why.

"I wish I could see that deed with my own eyes," Katie said, hoping there was still some way out of our predicament.

We even looked in the cellar one night, thinking that if her mother had hidden the gold there, she might have hidden the deed there as well. But we quickly realized that the damp, musty hole was not a likely place to keep such an important piece of paper.

One morning Katie took my hand and led me up the stairs.

"I'm going to try to open the safe, Mayme," she whispered. "Maybe I can find something that will help us."

"But, Katie, if the locksmith couldn't open it . . ."

"I know. But it's worth a try. You stand there by the window and watch for my uncle."

The picture was already off the wall from her uncle's latest attempt with the safe. Katie stood in the middle of the office and stared at it. She told me later she was trying to remember if she'd ever seen her mother or father open it. She did remember something . . . some memory of her father and mother talking in hushed tones. Katie thought they might have been talking about Burchard . . . and . . . someone else, another uncle . . . Uncle Templeton maybe? But she didn't think so.

Katie reached up and touched the dial, then quickly drew her hand back.

"How does it work?" I asked.

"I think you move it first one way, then the other, and back and forth like that. You have to stop on certain numbers."

"How do you know the numbers?"

"I don't know. I guess you have to memorize them. I wonder what numbers my mama and daddy would have used."

Katie's uncle Burchard had already scoured the place looking for a written combination—we knew that much. But he'd found nothing.

"They would have used some numbers that they'd never forget," said Katie. "What about . . . maybe their wedding anniversary? It was October 1, 1844." She excitedly began turning the dial. "Let's see. Ten," she said, then stopped. "One . . . and forty-four."

"What's supposed to happen now?" I asked when she stopped and withdrew her hand.

"I don't know, I think the door is supposed to open."

She tried the handle, but it was still locked. Katie exhaled a long sigh of disappointment.

"Try something else," I said, my own excitement growing.

"But what, Mayme?"

"I don't know . . . how about somebody's birthday?"

"Mayme, that's a great idea!" exclaimed Katie, bounding forward again. "Let's see, my daddy's birthday was December thirteenth . . . oh, but I forget what year he was born . . . hmm, was it eighteen-nineteen? I think so. I'll try that."

Again she began turning the dial with trembling fingers. But still the handle was locked.

"Uh . . . maybe my mother's," she said and tried again. But yet again the door didn't budge.

"It's no use," she sighed. "Why would it be a birthday . . . how could I possibly know what numbers they used?"

"Can they pick any numbers they want?" I asked.

"I don't know," said Katie. "I figured they could . . . but maybe not."

"What about yours?" I suggested.

"Why mine?"

"I don't know—you just had your birthday—maybe they thought of it just like I did. Maybe they got the safe after you were born. I don't know. Try it, Katie."

Again Katie reached out toward the dial. "Okay, then, May fourteenth, eighteen-fifty, so that's five . . . fourteen . . . fifty."

As she reached the last number we both heard a *click* inside the door of the safe. "Oh!" exclaimed Katie, drawing in a breath of surprise. "What was that?"

"Maybe that's it," I said. "Try the door!"

Katie tried to turn the handle, and this time it gave way. The door of the safe swung open toward her.

"Mayme!" she said in astonishment. "We did it!"

Then she paused and tears came to her eyes. "They used my birthday, Mayme," she said. "They used *my* birthday to hide their most important things."

"They must have loved you a lot, Katie . . . I know they did."

It was quiet a minute, and I knew she was missing her mama and papa all over again. But then finally she took a deep breath, straightened her shoulders, and stepped closer to the safe, swung the heavy door all the way open, and began to look inside the dim metal chamber.

Within a minute she was pulling out papers and envelopes and spreading them out on the desk.

"Help me look, Mayme. See if you see anything with the word *deed* on it."

Together we dug through the pile. Katie found birth certificates for each of her brothers and herself. She opened a small leather box and there was a beautiful ring inside with a red stone.

"Oh, Mayme! This ruby ring was my grandmother Daniels'. I forgot all about it. Mama showed it to me once and told me it would be mine when I came of age." Katie pulled the ring from the box and tried it on her finger. It was too big for her, so she pushed it onto her thumb for safekeeping. "Well, this surely doesn't belong to Uncle Burchard," she said.

We looked for another few minutes but found no trace of the deed. Then Katie's hurried search stopped. Suddenly her hand went to her heart as she picked up a large yellowed envelope. Written on the outside in old-fashioned script were the words, *Last Will and Testament*. Slowly she opened it. As she did, a single sheet of paper fell out. Two other folded documents remained inside. She picked up the paper and looked at it.

"This is my daddy's handwriting," she said, then began to read it aloud in a soft voice:

"To whom it may concern:

"With this letter, you will find the Last Will and Testament of my father, Adam Clairborne. In it, my father bequeathed the home and plantation known as Rosewood, County of Shenandoah, North Carolina, to me, Richard Clairborne, rather than to my elder brother and his eldest son, Burchard Clairborne. His reasons for doing so, I will in this letter attempt to explain.

"However, this present will, written in my father's own hand, though signed by him, was not witnessed by legal counsel prior to his death. In this same envelope you will also find his original will, drawn up some forty years ago, which names Burchard as

my father's heir. Because of these irregularities, a new deed for the property was drawn up and put into effect. However this deed for Rosewood is not in my name. It has been—"

Suddenly Katie's voice stopped. We glanced at each other with wide eyes. Heavy footsteps had just sounded on the stairs.

"Oh, Katie!" I whispered in alarm. "I'm sorry . . . I forgot to watch the window like you told me!"

Already Katie was scooping all the papers into her hands and stuffing them back into the safe. I ran to the hallway, thinking that maybe I could delay Mr. Clairborne. But he walked right past me without even looking at me. Katie had just closed the door of the safe when he walked in but hadn't had a chance to spin the dial to lock it again. When she heard his boots, she pulled her hand away and whirled around.

"Kathleen . . ." he said, "what are you doing in here?"

Katie stared back at him, and from where I stood in the doorway, I could see the guilt written all over her face.

He walked toward the desk and quickly surveyed its surface, then glanced over at Katie where she still stood beside the safe.

"I asked you a question," he said.

"Uh . . . just reminiscing, Uncle Burchard," Katie replied.

Her hesitant manner must have aroused his suspicion. He turned from the desk and walked toward her, then stopped right in front of her. He looked down at her with a mean look on his face. From where he was standing, he could have reached out and turned the safe handle right then and pulled the door open. Then his eyes drifted toward it.

"What have you been up to?" he asked slowly. "Are you getting curious about that safe there?"

I saw Katie force a smile on her face. "Uh, yes, Uncle Burchard," she said, like she was admitting something mighty foolish. "I was just thinking of giving it a try myself."

Oh no, Katie, I winced. *What did you go and tell him that for!*

But Mr. Clairborne seemed kind of amused, then began to chuckle. "You think you can open it when I couldn't!"

"I suppose it was a pretty silly idea," said Katie. "But suppose I did want to," she added, turning her back toward him and facing the safe. "What do you do— would I just turn the dial . . . like this?" She reached up and spun the dial a few times.

"That's right, missy—that's all you do!" laughed her uncle. "But just remember, anything you find in there is mine."

Katie kept spinning the dial. Then I saw her try the handle. I could tell she was nervous, and that she breathed a quiet sigh of relief when it didn't open.

"You don't even know how a combination lock works, do you, girl?" laughed her uncle.

"I guess not, Uncle Burchard. It was silly of me."

89

"Sometimes I don't know how you kept this place running, Kathleen," said Mr. Clairborne. "Didn't your mama and daddy teach you anything?"

Not to trust you, I thought to myself.

But Katie only shrugged and said, "Not enough, I guess." Then she turned and left the room and we walked downstairs together.

Downstairs, we talked quietly in the kitchen, all the while listening for Mr. Clairborne to come back down.

"At least you found out that Rosewood was supposed to belong to your papa and not to your uncle Burchard," I whispered.

"But I don't think it helps us, Mayme. If my uncle finds those papers, all he'd have to do is burn the new will and show the original one to Mr. Sneed. Daddy even said the deed wasn't in his name. I wonder why."

"Does that mean your uncle Burchard's name is on it?"

"I don't know, Mayme. I didn't even see anything in there called a deed. Wherever it is, let's just hope he doesn't get his hands on it."

FROM OUT OF THE PAST

15

We didn't know it at the time, of course, but about the same time all this was going on, a man was walking down the boardwalk of a busy street.

He paused at a store window to look at a pair of boots.

However, it was the stack of newspapers in a stand next to the window that caught his eye a minute or two later. He had merely looked toward it, absently glancing at the headlines. Then suddenly a brief article at the bottom of the page arrested his attention. The single word "Rosewood" jumped off the page and jolted him between the eyes. He grabbed the top paper and read the article even as he walked inside the store to pay for it.

By the time he emerged back out onto the street two or three minutes later, a sober expression had come to the man's face—sadness tinged with a shadow of guilt.

He knew what he had to do. And apparently he had better waste no time doing it.

FINAL NOTICE
16

A day finally came when Katie's uncle Burchard arrived, and he wasn't alone. There were several wagons and three or four other men following him.

We watched as they rumbled toward the back of the house and stopped by the barn. They all got down and Mr. Clairborne began pointing and giving orders to his men. One of them went and opened the barn doors, and for the rest of the day they were moving equipment around, taking some things out of the barn and putting in the new equipment they'd brought with them. More wagons arrived the next day, and for the rest of the week, full of machines and contraptions the likes of which I'd never seen in my life. By the end of that week, Rosewood was starting to look mighty different. Yet we didn't really have much choice but to go on with our work every day like always. We had to eat, and the cows had to be milked, and the pigs and chickens had to be fed. So we ignored the men, and the men ignored us. But it was almighty strange and sure didn't seem like it could go on forever.

We hardly ever talked anymore. Even Katie and I didn't talk. All we could do was look at each other and sigh, or look away to keep from crying. We didn't know what was going to happen. We had to do something . . . but what? In my own mind, I was trying to get up the gumption to talk to Emma and Josepha because I knew we would have to leave. But I just didn't have the courage to break Katie's heart again.

Then for a couple of days none of the men were around at all. I reckon it was their days off and maybe they'd gone back home. The place suddenly seemed so quiet!

Then Monday came and about the middle of the morning Katie's uncle rode in. He was alone this time. He went straight toward the house to talk to Katie. I wandered toward them. He glanced in my direction but didn't say anything. I guess he figured it didn't matter what I heard or didn't hear.

"I been patient with you, Kathleen," he said. "But it's just about over now."

"What do you mean, Uncle Burchard?" asked Katie.

"I mean that this is the end of things like they are. I filed all the papers and I've waited the sixty days. We both know your ma or nobody else is going to contest it because they can't. So this Friday the court order will take effect and Rosewood will become mine."

"This . . . *Friday?*" said Katie in a trembling voice.

"This Friday," said her uncle again. "I've tried to be fair, Kathleen, but Rosewood should have been mine a long time ago, and so on Friday it will be."

"What will happen then, Uncle Burchard?"

"Mr. Sneed will come out, with witnesses, of course, and will formally deliver the papers and enforce the court order. No contesting claims being made at that time, he will sign and issue a new deed to the property in my name—he is having it drawn up this week—and then Rosewood will be mine."

I stood there stock-still. It was deathly quiet. Finally Katie seemed to realize that there was nothing she could do to stop what was going to happen. I knew she was struggling, but could also see that she was determined not to cry in front of her uncle.

"What . . . what about everybody else?" said Katie after a minute. Her voice was so soft I could barely make out the words.

"Look, Kathleen," said her uncle. "I've been as patient as I can be. I gave you fair warning. I told you weeks ago to get rid of them. I don't want no darkies or kids around here. And come ten o'clock Friday morning, there won't be any, even if I have to pack them up and haul them off the property myself. Do you understand—if they ain't gone, then I'll pack them up myself."

"What . . . what about me, Uncle Burchard?"

"Why are you asking me these same questions all over again?" he said in exasperation. "I told you before, you can stay. You can do whatever you want, but I won't throw you out. You're kin and I reckon that counts for something. It's no nevermind to me what you do just as long as the rest of them are out of here by Friday."

"But, Uncle Burchard," said Katie, "Mayme's . . . Mayme's kin too."

"Who's Mayme?" he asked with a puzzled expression.

Katie glanced toward me.

He turned his head and his eyes came to rest on me where I was standing about thirty feet away. This time I did not so much feel hatred in his expression as disgust.

"Her?" he said after a few seconds, then turned back to Katie.

Katie nodded.

"What do you mean, she's kin?"

"My other uncle, my mama's brother . . . he's Mayme's daddy."

"The fellow that went to California?"

"No, my other uncle."

"The dandy?"

"I reckon," answered Katie.

"Yeah, I heard of him. Richard told me. A no-good

drifter, the way I heard it. What you're telling me is that he knocked up some slave of your pa's?"

Katie's eyes stung with tears and she couldn't answer.

"Can't imagine why your pa didn't horsewhip him, the trash. Well, none of that matters nothing to me. No bastard half-black girl's kin of mine, whatever your mama's side of the family wants to call such trash. You get rid of her with the others, you hear, Kathleen? You got till Friday. Then this place is mine, and they'll be gone one way or another."

He turned and walked to his horse, mounted, and rode away.

Katie and I just stood there for another minute, then slowly walked toward each other and embraced. There was nothing to say. I held Katie for the longest time while she cried. I was too angry to cry. Maybe I'd cry sometime later, but on that day I was angry. Katie was about the sweetest girl in all the world. How could anyone, let alone her own uncle, be so mean to her!

A DIFFICULT FAMILY TALK

17

Katie hardly said anything the rest of the day. If I'd thought it was quiet before, it was really silent now. She just sat and stared, or walked around with a blank expression on her face.

But by the next morning, a new look had come into

her eyes—a look of determination, like she'd made some kind of decision.

She got us all around the table in the kitchen as we were eating breakfast, and I knew she wanted to talk to us.

"Sit down, please, Josepha," she said as Josepha continued to bustle about with milk and bread and butter and eggs.

"I's jes' be gittin' dese eggs—"

"Josepha, please," said Katie in an insistent tone. "The eggs can wait. I want you to sit down and listen. I have to talk to all of you."

It was the first time Katie had ever spoken to her in that tone, and it seemed almost to shock Josepha. She put down what was in her hand and slowly walked to the table and eased herself into a chair. The rest of us were silent. We knew it was serious.

I looked around at all of us sitting there. Katie was so grown-up now. My, how she had changed since that first day! I wondered if I had changed as much in her eyes. Emma had grown-up some too. She wasn't nearly so scatterbrained as I'd thought her at first. Maybe that showed that I'd changed as much as her. William was sitting in the chair next to her on top of a box. He was playing with a string ball—unwinding it and then winding it up, over and over again. And next to him sat Josepha—a bit nervous, I could tell. She was always fine just so long as she was busy serving and helping others. But she didn't like to just sit still.

I guess I was pretty grown-up too. We weren't just a parcel of kids anymore. I suppose if someone had walked in right then and seen Katie talking to the four of us coloreds, they'd have thought she was our mistress giving her workers their instructions for the day. But how different from that it really was! We were a family.

"I . . . I don't know what to say," Katie finally began softly. "My uncle said that Rosewood will become his this Friday . . . so I guess . . . I guess it's over for us. I don't know what to do . . . it doesn't seem like there *is* anything to do. I . . . I want you to know . . ."

She tried to look around the table at each of us. The look on her face, with those big eyes of hers, was so sad, it was hard to return her look. She tried to smile.

"I just want you to know . . . that I love you all so much," she went on. "I don't know what I'd have done without all of you. . . ."

She glanced away. Emma was crying by now. I don't think Josepha was too far behind.

"But he says," Katie said, taking in a deep breath and struggling to continue, "he's going . . . to make you all leave. I'm so sorry . . . I don't have any choice. He's going to be the owner on Friday, and . . . I don't know what to do!"

At last Katie looked away and broke into tears.

"But what we gwine do, Miz Katie?" blubbered Emma through her tears. "I ain't got no place ter go!"

I saw that Katie couldn't reply. She felt terrible about what she was saying to us, but helpless too. It was killing her inside.

"It's all right, Emma," I said finally. "We're all family now, and it's not this house or this land that makes us a family but each other. So I won't let anything happen to you. I've already decided that I'm going north somewhere, you and me and William. We'll find some other coloreds somewhere—they'll take us in. You don't need to worry about a thing."

"Don't fergit 'bout me, Miz Mayme," said Josepha. "I's be goin' wiff you too, 'cuz I can't stay here neither, an' I shure ain't 'bout ter crawl back ter dat Mistress McSimmons, nohow."

"You see, Emma," I said. "We'll be all right together, and Josepha and I—we'll help you take care of William. Everything will be fine."

It was silent for a while. Katie managed to stop crying, and I saw that look of determination coming over her face again, though it was filled with sadness at the same time.

"Mayme," she began again, looking up at me, "you're right—we're a family. And not just you and Emma and Josepha. I'm part of your family too."

"Oh, Katie, I know!" I said. "You're the one that brought us all together. I only meant—"

"I know, Mayme," she interrupted. "I know what you meant. But, please, let me finish. What I was going to say is that if we are a family—*all* of us—then, why can't we all leave together? I don't want to stay here by myself. I could never stay here alone, with just my uncle Burchard and his workers. It won't be my home

98

anymore, and with all of you gone, well . . . it's just like you said, home isn't *here* . . . my home is with *you*. So I'm going with you."

We all looked at each other in surprise. My heart leapt to think that Katie would give up her life on a big plantation just to be with us. But almost as quickly I came to my senses.

"We'll be traveling around, Katie," I said. "We'll have to live with coloreds."

"If I can take you into my home, surely coloreds will take me into theirs," she said. "And besides, we've got money . . . we can pay."

"It isn't the money, Katie," I said. "It's just . . . a colored life is different than a white life. Sure, they would take you in . . . but . . . it's different . . . it's—"

"It jes' ain' dun, Miz Katie," put in Josepha. "Dat's what Miz Mayme's tryin' ter say. Jes' wouldn't be right, dat's all."

"But why, Josepha?" said Katie. "*Why* wouldn't it be right? Blacks don't mind what color anyone is, do they?"

Again it was quiet. Josepha didn't have an answer. But I knew what she meant.

It would be hard, maybe one of the hardest things I'd ever done. But I knew what I had to say.

"Katie," I began, "this . . . this life here at Rosewood—you've let us all live a dream. That's what it's been like, a dream come true. You've been kinder than anyone could have ever been. You've shared everything with us and even let us feel that in a little way Rosewood belonged to us too. You've let us live like whites and you've treated us with respect and kindness. You're just about the most wonderful person in the whole world, and you know how much I love you. I won't ever forget what you've done for me, and I know Emma and Josepha won't either, or Aleta, though she's already gone."

I paused. Katie was starting to cry again and it was all I could do to keep from crying myself.

"But, Katie," I continued, "this isn't like the rest of the world really is. Like I said, this is a dream. Even if we call ourselves a family, and even if you and I are cousins and kin, the fact is, you are white and I am black. Emma and Josepha are black. Nothing can change that, and life will always be different for us. Life is different for coloreds, Katie."

"Miz Mayme's right, Miz Katie," nodded Josepha. "Dat's what I wuz tryin' ter say. Dis here's been da bes' time er my life too, but you's white an' dat makes things different fer you."

"This has been the most wonderful time of my life too, Katie," I said. "But down inside I knew it wouldn't last. You know that, because that's why I tried to leave a couple times."

"But I still don't see what any of this has to do with me," moaned Katie. "We can leave together and keep being a family."

"Katie," I said, "you have a life ahead of you, and you've got to live it. You can do things that we will never be able to do. You can go to school and you will meet a young man someday and get married and have children and maybe have another nice house of your own. None of that will happen if you come with us. We don't have a future like that, and no white person traveling around and living with coloreds can either. They would call you poor white trash, Katie. And even if it means leaving you, I would never let that happen to you. You have no idea how coloreds live. Emma and I and Josepha, we know what it's like to be black. We can handle it. But I don't want you to have to live that kind of hard life. I want you to have the kind of life you deserve. And you can't have it if you come with us."

My words even sobered Emma. And I think I'd finally gotten through to Katie. Our hearts were all breaking to realize that in a few days we were all going to have to say good-bye to each other. But I think at last Katie realized it too. I just hoped she knew it wasn't because I didn't love her that I'd said what I did, but because I knew what was best for her.

I don't think anyone could love a friend more than I loved Katie.

After another minute, without saying anything more, she got up and walked outside.

18

I hardly talked to Katie the rest of that day. I saw her in the distance walking about the place and I knew what she was doing. She was thinking about all the times we'd shared here. I have to admit, I had been doing a lot of that lately too. And if I wasn't mistaken, Katie probably spent an hour or two in her secret place in the woods, probably praying. I spent quite a bit of the day on and off in prayer too, and reliving all over again—from that horrible day we met, Katie in a daze with blood on her nightgown, and me having no idea what kind of place I'd stumbled into, right down to the day not so very long ago when we'd found out that we were cousins.

There were so many memories! As horrible as it was to lose our families tragically like we had, I would never say that it was *worth it* to get to know Katie, but getting to know her and having a best friend and cousin like that almost made up for the grief and pain. *Nothing* could ever make up for losing a mama. That was a heartache Katie and I would always share, that we would never see our mamas again in this life.

But we had each other, and that sure helped!

Or at least it *had* helped. It looked like that was going to be taken away from us too. But nothing could take away the memories . . . or the friendship. And somehow, even if we were separated, I knew we would always be friends. Nothing could change that.

The next morning Katie came downstairs all dressed up and said she was going into town. I didn't ask why. I knew Katie would tell me when she was ready to. Even Emma didn't say anything and wasn't blabbing so much anymore. She too seemed to realize something special was coming to an end. We were all close to tears. We couldn't help it.

Katie left for town in the small buggy and all the rest of us quietly kept to ourselves. We didn't know what else to do but to keep puttering around with our chores. It didn't seem like there was much use in doing anything, but what else could we do? And cows had to be milked twice a day no matter what. But we couldn't help thinking that whatever Katie was doing in town, it must have something to do with our own fate.

When she got to Greens Crossing the first place she went was to the bank. She said Mr. Taylor didn't seem surprised to see her and wasn't particularly friendly.

"So, Kathleen," he said in a snappy voice, "you were lying to me all along every time I asked you about your mother."

"I'm sorry, Mr. Taylor," said Katie. "I didn't know what else to do. We had to have money to keep Rosewood going. Maybe it was wrong of me . . . but I didn't know what else to do."

"Well, a lot of good it did you. As I understand it, you are going to lose it now anyway."

"That's why I want to take out all our money."

He looked at her as if she must be joking. I guess bankers don't like people taking all their money out of their banks.

"Take it out . . . all of it?"

"Yes, sir."

"But why?"

"I need it."

"*Need* it . . . need it for what?"

"All right, then, maybe I just want it. And maybe what I want it for is my own business."

"You must know, Kathleen, that technically it's not really your money at all. The account is in your mother and father's name."

"But they're dead, Mr. Taylor. Who else could the money belong to but me? Besides, I'm the one who brought you the money from our cotton, and from the gold. My mama didn't give it to you, I did. And I want it back."

"Yes, well . . . yes, that makes a certain amount of sense," he said, a little annoyed at her attitude, Katie thought, but what else could he do? "I, uh . . . I'll check your account," he said.

He rose and left Katie sitting at his desk. When he returned a minute later, he seemed to have recovered a little of his poise.

"The balance in the account is two hundred and seventeen dollars," he said, sitting down again. "How much of that do you need?"

"I told you, Mr. Taylor," said Katie. "I want it all."

"But what could you possibly want with all that money?"

"That's my own business," said Katie. "If Rosewood is going to be taken away from me, at least I want the money Mayme and I made ourselves. It's ours, Mr. Taylor. I just want to make sure that my uncle doesn't somehow get his hands on it. And we might need it to live on when we have to move away from Rosewood."

"It was my understanding that you would be staying."

"I don't know, Mr. Taylor. But I want to withdraw our money . . . all of it."

The bank manager stared back at Katie for another few seconds. Finally he seemed to realize how serious she was. He sighed and rose again. When he came back three or four minutes later, he was carrying an envelope full of twenty- and ten-dollar bills and some smaller money to make up the total.

"Here it is, Kathleen," he said. "Be careful. This is a great deal of money. Does this mean you want me to close the account for good?"

Katie stood and thought a few seconds as she held the envelope. "I don't know, Mr. Taylor," she said. "I don't know what's going to happen to me. If we can find somewhere else to live, maybe I'll bring some of it back. Otherwise . . ."

She stopped, realizing she had nothing else to say.

"I just don't know, Mr. Taylor," she added. "You can close the account or leave it open for a while longer, whatever you think best. But I'm sure my uncle will open a new account for Rosewood."

"Yes . . . yes, of course. He, uh . . . he already has, actually," returned the banker, who knew far more about Burchard Clairborne's activities than Katie realized.

"Thank you, Mr. Taylor," said Katie, then turned and left the bank. As she went, the few other customers and the rest of the bank people nodded and smiled and a few spoke greetings to her. Suddenly in their eyes, little Katie Clairborne had become a woman, and they could not help feeling admiration for her after what they had heard she had done after the death of her family. Though no one in the town had known the Clairbornes well, they were liked and respected. News of the massacre had stunned everyone who had heard it. That was probably why the newspaper article written about us, which we still knew nothing about, was generating such interest—in other parts of the country even more than in Shenandoah County. And so, except for a few people who were a little annoyed to think that Katie and "that darkie girl of hers" had fooled them, most people in Greens Crossing were respectful and kind and spoke to her in a new way that showed how much she had suddenly grown up in their eyes.

Of course, there was one person in town who wasn't about to give Katie the satisfaction of any show of respect. Katie's last stop before coming home was at the general store.

"Hello, Mrs. Hammond," she said as she walked in.

"So, you dare show yourself in town," said Mrs.

Hammond, her nose inching a little higher in the air than usual as she eyed Katie walking toward the counter.

"Yes, ma'am," said Katie.

Katie said Mrs. Hammond sniffed a bit and looked Katie over up and down, with her eyes squinting a little.

"And you were lying the whole time," Mrs. Hammond went on.

"Yes, ma'am," said Katie, looking down.

"I would think you would be ashamed to show your face, deceiving everyone with your poor mama lying there cold in her grave."

"Yes, ma'am . . . I'm sorry, Mrs. Hammond. I didn't know what else to do. But it doesn't matter now—my uncle's making everybody leave."

"The way I hear it, only the darkies have to leave."

"Yes, ma'am. But I can't stay without Mayme."

"Humph!" she snorted. "You mean that ugly one who's always coming in with you?"

Katie didn't say anything. I didn't mind people calling me ugly because they always had. When you grow up colored in a white man's world, you get used to that sort of thing. I just figured all black folks look ugly to whites, except for a few like Emma, who are so pretty nobody could call them ugly. But Katie didn't like her saying it. For a second or two she flared up inside and almost blurted out something that might not have been the kindest thing in the world to say. But then she caught herself and didn't.

"Well, it's no business of mine," said Mrs. Hammond,

who obviously thought it was, "but if you ask me, young ladies who aren't grateful for what they've got will come to no good, and you ought to thank your lucky stars that your uncle is being so kind to you as to let you stay."

"Yes, ma'am."

"Well, what do you want, Kathleen? I assume you came in for some supplies."

"Uh . . . no, ma'am," said Katie hesitantly.

"What, then . . . what do you want?"

Still Katie hesitated, looking down at the floor.

"I . . . I, uh . . ."

"What is it, girl?" said Mrs. Hammond, standing staring at her like an impatient schoolmistress. "Out with it."

"I wondered, Mrs. Hammond," Katie began, "that is . . . I wanted to ask . . . well, I need a job, you see, if I am going to leave, and . . . do you have any work that I could do for you, Mrs. Hammond?"

"What! You mean . . . for pay?"

"Yes, ma'am."

Mrs. Hammond began to laugh at the thought of such a thing. "Certainly not!" she said. "You're just a girl, and a lying one at that. Do you honestly think I would trust a girl to work in my store who would as soon steal from my cash box when my back was turned as anything? No, Kathleen, it's out of the question."

"I would never do that, Mrs. Hammond," said Katie softly.

"So you say. But if you would lie, why wouldn't you

steal? And you've already admitted to lying, haven't you, Kathleen?"

"Yes, ma'am."

"Well . . . there you are."

"Thank you, Mrs. Hammond," said Katie in hardly more than a whisper. She turned and hurried from the store with her eyes stinging.

THE ARTICLE

19

When Katie got back to Rosewood, she didn't tell us about the money or Mrs. Hammond. The rest of that day, and the next, continued just like it had been—quiet and sad. Katie and I had so *much* to say to each other, we couldn't bring ourselves to say anything. I reckon that's sometimes the way it is, that love itself is too big a thing to be contained in words.

So though our hearts were bursting . . . there was nothing to say. I suppose we knew that if we tried to start talking about it, we'd only start crying.

The next day, which was Wednesday, I went upstairs one time when Katie was out walking somewhere and slowly started packing up a few of my things. I didn't want to save it all until the last minute just in case something happened and Katie's uncle came unexpectedly and we had to leave earlier. And besides, the last minute, which was Friday, was only two days away. So it was high time we were getting ready.

Emma seemed to sense what I was up to. While I was sitting on the bed looking through some of the things Katie had given me, wondering what I should take, I heard a sound and looked up and saw her standing in the doorway.

"What you doin', Mayme?" she asked.

"I'm just starting to pack up my things, Emma," I said. "You'd best be thinking of what you're going to take too. We'll be leaving day after tomorrow."

"I been thinkin' 'bout it," she said. "But if I's got ter be luggin' William, I ain't gwine be able ter take nuthin' mo den him."

"I'll help carry your things," I said. "We don't have much anyway. You and I arrived at Rosewood with nothing but the dresses we were wearing, so I don't reckon we've got any business leaving with much more than that."

"You think Miz Katie's mind effen I take dose dresses she gib me, an' da nice shoes?"

"No, Emma," I said smiling. "I know Katie will want us to take whatever she's given us. But we can't take more than we can carry. So we'll have to leave a few things behind. We may have to do a lot a walking."

"Where's we gwine go, Mayme?" asked Emma, a hint of fear in her voice.

"I don't know, Emma. But don't worry, we'll keep away from the McSimmons place. We'll leave in the other direction and head north, and then we'll see where our steps take us."

Josepha must have heard us talking, because now

she walked into the room.

"I's practically ready ter go, Mayme," she said. "I dun wrapped up what I come wiff, though I made shure Miz Katie din't see me 'cuz I don' want ter make her no sadder den she is, an' dat po girl's heart is breakin', dat much is plain enuff. When you figger on us leavin'?"

"On Friday when Katie's uncle comes back, I reckon, Josepha," I said. "Unless he comes sooner, which is why I thought we ought to be getting ready."

"Dat's a good-soundin' plan all right."

"Den I'll git me an' William ready too," said Emma. "We's be ready wheneber you says, Mayme."

"But do it when Katie's not in the house, like Josepha said," I said. "We don't want to talk about leaving around her. Then when Friday comes, we'll say our good-byes and just go. That will be the easiest way."

The other two nodded and left the room, leaving me alone again with my preparations, and with all the memories every little thing brought back to my mind.

As I made my preparations and was wandering around the second floor of the house, chatting occasionally with Emma and Josepha, looking at things, I peeked into the room Katie's mama had used for an office, the room with the safe. Her uncle Burchard was still using that room whenever he came around, snooping through the secretary, still looking for the combination.

I don't know why I wandered in like I did. I was just quietly looking at everything in a sad and pensive way.

The top of the secretary was open from the last time Mr. Clairborne had been here, with papers and things on it. On top of the stack of papers sat a folded-up newspaper. I still couldn't read as good as Katie, but I could read well enough to glance over it. And then suddenly my eyes stopped on some big words at the bottom of the page that shocked me like nothing I'd ever read in one of Katie's McGuffy Readers!

The words said: *Two Girls At Rosewood Fool A Town and Run A Plantation Alone.*

I picked it up and ran downstairs looking for Katie.

"Katie, look at this!" I said when I found her outside.

A minute or two later all of us were clustered around the kitchen table.

"Read it, Miz Katie," said Emma. "Please, read it out loud."

Katie looked up and smiled kind of sadly. To read what other people were saying about us couldn't help but make us feel proud of what we had done. But it was hard to feel much happiness along with the pride because it was all going to be over in two days.

Katie drew in a deep breath, then started to read aloud:

"*Shenandoah County, North Carolina, has harbored a secret for the past two years—a secret shared by two sixteen-year-old girls—one white, the other colored. The families of the two young women, on different plantations, were both massacred by the gang known as Bilsby's Marauders. The girls, however, hiding from the tragedies, managed to survive.*

"After Bilsby's rampage through the South in the month following the war, Kathleen Clairborne, daughter of Richard Clairborne, owner of the plantation known as Rosewood near the town of Greens Crossing, and a former slave girl by the name of Mayme Jukes, suddenly found themselves together . . . but alone.

"The unlikely pair, whom fate brought together quite by accident in the days following the massacre, decided to make a life for themselves at the Clairborne plantation. Their plan was to pretend that everything was perfectly normal, and thus to escape detection.

"For the next two years the two did precisely that, devising various charades to make Rosewood look busier than it was. They not only survived together, they succeeded in bringing in two harvests of cotton without help from the outside world. In almost two years, only a handful of people discovered their secret.

"The truth, however, was recently learned by an uncle of Miss Clairborne's from Charlotte. Richard Clairborne's brother has now filed for ownership of the plantation, and transfer is scheduled to take effect later this month."

Katie set down the paper with a sigh. There wasn't much more to be said.

20

Though we hadn't wanted to talk in front of Katie about the rest of us leaving, we finally did, though it was Katie who brought it up. On Thursday evening, as we were eating our last supper together, she got real quiet, even more than usual. Pretty soon the rest of us quieted down too, and waited. It was obvious that she was wanting to say something.

Finally Katie spoke up.

"I want to talk to all of you," she said slowly. "This is our last night together here at Rosewood, and there are some things I want to say."

She paused and took in a deep breath.

"There's too much to say and I don't know how to say it," she went on. Her voice was strong, not as if she was about to cry like we'd been doing all week, though I know it was still hard for her. "So I will just say thank you to you all. I couldn't have kept Rosewood going all this time, or paid off my mama's loans at the bank, without your help. I love you all. I wish it didn't have to be like this, but I suppose it is and there's nothing any of us can do about it."

She stopped, then got up and walked over to the sideboard and pulled out a drawer and took out an envelope. It was the same envelope from the bank, though we didn't know it.

She brought it back over to the table and sat down.

"I don't know what it's going to be like after tomorrow," she said. "I've been thinking about it all week, although I can't think about it at all without making myself so miserable I can't stand it. The only conclusion I've come to is that I can't stay here without the rest of you. Rosewood could never be home again to me without you. I lost one family here, and I don't think I could stand to lose another one."

She stopped and took in a couple of breaths. Occasionally as she talked she glanced toward Emma and Josepha. But she didn't look at me. I kept my eyes mostly down on the table too. I don't think we could have stood it to look into each other's eyes.

"So if you won't let me go with you," she went on after a minute, "then I'll have to go someplace else. All I know is that I can't stay here. I don't know where I'm going, but I have to go somewhere. I'll rent a room or a house, or I'll get a job, or maybe I'll go up north to Philadelphia and try to find my aunt and see if she'll have me, I don't know. But when the rest of you leave tomorrow, I'm going to leave too."

She stopped again and pulled the envelope out from her lap and set it on the table. Then she reached inside and started pulling out the money that was inside. I glanced over and saw Emma's eyes getting wide as saucers. It reminded me of Katie when we'd first met. She set the bills into four stacks, then handed one to Emma, one to Josepha, and finally shoved one across the table to me.

"You all helped earn this money," she said. "It's yours just as much as it's mine. Wherever you go, you're going to need it just as much as I will, and I want you to have it."

"Laws almighty, Miz Katie!" exclaimed Emma.

Josepha just sat there dumbfounded, looking at the money in her hand like it wasn't real.

I guess I was still the practical one. I took the small stack in front of me and counted it.

"But, Katie," I said, "there's fifty-five dollars here! No colored person in the world's ever had that much money! I can't take this."

"It's yours, Mayme," she said. "You picked more of that cotton than I did. If anyone deserves it, you do. And you should go get the money of yours that's in the bank too."

"But where we're going, we won't need money. Other colored folks will take us in."

"You might need money, Mayme."

"Then let me take five dollars. That will be enough. If you're going to rent someplace new to live, or take a train up north, you need this money."

"Nothing you say will make me change my mind, Mayme," said Katie determinedly. "I knew you would try to talk me out of it and that's why I made up my mind ahead of time. None of you have to take the money if you don't want to. But if you don't, it's going to stay right on the table there. Because when I leave here tomorrow, it's going to be with my own fifty-two dollars. If you don't take what I gave you, it will just sit there on the table for my uncle Burchard to find when he comes and moves in tomorrow."

She got up from the table, holding her own portion of the money. It hadn't even dawned on me yet that she'd given each of us *more* than she'd kept for herself.

"Now I'm going to go upstairs and start packing a suitcase. I have the feeling Uncle Burchard will be here bright and early in the morning."

Finally I couldn't stand it any longer. I got out of my chair and went around to her, and the next minute we were in each other's arms. Finally the dam burst and we cried and cried, and before we knew it Emma and Josepha were hugging us and crying too, and we were all telling each other how much we loved each other. All three of the stacks of money except Katie's, which had fallen on the floor, were still sitting on the table.

Money was the last thing we were thinking about right then.

Henry and Jeremiah came out that evening to say their good-byes. Ever since all this had been happening, Henry had been sorely grieved about our talk of leaving. But he didn't know what else to suggest either. He and Jeremiah didn't have room to take us in. Henry just rented two small rooms behind the livery from Mr. Guiness, the man he worked for. There wasn't room for us. They were men, and we were three women and a baby, besides. Mr. Guiness would never have stood for it, not to mention the townspeople. Blacks may have been free, but that didn't mean they could just do anything they wanted, and if the whites around had seen anything like that, they'd have had a fit and probably strung us all up. So Henry had no better solution to our dilemma. He didn't think Katie ought to leave, just like I'd told her, especially since she needed to be around when my papa, her uncle Templeton, came back. He agreed it wasn't wise for her to come with us.

But if she was determined not to stay at Rosewood after her uncle Burchard became the new owner, at least, Henry said, he would keep an eye out for when Papa came back so he could tell him what had happened and where we all were. So we all promised to make sure we kept in touch so we'd all know where the others were. It was still plain that Henry and Jeremiah didn't like the idea of us leaving. But what else could we do?

Jeremiah and I went for a long walk. But it wasn't anything like the ones we'd had earlier because we knew we were saying good-bye and might not see each other for a long time. I think Jeremiah wanted to ask me to marry him, and might have been fixing to. But he didn't, and I was glad. There wasn't any way I could leave Emma, not now, not the way things were. And Josepha'd never be able to take care of her alone. I think down inside Jeremiah knew it too, and didn't ask me 'cause he knew I'd have to say no. It wasn't that we didn't love each other. We did, at least I knew I loved him and I was pretty sure he loved me too. But sometimes life gets in the way of love. And sometimes being black gets in the way of how you wish life could be.

So it was a pretty quiet walk. There wasn't much to talk about, any more than there was with Katie. My heart hurt. I never thought I'd be so full of love. But knowing I was going to have to say good-bye to Katie the next day, and that I was saying good-bye to Jeremiah tonight, made me feel so full and so sad at the same time that I thought I would burst.

Of course, we talked about when we'd see each other again. But you never really could know about such things. Life didn't always go the way you hoped it would.

TOO MANY GOOD-BYES, TOO MANY TEARS

21

W hen Friday morning arrived there were three rolled-up blankets and three pillow slips stuffed full of our things sitting on the kitchen floor.

Emma and Josepha and I had already had several quiet private talks amongst ourselves about our plans and what we would do and which way we would go. Josepha said she knew of some free coloreds about fifty miles north, and we decided to try to find them first. The money Katie had given us kept sitting on the kitchen table for more than twenty-four hours after we'd talked about it. I knew Katie was serious and that if we didn't take it, it would still be sitting there when her uncle came. So finally I took all three stacks and gave Josepha hers, and put Emma's and mine in my bag. I figured Emma's would be safer if I kept it for her.

Sometime after we'd gone to bed the night before, Katie's suitcase appeared on the floor sitting next to our three bags. I don't know when Katie brought it downstairs, but it looked like she was serious about leaving too. I didn't know what her plans were, if she was still determined to come with us or go someplace else.

When I first saw Katie that morning, her eyes were red from crying. She walked past me without looking in my direction and began bustling around in the kitchen, as if by staying busy she could avoid the painful good-bye that was hurrying our way. I just stood there in the kitchen doorway and watched her until she finally turned around. We looked at each other for a long moment, then we crossed the room and embraced. We stood in each other's arms for the longest time.

"I love you, Mayme," Katie finally whispered in my ear.

That did it. I started blubbering like a baby and cried and cried.

"Oh, Katie," I said. "I love you so much. I'll never forget you."

"Whatever happens," she said, "write to me at Mrs. Hammond's or Rosewood. Wherever I go, I'll be sure to keep in touch with her and Uncle Burchard. They'll keep my mail for me."

"I will, Katie," I said. "As soon as me and Emma and

Josepha are settled someplace, I'll let you know where we are. I promise. But . . . but what are you going to do?"

"I don't know," said Katie. "I think today I'll walk to Oakwood, unless Uncle Burchard will let me keep one of the horses. I've got the fifty dollars. I'll stay in the hotel there for a night and maybe try to find a job or something. You said there was a job there once. I'll learn to work, Mayme. I'll work hard. And if I can get a job, maybe I'll rent a room somewhere and wait until Uncle Templeton comes back. If I can't find anything to do, I'll go to Charlotte and try to find a job there."

"What about Papa, then?" I asked. "How will he find us?"

"After I leave, I'll talk to Henry and Mrs. Hammond," said Katie. "When Uncle Templeton comes back, whenever that is, he'll ask questions and I'll make sure they know where I am. Then once he and I get together again, I'll tell him what happened and we'll come find you. That's why you have to make sure that Henry and Mrs. Hammond know where you are. Then we'll all get together again. Uncle Templeton will know what to do."

22

We would never have guessed that at the very time we were talking about Henry and Mrs. Hammond, Henry and Mrs. Hammond were thinking mighty hard about us too. Because at that very hour, as we would soon discover, Henry was in Mrs. Hammond's store, buying a few things he hoped to give to us girls, a sort of good-bye present, or something to help us get along on the road. When he had entered the store, Mrs. Hammond barely acknowledged him, grumbling that she had only opened so early to take care of a few things before heading out to Rosewood with a number of the other townspeople, for the doings there later that morning.

But just as Henry was looking at those shelves of pretty things, Mrs. Hammond's eagle eye watching him with suspicion, someone walked into the general store who drove all other thoughts from his mind.

Mrs. McSimmons, mistress of the large McSimmons plantation, strode through the door of the general store. And it was plain from the determined look on her face that she had something on her mind besides dry goods or food or any of the notions lining the shelves.

Even though the plantation owner's wife wasn't a regular customer in Greens Crossing, seeing as she lived closer to Oakwood, Henry recognized her the moment he saw her. It seemed that Mrs. Hammond did too, because the lady straightened up right smart and smoothed down her apron. Henry did notice, however, that even though Mrs. Hammond's eyes left him, her expression of suspicion remained.

I suppose Mrs. McSimmons was the kind of lady everyone for miles knew of. Although I reckon you could say the same thing about Mrs. Hammond. And it soon became clear why Mrs. McSimmons had come to her store almost at the crack of dawn on this day—she knew what everyone knew about Mrs. Hammond, that if there was any gossip about anyone afoot in Shenandoah County, she would know it and wasn't above letting it be coaxed out of her.

"You are Mrs. Hammond, I take it," said Mrs. McSimmons without smiling as she walked toward the counter.

"That's right," replied the shopkeeper. "Good day to you, Mrs. McSimmons."

"We'll see what kind of day it is, depending on what you tell me."

"About what?" rejoined Mrs. Hammond a little curtly, clearly perturbed at her visitor's tone of voice. Mrs. Hammond was not used to people talking down to her. That's how she usually talked to other people.

"They say there's a houseful of urchins around here someplace. I want to know where it is."

Mrs. Hammond paused, eyeing the lady. "I'm not sure I know what you're talking about, Mistress McSimmons."

Henry was surprised at her answer. He had no doubt that Mrs. Hammond knew well enough who Mistress McSimmons was talking about, since the shopkeeper had done more to spread the Rosewood rumors than anyone.

"Come now, Mrs. Hammond. Everyone says that you know everything that goes on in Shenandoah County. Do you mean to tell me you have heard nothing about a place where someone's taking in strays and runaways? Darkies, I mean. If I have heard about it, surely you have."

"Well, let me think . . ." And Mrs. Hammond appeared to be searching her brain, likely enjoying the attention. And Henry wondered if by some miracle she would keep the information to herself. He was sure praying she would.

But it seemed Mrs. Hammond's natural tendency to ingratiate herself to the most wealthy of her clientele began to moderate her temporary annoyance at Mrs. McSimmons' manner toward her.

"There's young Kathleen Clairborne," Mrs. Hammond offered, "over at the Rosewood place about six miles from here. She's the one whose family was killed."

"Is she the one taking in strays?"

"I've only seen one other girl with her, an ugly darkie who seemed more thickheaded than the Clairborne girl herself."

"That must be it—that's got to be the place!"

"Wouldn't surprise me. That Kathleen Clairborne is

nothing but a dimwit herself. Although they say she kept the plantation going on her own somehow—until today, that is."

"What's today got to do with it?"

"Her uncle, who now owns the place as I understand it, is assuming ownership of the plantation today. But"—Mrs. Hammond paused, lowering her eyes modestly—"as to the houseful of urchins, Mistress McSimmons," she began, "there have been a few rumors, of course, but I must confess I've seen nothing with my own two—"

"Never mind all that," interrupted Mrs. McSimmons. "Just give me directions how to find this place."

Henry didn't stay to hear the directions. He left the store as quickly and quietly as he could. Neither woman paid him any mind.

Then Henry ran up the street to the livery.

AWAY

23

Not knowing that we had more people to worry about than Katie's uncle Burchard, Emma and I and the others were still getting ready to leave. Katie made all of us eat a big breakfast to tide us over on the road. She was mothering us all she could, it seemed, one last time.

Although Katie's uncle had said ten o'clock, it wasn't much past eight in the morning when we started hearing wagons rumbling in.

"I reckon it's about time the three of us were off," I said in a husky voice. "It looks like your uncle's here."

Katie tried to smile, but there were tears shining in her eyes.

Emma and Josepha stood and picked up their things. They'd heard the wagons too and knew it was time to say our final good-byes.

Katie's uncle walked into the kitchen then, his face stiff. But when he saw us obviously getting ready to leave, he decided not to say whatever he had been about to and just turned around and left the house again.

Finally there was nothing else to do but just go. The moment had finally come.

I couldn't stand it, but I went over and picked up my blanket and pillow slip.

Emma was blubbering and telling Katie how wonderful she was. "Good-bye, Miz Katie . . . I love you, Miz Katie . . . thank you, Miz Katie . . . good-bye." Josepha was holding William and wiping at her eyes with the fat back of her free hand. Then Katie looked up and saw me on the other side of the room, holding my bag and waiting for the other two.

"Oh, Mayme!" she said, her eyes flooding with tears again. Slowly she walked toward me and opened her arms. I dropped the bag and fell into her embrace.

"Aren't you going to wait for Henry and Jeremiah?" Katie asked. "They said they'd be back out this morning."

"I couldn't bear it," I said. "It'll make everything easier for everyone if we're just gone. You've got enough to worry about with your uncle and all."

Katie nodded and we just stood a few seconds holding each other tight.

"I love you so much," I said softly. "I'll never forget you."

"Oh, Mayme, don't talk like that! We'll see each other again real soon. Uncle Templeton will come back, and you write me a letter to Mrs. Hammond's store telling me where you are and when you find those people of Josepha's. Then we'll come and get you."

I just nodded.

"I love you, Mayme," Katie said.

We stood back from each other. Our eyes were both wet, but at last we looked each other in the eyes and smiled.

Then I took a deep breath, picked up my blanket and bag again, and slowly walked toward the parlor. Emma and Josepha followed.

"You all write to me as soon as you find those people," said Katie. "As soon as Uncle Templeton gets back, we'll come!"

Slowly the three of us, Josepha still carrying William, walked out the back door.

Suddenly we heard the sound of horses' hooves coming fast down the road. We looked up and saw a cloud of dust rising above the trees even before we could see who was coming. I felt that old fear of discovery we always felt when anyone had approached

Rosewood over the past two years. My muscles tensed, as if ready to run down to the slave cabins to light the fires that were no longer there. I looked at Katie and our eyes met, and we shared a sad smile, knowing we were both seeing those same memories in our minds. But those days were over. The only people we needed to hide from were the McSimmons. For Josepha's sake, yes, but mostly for Emma's and William's. For their safety, we were planning to take the road away from Greens Crossing. But it never crossed our minds that anyone from the McSimmons plantation might be riding toward us at that moment. Looking back, it was mighty foolish for us to just stand there, out in the open like that, waiting to see who was coming. I suppose we were hoping it was Papa.

It wasn't.

INTERROGATION

24

W hen the rider broke into the yard, dust flying, we were all surprised to see Henry. I knew something was wrong. Jeremiah wasn't with him. I don't know if I was more disappointed or relieved not to have to say another good-bye to him.

Henry jumped off the horse before the animal had even come to a full stop.

"You girls better git," he called, turning his head to search the road behind him. "Mistress McSimmons is on her way out here right now. She was still at de general store w'en I lef'. Now, hurry on outta here."

"Miss Katie, what should I do?" asked Emma frantically. "Should I go hide me an' William in de cellar agin?"

Katie thought a moment. "No, Emma. We can't take that chance now with my uncle around. Henry's right. Go, all of you, as fast as you can at least until you reach the trees."

"But what about Jeremiah—" I began.

"He's on his way out," interrupted Henry. "I passed him on my way. But you can't wait fer him. You's gotter git."

Swallowing hard, I tried not to show my disappointment, and we all began moving away from the house. Then I ran back and hugged Katie one last time, my eyes hot with tears, then ran to rejoin the others and led them quickly away.

As we went, I knew Katie was standing on the porch, watching us leave.

We hurried away, and I took William, since Emma already had a heavier bag with belongings for William and herself. Josepha huffed and puffed, but I think the thought of facing Mistress McSimmons again kept her moving. I wouldn't have thought a woman her size could move so fast. Finally as the road began to bend into the woods, I stopped and turned back. I could barely make Katie out in the distance, but she was still there. I raised my hand and waved. I saw her wave back.

A chill swept through me, a chill of fear that I might never see her again.

"Good-bye, Katie," I whispered to myself. "I'll never forget you."

Almost that same moment a buggy came careening into the yard, sending dust in every direction.

Katie quickly dropped her hand, pulled her eyes away from our retreating backs, and went into the house.

"You'd better get out of sight, Henry," she said as she went.

As the door closed behind Katie, Henry disappeared in the direction of the barn.

The woman inside the buggy kept yelling and whacking the reins on her horse's back until she practically skidded to a stop by the kitchen door at the back of the house.

Mr. Clairborne had been expecting the lawyer, and Katie watched from the window as he walked toward the buggy.

When the lady stepped to the ground, he looked surprised and quickly reached for his hat, but it was soon obvious that his visitor wasn't interested in niceties.

"I'm looking for the Clairborne girl," she said.

"She's inside, ma'am," said Katie's uncle. "But if you—"

"Are you the new owner?" she interrupted.

"I am," replied Katie's uncle, clearly irritated at the woman's demanding tone.

"Then perhaps you can tell me if it's true what they

say's been going on around here—that strays and run-aways and coloreds have been hiding out here."

"There were a parcel of 'em, all right," replied Mr. Clairborne, "—kids, couple of darkies, a little girl—But don't worry—I ran them off."

"You what!"

"I told my niece to get rid of them. This is my place now and I didn't want them around."

"You fool!"

"Look, lady—I don't know who you are, but you got no cause to talk to me like that. This is my place, and if you don't show some civility in that tongue of yours, I'll run you off too. The truth is, I don't like you much."

"I apologize," said Mrs. McSimmons, flustered but obviously realizing she'd let her anger get the better of her. "Tell me, then, when did she leave—the darkie girl?"

"The little girl was white, ma'am. But I ain't seen her around the place in a long time."

"I'm not looking for a white girl. I'm looking for a runaway nigger, skinny as a post. Good-looking . . . with a baby."

"Don't know, ma'am . . . yeah, she might have been here. I didn't pay that close of attention to what they all looked like. All I wanted was rid of 'em. And like I say, they're gone now."

"Then, where's the other girl, the Clairborne girl they say's not too bright?"

"That's my niece. I think she's inside. She—"

But already Mrs. McSimmons had turned and was

walking toward the house.

Katie was still watching from the window, praying desperately that Mistress McSimmons wouldn't glance in the other direction before we disappeared from sight.

Now Mistress McSimmons was walking straight toward her with a determined look on her face, and Katie began to tremble. She took a deep breath, wanting to appear calm, then went to the door and stepped outside to await her visitor. Katie allowed herself one quick look in our direction. She saw me disappear behind a tree. When she turned back, Mrs. McSimmons' eyes were on her. Katie swallowed. Mrs. McSimmons looked in the direction we'd gone and Katie held her breath, but then the woman looked back at Katie, eyes narrowing. Whether the wife of little William's father recognized her at first, Katie could not tell. She just stood for a moment looking her up and down.

"You had a darkie girl here," she said in a demanding voice. "Where is she?"

"Who, ma'am?" replied Katie.

"Is everyone around this place dense!" exclaimed Mrs. McSimmons. "The colored girl you were hiding."

"There have been a lot of people here, ma'am. My cousin Mayme was here for two years—she's half colored."

"Did she have a baby?"

"No, ma'am."

"What about the others?"

"There were some others too, but they've . . . uh, been gone for a while."

"Where did they go . . . why did they leave?"

"My uncle made them."

"How long ago?"

"Uh . . . the little girl's been gone a few weeks."

"Where did she go?"

"Home."

"Another darkie?"

"No, ma'am—she's white."

"I am only interested in the darkies you had here! How long have the rest been gone?"

"A while, ma'am."

"Where did they go?"

"I don't know."

"And you're the only one left now . . . besides your uncle, I mean."

"Yes, ma'am. I'm the only girl here."

Mrs. McSimmons glanced around in annoyance, seemingly debating inside herself whether she ought to search the house in spite of what Katie said. Then she looked at Katie again and decided not to.

"If I find out you have been lying to me, young lady," she said, "you will regret it. In the meantime, I intend to make further inquiries . . . then I will be back."

She turned and stepped down off the porch.

Clearly exasperated, Mrs. McSimmons climbed back into her own buggy, turned her horse, and rode back toward town more irritated than ever.

By this time, Josepha, Emma, and I were around the bend where the shadows of the trees fell across the road. I don't know why I glanced back again, because I knew the house was out of sight.

Then I turned toward the road again, and we slowed our pace a bit, to catch our breath. We kept walking, though, because wherever we were bound and whatever our future held, it was high time we got on with it.

We hadn't brought along much water, both because it was heavy to carry and there were enough streams and small rivers everywhere that we'd be able to find all we needed. So we stopped every so often to drink and rest. Most of the weight in our bags was food we'd brought along—enough for about a week, we figured, if we didn't eat too much. We didn't know how long it would take us to find the folks Josepha knew—probably longer than that.

I didn't really care how fast we went, I just wanted to get far enough away from Oakwood and Greens Crossing that we didn't have to worry about anyone connected to the McSimmons place seeing us. I'd start to feel more comfortable once we were ten or fifteen miles from Rosewood in the opposite direction. Then we could relax a bit.

We didn't get along too fast. Lugging William in the heat was a chore because he was fat and heavy. We took turns carrying him, but Emma and Josepha were sweating and tired in less than an hour. I began to wonder how we'd *ever* make it. William could walk a little by himself, but he tired out faster than the other two and then started begging to be carried again. Even without William, walking like this was mighty hard work for Josepha.

So we did a lot of stopping and resting and I didn't know if we'd gone more than three or four miles before ten or eleven or whatever time it was getting to be. And I was still nervous and listening and looking out for anyone who might be following us. Still, I suppose, three or four miles from Rosewood meant that we were six or eight miles from the McSimmons place, and by the time we stopped somewhere to sleep for the night, we'd likely be ten or twelve miles away. So we were probably safe from anyone seeing us who shouldn't.

A CUP OF COFFEE WITH FRIENDS

25

Katie watched until Mrs. McSimmons rode from sight, then turned back in our direction, as if to assure herself—and convince herself—that we were really gone. Katie stood there and cried for a few minutes, relief and grief mingling in her tears. Then she wiped her eyes and walked across the yard to where her uncle was standing while his men unloaded two wagons.

He glanced up as she approached.

"They're gone, Uncle Burchard," said Katie.

"Who's gone?" he said gruffly.

"Mayme and the others—they've left."

He glanced about, then peered down the road toward town.

"I didn't see anyone," he said.

Katie said nothing.

"Well, no matter," he added, "as long as they're gone. I'm glad to see you came to your senses and decided to stay. Be a plumb fool thing to leave a good life here just for some no-good niggers—"

A reply that would not have been kind rushed to Katie's lips, but she held it back.

"—I'm offering to let you stay and do as you please," her uncle continued. "Ain't too many girls with no family and no money that have it so good. So I hope you're grateful."

"I won't be staying, Uncle Burchard," said Katie.

"What are you talking about?"

"I'm leaving too."

"With the niggers?"

"No."

"Where are you going?"

"I don't know, just away from here."

He kept looking at her, then shook his head almost as if in disgust.

"Well . . . suit yourself," he said. "Sounds like a fool thing to me, but I ain't going to make you stay. Don't expect me to nursemaid you."

"No, sir. I don't, sir."

Again Burchard Clairborne glanced toward town and this time frowned. Katie followed her uncle's gaze and saw Jeremiah walking toward them along the road.

"What is he. . . . It's that colored boy from town—what does he want?"

"He and his father are friends of mine, Uncle Burchard," said Katie.

"Friends . . . of *yours?*"

"Yes, sir."

"What in blazes . . . are all your friends colored! How'd your mama raise you, girl?"

"To show respect to everyone, sir," said Katie a little crossly, her feelings at last getting the better of her.

She turned and walked toward Jeremiah. "They're already gone," she said to him.

"Gone!" exclaimed Jeremiah. "You mean Mayme and the others?"

Katie nodded. "Mayme said they'd already said enough good-byes and thought it would be easier this way."

"Dangnashun!" said Jeremiah under his breath, glancing about in every direction. "How long ago?"

Katie sighed. "Just long enough. Mistress McSimmons was just here."

"So dat's who was in dat buggy! She din't see dem, did she?"

"No. They left just in time. Your papa rode out to warn us."

"So dat's what my daddy was shoutin' bout back dere when he passed me on de road."

They walked past her uncle and his men toward the house. Katie felt her uncle watching her from the corner of his eye. She did her best to ignore him and led Jeremiah toward the door. Henry had seen Jeremiah arrive and had been ambling toward them. He now followed.

"Wha'chu gwine do, chil'?" Henry asked when all three entered the kitchen.

"I thought I ought to wait until Uncle Burchard and Mr. Sneed do whatever they're going to do at ten o'clock," said Katie. "Then I'll go to Oakwood and see if I can find a job. My suitcase is all packed," she said, nodding toward the last remaining suitcase on the floor. They all stared at it for a moment, saddened at the sight.

"Well, we's stayin' wiff you as long as you like, an' den we'll go inter town tergether. We'll carry dat bag er yers, Miz Kathleen. Don' seem right fo' a girl like you ter hab ter carry hit yerse'f."

"Thank you, Henry, but I am sure I will manage. I have to get used to living on my own."

"Still don' seem right. But effen you's determined ter go ter Oakwood, leastways let us take you dere in one ob da livery's wagons. Dat's a long way ter walk."

"Would you like one last cup of coffee here with me?" asked Katie as the three of them sat down at the table.

"Soun's right fine ter me, Miz Kathleen." Henry nodded.

But Katie had barely begun to boil the water when the door opened behind her and her uncle walked in.

"What are these two darkies doing in my house?" he said angrily.

"They're my friends," said Katie. "I'm fixing them some coffee."

"I thought you understood me, Kathleen, that I wanted no darkies around. You said the others were gone, and—"

"Uncle Burchard," Katie interrupted, now getting angry herself. "This is still *my* kitchen and *my* house, or at least my mama's and daddy's. And it will be mine until Mr. Sneed tells me otherwise. Then I will leave and it will be yours. But until then, it is mine and my friends are welcome in it. And if you don't treat them with a little more respect, I just may ask *you* to leave."

Her uncle stared at her, clearly dumbfounded that she would speak that way to him. He turned around and left, fuming but silent.

LEGAL TALK

26

At a little after nine-thirty, Mr. Sneed rode into Rosewood in his buggy.

Other people also arrived, including Mr. Taylor from the bank, who Katie's uncle had asked to be present as a witness to the proceedings. Then Mrs. Hammond was there, though what business it was of hers I didn't know, and a few other people from town that Katie recognized. I'm not sure exactly why, but I guess when things like this happen, they have to announce it to the public to make it legal or something so that people have a chance to speak up or say if Rosewood has any debts they haven't paid before there is a change of ownership. Some folks were probably there for that, although most, like Mrs. Hammond, were just almighty curious after all they had heard.

Anyway, that's something like it, and because of those announcements that Mr. Sneed had posted in both Greens Crossing and Oakwood, and had put in the Charlotte newspaper, there were ten or fifteen other people who came, most of whom Katie didn't know.

Mr. Sneed was dressed in his business suit as usual, and carrying his briefcase with the papers in it. After he arrived, everybody gradually started clustering around and moving toward the front of the house, around the other side from the barn where they'd been unloading the wagons.

Katie got her suitcase and carried it out of the kitchen and set it down outside. She wanted to be ready to leave as soon as it was over, and not have to go back into the house once it officially became her uncle's. Then she and Henry and Jeremiah followed the small crowd around to the front of the house. Some of the people glanced toward her now and then, wearing expressions she couldn't altogether understand. Were they glad to see the place taken away from her after she'd fooled everybody, including them? Katie couldn't tell.

Mr. Sneed and her uncle were already standing up on the porch, and Mr. Sneed had opened his briefcase and began talking to the small gathering of people standing listening. Katie and Henry and Jeremiah stood in back.

Mr. Sneed and her uncle paid no attention to them, but every once in a while Mrs. Hammond or one of the other people from town glanced back at Katie. Katie couldn't tell whether they were sorry for her, or just curious what she was thinking.

". . . all for coming today," Mr. Sneed was saying. "We are here to comply with certain legalities connected with the papers filed by Mr. Burchard Clairborne for the disposition of the estate known as Rosewood in light of the tragic death of its owner, Mr. Richard Clairborne, brother of the filer in these proceedings.

"As part of that process," he went on, "the law requires that the opportunity be given to any and all persons who may have claims to put forward in the matter of unpaid loans, debts, or other encumbrances on the property or incurred by the owners or his heirs, including, I might add," he said, glancing for the first time to where Katie stood, "any and all of those, of whatever race, who have been living here and operating the plantation since the unfortunate deaths of Mr. Richard Clairborne and his wife and sons.

"This will provide a final opportunity for any and all interested parties to set forth the claims to which they consider themselves entitled, after which time the court documents that have been prepared, along with a new deed to the property, will be enforced as per the instructions of the court, and title will officially be granted and turned over to the brother of the deceased, Mr. Burchard Clairborne."

Mr. Sneed paused briefly, cleared his throat, put on a pair of reading spectacles, and then began to read from the document he was holding in his hand.

"Whereas the land and real property known as Rosewood and situated near Greens Crossing in Shenandoah County, North Carolina," he began, continuing on with a lot of legal-sounding talk and descriptions, with words like *wherefore* and *insofar as* and *lien* and *deed* and *encumbrance* and *encroachment* and *just cause* and *due notice* and *failure to comply*. Katie couldn't understand more than a dozen words of most of it. And if she didn't understand any more than that, how much less did Henry and Jeremiah understand as they stood there with her at the back of the small crowd.

Henry leaned close and whispered, "Don' seem dat dese yere lawyers kin speak a word ob real English nohow!"

Katie nodded, thinking that no matter how highfalutin' Mr. Sneed made it sound, all his fancy words didn't change the fact that they were taking her home away.

But the three of them stood patiently listening, waiting for Mr. Sneed to get finished. Then they would leave.

Nobody said anything, even after Mr. Sneed paused to give them the chance to say if Rosewood owed them anything or if anyone objected or had any kind of what he called a claim to put forward. Katie wondered why they'd all come if they didn't have anything to say. But if Mrs. Hammond was anything like the rest, they probably came just to get a look at the place and to snoop around, and maybe see the new owner after all they'd heard about Katie and me and what we'd done. They tried to pretend they weren't interested and didn't notice, but they stole glances at Katie now and then. Whatever it was they were thinking, the fact was that we'd been written about in the newspaper and those who'd heard about it, and even those who'd just heard all the gossip about us, couldn't help being mighty curious about the girl Kathleen Clairborne, who had grown up to be a fetching young woman but who, folks said, seemed to take to coloreds more than was natural for any white person. And as she stood there with Henry and Jeremiah, everything they'd heard seemed to their own eyes to be true enough.

AN UNCLE SEALS OUR FATE

27

M r. Sneed put down the paper he'd been reading and adjusted his spectacles. The people shuffled about where they were standing as if they were getting bored with it just like Katie was.

Then Mr. Sneed picked up another single sheet of paper.

"I have here a new deed to Rosewood," he said. "In the absence of the original deed to the property, which we have unfortunately not been able to locate, and as authorized by the court and the laws of the United

143

States government and the state of North Carolina, a new deed has been executed and duly witnessed, and will now be issued to Mr. Burchard Clairborne, and, with his signature, will entitle him to full legal ownership, and with all the incumbent rights and privileges therein, to the—"

It had been so quiet for so long, with no sound but the droning of Mr. Sneed's voice, that when the hooves of a galloping horse intruded into the proceedings, everyone noticed the sound immediately and began turning their heads to see where it was coming from. It even startled Mr. Sneed enough that he stopped what he'd been saying in midsentence.

But no one saw the horse coming on the road from town on the other side of the house, even though they heard clearly enough that whoever it was, was riding fast, and coming their way.

Just as Mr. Sneed had decided to try to start speaking again and finish the transfer of ownership, suddenly the horse and rider tore around the corner of the house in a tumult of sound and commotion, sending Katie and Henry and Jeremiah and the rest of the small crowd scurrying to get out of the way.

A man was yelling and whipping his horse into as much speed as it had left, even though the poor thing was exhausted and sweating and frothing from coming a long way.

With a great flurry of whinnying and hooves and dust and the sounds of leather and a few shouts from the onlookers, the wild-looking rider reined in right in front of the porch where Mr. Sneed and Burchard Clairborne stood. The horse, agitated from so suddenly finding itself surrounded by people, continued to prance and stamp and snort. Every eye looked up to the strange rider who had thrown the proceedings into such a frenzy. He wore plain work clothes, a dirty brown hat that looked like it had been on his head at least twenty years, and a growth of beard that was probably a week old. Not a single person present, including Katie, had any idea who it might be.

"What is the meaning of this?" demanded Mr. Sneed in a loud voice. "We are in the middle of a formal legal proceeding."

"That's why I'm here," said the man, still sitting on his horse and trying to calm the animal down. "You be the fellow they call Sneed?"

"That's right. I am Leroy Sneed, attorney at law."

"Yeah, they told me in town I'd find you here. The minute I mentioned Rosewood, your name came up and that's when I figured I oughtn't to waste any time getting out here. I just hope I ain't too late."

"Too late for what?"

"For the deeding. Someone told me you'd drawn up a new deed to this place."

"That's right. I'm holding it here in my hand. It's all perfectly legal, I assure you. I certainly don't see what possible interest you could have in the matter such as to justify all this commotion you have caused."

"Just this, Mr. Sneed," said the man. "That deed of yours might not be as legal as you think."

"What are you talking about? Are you a lawyer too?"

"No, I'm no lawyer."

"Then who are you, and what right do you have—"

"I'm the owner of this house and this land and this whole plantation, that's who I am."

"What! That's preposterous. I demand to know what this is all about!"

"I'll show you soon enough, if you'll just give me the chance," said the man, now dismounting and tying his horse to a rail. "What I've got in my saddlebag here," he went on as he began opening the leather satchel hanging to the side of his saddle, "is the *proper* deed to Rosewood."

"What—that's impossible!"

The man pulled out a folded paper that looked old and kind of ragged, then walked forward and handed it to Mr. Sneed.

"I think you'll find that it's more legal than that one of yours," said the man.

Mr. Sneed unfolded the paper and quickly looked it over. The expression on his face gradually changed. The shock in his eyes made it clear that he no longer felt inclined to argue the point.

"But . . . but I don't understand," he said. "Where did you get this . . . how does it come to be in your possession . . . and just who are you?"

"My name's Ward Daniels," said the man. "And that deed was transferred to me by the owner of Rosewood, my sister Mrs. Rosalind Daniels Clairborne."

STUNNING AND UNEXPECTED
DEVELOPMENTS
28

Katie had been just as bewildered as everyone else as she stood listening to the strange turn of events.

At the words *Ward Daniels,* however, her mouth dropped and her eyes opened wide. To no one else present, did the name carry the slightest significance. But to Katie, the two words were filled with worlds of meaning. And not because of what he had said about being the rightful owner of Rosewood. For the moment the importance of that fact was lost on her. It didn't enter her mind that this suddenly changed everything, only that in front of her stood the uncle she had thought was dead. She just stared at him in a daze, unaware of what it meant, unaware of the looks and gradual murmurs of the townspeople and others that began to be directed toward her to see what she was going to do.

Then slowly she found herself walking forward through the small crowd. The people stood aside as she passed, whispering amongst themselves. By the time she reached the porch, nearly every eye was on her. Even if Katie herself didn't, everyone else certainly realized the significance of this sudden change.

Mr. Sneed saw Katie approach. He glanced up, and as he did, the newcomer followed his gaze and turned to see a girl standing three feet away.

His face went pale. Visibly stunned at the sight of her, he stood speechless.

"Hello, Uncle Ward," said Katie. "I'm Kathleen."

Still he stood, as if the name didn't register. Then gradually he began to nod. "Kathleen . . ." he said, "you . . . you look so much like your mama. I . . . I almost thought you were her for a second."

"My mama's . . . she's dead, Uncle Ward," said Katie.

"Yes . . . I know, Kathleen. I heard. I'm sorry. That's why I came. I came as quickly as I could after I heard what happened."

In the few seconds that had passed since he had heard the name Daniels, Burchard Clairborne's brain seemed to have gone numb. But he quickly recovered himself and now stepped forward.

"Now, hold on here just a minute," he said. "Whoever you are, mister—and I ain't got no call to say you ain't who you claim—but you must've gotten hold of some bad information somewhere. This house and this property was my brother's, and now that he's dead, as we all know by now, it belongs to me. That's what this man here's doing. That's a new deed he's holding, and it's legal and it's in my name."

"And just what would that name be?" asked Mr. Daniels.

"Clairborne . . . Burchard Clairborne—brother of the deceased."

"Oh . . . so you're Kathleen's uncle too?"

"That's right. So you see, that makes me the new owner of Rosewood now."

"Not so fast. The fact is, this place didn't belong to your brother at all."

"What are you talking about?"

"As you can see from that deed there," said Mr. Daniels, nodding toward Mr. Sneed, "the ownership of this property was transferred to my sister."

Both men looked at Mr. Sneed, who was still perusing the paper.

"I am afraid he appears to be right, Mr. Clairborne," he said slowly. "I don't understand it, and this comes as a big shock to me, as I am sure it does you, but this deed was drawn up in the name of Rosalind Clairborne and was recorded according to all the proper legalities."

"But there's got to be some mistake," objected Burchard. "It's a forgery!"

"I don't think there's much chance of that, Mr. Clairborne," said the lawyer. "In my considered opinion, this is a perfectly legal document, and obviously it precedes and supersedes, and I would have to say invalidates this new deed I have drawn up. I am afraid there is nothing I can do about it."

"Well, that deed may be in Rosalind Clairborne's name, but she's dead. Don't that mean the deed's no good?"

"Without a will," began Mr. Sneed, "the next of kin would have to be determined."

"Which is me!" said Burchard.

"Not necessarily, I am afraid, Mr. Clairborne," said Mr. Sneed. "If this man is indeed her brother, and can prove his identity, and with her daughter also here, I am

149

afraid that you, as merely the deceased woman's brother-in-law and not actually related by blood, would not be in a legal position to file a convincing—"

"This is ridiculous!" boomed Burchard, interrupting the lawyer in an angry voice. "This place ought to have been mine in the beginning and it's mine now. If you won't enforce the new deed, I will go to someone who will!"

"There is one other fact," Mr. Daniels now said. "If you'll look on the reverse of that deed, you'll see that my sister signed it over to me ten years ago."

Mr. Sneed turned the paper over, adjusted his spectacles again, and read over what had been written there in hand.

"Rosalind told me that her husband was concerned about you, Mr. Clairborne," Mr. Daniels went on. "She said that Richard was worried that if anything ever happened to him, you would try to get your hands on Rosewood however you could, something about bad blood between you and him over a family inheritance or something. I don't know more than that, except that he put Rosewood in her name just to keep you from being able to get your hands on it like this. Then when I got back from California, she signed it over to me in exchange for some gold I gave her to keep for me. I never thought much about it and never considered Rosewood mine—it was just her way of giving me a promissory note for the gold."

At the word *gold,* murmurs began again from the crowd. Of course, Mrs. Hammond and Mr. Taylor already knew a little about it, but now suddenly things that had been a mystery to them, especially with Katie showing up in town with gold coins and nuggets, were beginning to make sense.

The word also woke Katie out of the reverie she'd been in while listening to her two uncles dispute about the deed.

"Oh . . . oh!" she exclaimed. "Uncle Ward . . . the gold . . . I'm sorry, but . . . it's gone . . . I spent it."

He glanced away from the other two men, at first not grasping what Katie was talking about.

"Rosalind gave it . . . to you?" he said.

"No . . . we found it! Mayme and I found it. But Mama had two loans at the bank, and it was the only way to keep the bank from taking Rosewood."

Mr. Taylor squirmed a little uncomfortably where he stood. Throughout the whole situation between him and Katie, he had intentionally kept the affair quiet. It unsettled the people of a small community to hear about foreclosures and he hadn't wanted word of it to get out.

"Ah . . . right," said Mr. Daniels, nodding. "Don't worry about the gold, Kathleen," he added. "Wasn't that much anyway. I didn't come back for the gold. You can tell me all about it later."

"Wait a minute!" Burchard now said. "Mr. Sneed, I want to know what you are going to do about my claim, and the new deed to Rosewood in my name."

"I am afraid there is nothing I can do, Mr. Clairborne," replied the lawyer. "This man is in possession of what to all appearances is a fully legal deed to the property. He is also the next of kin to the deceased legal owner of Rosewood, which appears to have been Mrs. Rosalind Daniels Clairborne, not Richard Clairborne at all. In light of these facts, it would seem that you have no claim to make, that the new deed is invalid, and that my business here today is concluded."

He handed the original deed back to Mr. Daniels, took off his spectacles, then began putting the other papers and documents back into his briefcase.

"You are, of course, free to pursue your claim through the courts," he added. "But at this point, I will bid you all a good morning."

He walked off the porch and around the house to where his horse and buggy were tied, while the onlookers, still talking amongst themselves in astonishment, slowly began also to disperse and wander back to their horses and carriages. A flustered and angry Burchard Clairborne disappeared around the house.

UNCLE AND NIECE

29

Katie and Mr. Daniels were still standing at the foot of the porch as everyone around them slowly walked away, glancing toward them now and then and still murmuring and talking. Suddenly Katie began to get nervous. She realized she didn't know her uncle Ward any better than she did her uncle Burchard.

"Uh . . . what do you want me to do, Uncle Ward?" she asked.

"What do you mean, Kathleen?" he replied, placing the deed back in the bag of his saddle and untying his horse's reins from the rail.

"I mean . . . do you want me to leave, or stay . . . or, I don't know . . . I was getting ready to leave."

"Leave . . . why would I want you to leave? Was that other fellow—your uncle on your pa's side—was he kicking you out of here?"

"No, he said I could stay, but I didn't want to . . . I—"

"Well, it's all right by me if you stay too. I ain't got no plans. Heck, it's your place more than it's mine. You got more of a right to be here than anyone."

"Uncle Burchard was going to take Rosewood over and made everyone else leave. So I didn't see how I could stay. He wasn't too nice to me."

"Yeah, well . . . from what I've seen, that doesn't exactly surprise me."

"Are you . . . are you going to take over Rosewood . . . like he was?"

Mr. Daniels laughed. "I ain't got no intention of being a plantation owner," he said. "I just figured I oughta come see what was going on, pay my respects and all. I had no idea what I was walking into till I got here, other than the little I read about in the newspaper. Soon as I saw that I knew I'd better get down here. But it's like I said, the way I figure it, you got more right to this place than me."

He got serious, remembering again why all this was happening. "I'm sorry about your ma, Kathleen," he said. "I'm sorry I didn't come back and never saw her again."

Katie nodded. "So . . . you really mean you don't mind if I stay?" she asked.

"Course not. I want you to stay, Kathleen. 'Course I want you to stay. What else would I want?"

"I . . . I don't know . . . I just . . ."

Katie's eyes began to fill with tears.

"This ain't my place now any more'n it ever was," said her uncle. "The way I hear it, you been running the place without anyone's help anyway . . . except for that colored girl I read about—what's her name?"

"Mayme," said Katie.

"Right . . . where's she at anyway?"

Suddenly Katie's mind filled with new thoughts. *Thoughts about me and Emma and Josepha! We had been gone more than an hour, maybe close to two. And she didn't even know where we were!*

"Can the others stay too?" Katie asked excitedly.

"What others?"

"Mayme and the others who were helping us and living here with us!"

"Sure . . . I reckon so . . . where are they?"

"They left. Uncle Burchard made them leave."

By now most of the townspeople were on their horses and in their buggies and starting back toward town, though still buzzing about the sudden turn of events they had witnessed. And thanks to Mrs. Hammond, the whole community would know about it soon enough.

Mr. Sneed and Mr. Clairborne had talked awhile longer on the other side of the house, Mr. Clairborne angrier than a wet hen. Then Mr. Sneed left and Mr. Clairborne and his men started loading up some of the wagons with the stuff they had unloaded earlier.

Seeing what had happened and happy for Katie, Henry and Jeremiah had wandered off with the rest of the people. But now Katie's brain was moving at full tilt.

"Henry . . . Jeremiah!" she called, running after them while her uncle stood still holding the reins of his horse. "Stay here, will you . . . until we get back. Jeremiah, would you please go saddle my horse—hurry!"

Jeremiah dashed off toward the barn.

"What you want me ter do, Miz Kathleen?" asked Henry.

"Nothing, Henry," she answered. "Just stay here and keep a watch out. I don't want to leave Uncle Burchard here all by himself. He's so mad I don't know what he might do. My uncle Ward and I will get back as soon as we can."

"But, Miz Kathleen, where's you—"

It was too late. Already Katie was running back to where her uncle stood watching her with a look of perplexity on his face.

"Uncle Ward," she said hurriedly. "You've got to come with me—I hope it's all right! It's terribly important. And we've got to ride fast to catch them! I'll be back in a minute with my horse!"

Again Katie ran off and disappeared in the direction

of the barn. She ran right past where Mr. Sneed was just climbing into his buggy and her uncle Burchard, still fuming, was standing with two of his men. She was afraid to glance up at him, but heard him yell as she ran past.

"Don't think this is the end of it, Kathleen," he said. "I'll be back with an attorney who's not a spineless woman like Sneed! Then we'll see just how legal that deed of your ma's really is."

When he next saw Katie a minute later, she was riding out of the door of the barn, leaning low against her horse's neck till she was clear of the overhang, Jeremiah running after her on foot. The instant she was in the yard, she yelled a command and galloped around to where her uncle Ward was waiting.

"Are you ready, Uncle Ward!" shouted Katie as she rode up.

"I reckon, but I still don't know what for."

"Just come with me and I'll explain it on the way . . . we've got to catch them! And do you have the deed? You've got to bring the deed."

"Yeah, it's still safe and sound. But what do you want with that?" he asked as he mounted his horse.

"Mayme will never believe me if she doesn't see it. She can be stubborn sometimes when she thinks she's acting for my best. And once she's made up her mind about something, we'll never change it unless she sees proof of what we say!"

She galloped off in the direction we'd gone, and her uncle, still more than a little confused, followed her.

"Hey, Kathleen . . . hey—wait," he called after her. "This poor horse of mine's bushed. At least let me give him a drink."

"There are plenty of streams along the way!" Katie shouted back over her shoulder. By now she was halfway to the trees, and her uncle dug his heels into his horse's flanks, shouted a couple of commands, and did his best to catch up.

COMING AFTER US

30

By the time it had got on to eleven o'clock, the sun was high and we were tired. Poor Josepha had been slowing down for a while and was sweating a lot. We'd only just left and I was already getting worried. How we'd ever make fifty miles I couldn't imagine. Emma and William were about tuckered out too. So we walked off the road by where it crossed a good-sized stream, found a nice shady spot under a big oak, and sat down to rest and have something to eat. We all drank our fill from the stream, and after some bread and cheese and another drink, it didn't take long for a few folks to get sleepy. In fact, in about ten minutes both Josepha and William were sound asleep, and Emma and I weren't far behind them. A warm day always seems to put you to sleep.

Katie rode hard. She and the new uncle she'd just met

didn't have the chance to talk much as they went, so whatever explanations she'd intended to give him had to wait until later. Whatever he thought, he didn't object too much and kept following, though who could tell what he was thinking.

From what she'd overheard Josepha and me saying, Katie had a pretty good idea which way we'd be going, though once the road north passed the Thurston plantation it went in two directions. The way they went at first didn't happen to be the same way we'd gone, and so they saw nobody, and after about twenty minutes of fast riding Katie was sure we couldn't have gotten that far. They turned around and retraced their way back to where the road split and this time took the other road.

They stopped a couple of times for their horses to drink, though by now Katie's uncle's horse was showing signs of slowing down regardless. But still Katie kept riding at a gentle gallop as hard as the two horses would go.

I don't know how long we slept, probably not too long. It was such a warm day, and with the sound of the stream and a gentle breeze in the oak leaves above us, it was just about as nice and as peaceful as you could imagine. But we had such a long way to go, and we'd never get there if we slept four hours every day. And besides, we had to get far enough away so we wouldn't have to worry about still being in the vicinity of the McSimmons place. So when I woke up and remembered where we were and what we were doing, as peaceful as it was, I knew we had to be getting on our way.

"Emma," I said, shaking her gently where she lay next to me. "We gotta be going . . . Josepha, time to get on our way."

Slowly we all roused ourselves. As I was coming back from the woods from doing my necessaries, all at once I heard the sound of horses. I listened real intently and realized there was more than one. I ran back to the others.

"Horses coming," I said. "I think there's several. Let's get out of sight behind that shrubbery and everyone keep quiet. Can you keep real still, William?" I said as I hurried them out of sight of the road.

Ten or fifteen seconds later, the sound of two horses echoed on the wooden bridge over the stream that we'd crossed a while earlier.

We waited till they were by, but then Emma stuck her head up and glanced toward the road.

"Emma!" I whispered. "Get down."

"I jes' wanted ter see who it—"

Suddenly she jumped to her feet. "It be Miz Katie!" she cried. "Look . . . hit's Miz Katie!"

Before I could even think about what she'd said, Emma was off like a shot, running up onto the road and shrieking at the top of her lungs.

I ran after her, and by then Josepha had struggled to her feet too. By the time we reached the road, the two horses were well past us. But Emma was making such a racket that not even the sound of horses' hooves could drown it out. I saw the second rider rein in and look behind him. I didn't know him any more than he knew any of us. A strange look came over his face as he saw two colored girls chasing after him and yelling what he could hardly make out a word of. And when a huge colored woman waddled up out of the brush after them, I can't imagine what he must have thought!

By then Katie had heard something too and realized that her uncle had stopped. She reined in and spun her horse around, and the next instant was galloping back past him and straight up to us.

"Mayme . . . Mayme!" she cried excitedly. Dust was flying all over and the horse pranced about as she jumped off, not even bothering with the reins. "You'll never guess what happened!" she went on as she ran to meet us. "This is my uncle . . . the uncle I thought was dead, my uncle Ward! He came right when that lawyer was about to turn Rosewood over to Uncle Burchard, and everything stopped and he pulled out the deed to the property. You remember the deed they were looking for but couldn't find . . . Uncle Ward had it! My mama gave it to him . . . Rosewood belonged to my mama not my daddy, and she gave it to Uncle Ward when he gave her the gold . . . and so he owns it . . . and he still owns it, not Uncle Burchard . . . and he said we could stay!"

Katie was nearly out of breath from talking so fast. I had only understood about half of what she'd said, but the expression of happiness on her face told me everything there was to know. By then we were all clustered around, and her uncle had ridden up slowly behind us. I glanced up at him and saw the resemblance between him and my papa right off. I smiled and he smiled back.

"You must be Mayme that Kathleen's been telling me about," he said.

I nodded. "And this is Emma and Josepha," I said, pointing to the other two.

"An' William!" added Emma, because just then William, who'd been suddenly deserted down by the stream, trundled up behind us.

"Well, I must say, Kathleen," said Mr. Daniels, "this is quite a little troop you've got here. Maybe now I understand why your other uncle back there made them leave—they're all colored."

"Yes, sir," said Katie.

"Well, that don't matter none to me. Takes all kinds to make a world, I always say. Heck, I ain't even sure how long I'll be staying myself. I just came for a visit after hearing what had happened."

Now that the dust had settled, so to speak, although it was still dusty where we were standing, Katie and her uncle had a little more chance to talk about what had happened.

"How did you hear about what was going on, Uncle Ward?" asked Katie.

"You don't know?"

"What do you mean?"

"I read about the two of you in a paper up north. That's how I found out Richard and Rosalind were dead, and I figured I ought to come down and see if there was any way I could help out, you being kin and all."

"Did you know about Uncle Burchard's saying Rosewood was his and having a new deed drawn up and everything?"

"There was just a mention of a brother of Richard's in the paper taking over ownership. But I didn't know any more than that till I got to Greens Crossing. I saw a notice up on a signboard and I asked somebody about it. That's when I figured I'd better hightail it out there so I could have a say in the matter."

"I'm sure glad you did!" said Katie.

"And just in the nick of time, by all appearances of what was going on," he said, now getting down from his horse and walking it to the stream. "So that was your pa's brother, huh?"

Katie dismounted too and we all followed. "But I still don't understand about the deed, Uncle Ward," she said as she led her horse after her uncle. "Why did Mama give it to you and sign it so that Rosewood would be yours?"

"She and Richard were always a mite worried about that Burchard fellow. And then when I got back from California and asked her to keep my gold for me, she figured it was only right to give me something in exchange. I told her she didn't need to, but she insisted. She said it was only fair, something like giving me a note in exchange for the gold, and she wouldn't take no for an answer."

"I'm sorry about us using up all the gold, Uncle Ward."

"I already told you, I didn't come back for the gold. But tell me again what happened with it?"

"We used it for Rosewood," answered Katie. "My mama had taken out two loans when my daddy was away at the war, and after they were killed the loans came due. Mayme and I found the gold and paid off the loans."

"Well, no matter. I'm glad it got put to good use. I came back to see if you were okay and to tell you how sorry I am about your ma. If my hard work in California helped save the place from some banker, well, then, I figure maybe that's worth it."

"He kin hab dat fifty-five dollars you dun gib me, Miz Katie," Josepha now said. "I don' need it. Lan' sakes, dat's more money den mos' black folks eber see in dere lives!"

Katie and I looked at each other and laughed. Her uncle looked back and forth between us, then started to chuckle too.

"We've got about two hundred dollars between all four of us, Uncle Ward," said Katie. "You can have it if you want. I split up the money between us all before they left, since they helped pick the cotton. It won't make up for the gold, but it's something."

"You picked cotton too!"

"Yes, we made over four hundred dollars."

"That's a lot of money! But I don't want your two hundred dollars, Kathleen.—That's just about more

163

money than this white man has ever seen in one place either, ma'am!" he added to Josepha.

Josepha's eyes went wide and she just stared back at him. It was the first time she'd ever been called *ma'am* by a white man.

"And I ain't so sure a plantation's what I want either," Katie's uncle added. "I just kept the deed all this time out of respect to Rosalind and figured one day I'd sign it back to her whether she liked it or not. So maybe I ought to just sign it back to you, Kathleen. Then Rosewood will be yours and nobody can take it away from you."

I glanced over at Katie and there were tears in her eyes. I knew she wanted to give the man in front of her a big hug. But she barely knew him and couldn't quite bring herself to it. But it didn't make what he'd said any less important.

"What about Uncle Burchard?" said Katie. "Aren't I too young? Couldn't he come back and make trouble again later?"

"You might be right. How old are you, Kathleen?"

"I just turned seventeen."

"All right, then, we'll wait till you're eighteen, and then I'll sign it over to you . . . or twenty-one if you like. We'll do it all legal-like so he can't do nothing to bother you.—But what are we all standing around here for? Didn't we come find these folks so you could take them back to the house with you?"

"Yes, but—" Katie began, then stopped and looked around at all of us. "But what are we going to do—

we've only got two horses. We'll have to go back to get a wagon."

"You want me to go?" said her uncle.

"Can you find your way?"

"I reckon so."

"Henry—he's the black man who was there that I was talking to—he should still be there. Tell him what we're doing and that I asked him to help you. He'll know which wagon is best, and can hitch it to one of our other horses so that yours can rest. Henry will know what to do. You can take my horse if you want."

"And you want to wait here with them?"

Katie nodded.

"All right, then." He paused, glanced briefly at me, then back at Katie. "She didn't ask to see the deed," he said with kind of a twinkle in his eye, nodding in my direction.

"What is he talking about?" I asked.

Katie hesitated. An embarrassed expression came over her face. "I told him you wouldn't believe me about what had happened if we didn't have the deed to show you."

"I don't suppose I had any reason to doubt it," I said. "But I reckon I would like to see it."

Her uncle opened his saddlebag and handed Katie the deed. She showed it around to the rest of us. "You see," she said, "it was in my mama's name, not my daddy's. So that means that Uncle Burchard's got nothing to do with it. And then when Uncle Ward gave mama the gold to keep, she signed it here—see, there's her signature signing the deed over to Ward Daniels."

"That's me!" said her uncle.

"So Uncle Ward's the legal owner of the plantation. And he says I can stay, and all the rest of you can too."

"We's mighty thankful, Mr. Daniels, sir," said Josepha. "I's Josepha Black, an' I'm right proud ter mak yer 'quaintance." She held up a big fleshy hand. Katie's uncle shook it and smiled. "I's try ter please you, sir," said Josepha, "an' I's work jes' as hard as I dun fer Miz Katie."

"And this is Emma," said Katie. "She and William have been staying with Mayme and me right from the beginning."

"And what about you, Mayme," he said, turning to me. "I read in the story in the paper that you lost your family too, just like Kathleen. You want to stay on at Rosewood too?"

I looked up at him, realizing for the first time that he was my uncle too.

"Yes, sir, Mr. Daniels," I said. "Rosewood's my home. This is just about the only family I've got left."

"Well, I'm glad all that is settled," he said. "So I guess I'd better get going so I can return with that wagon and take you all back to the house."

He took Katie's reins and handed his to her, then led his horse up onto the road, mounted, and a few seconds later was galloping away.

ANOTHER HOMECOMING

31

We were too excited about the sudden change to be able to go back to sleep on the ground while we waited, even though we were still tired. Suddenly our fortunes and our futures had changed again! Though we weren't altogether sure yet what it would all mean.

We talked and talked excitedly and Katie told us all about what had happened and about how her uncle had ridden up right at the last minute and about how mad her uncle Burchard had been. We all laughed and asked so many questions that the time went by quickly. Before we knew it we heard the sound of the wagon coming along the road. And there was Jeremiah sitting beside Katie's uncle on the seat board! Now I was even happier than ever!

He turned the wagon around, and we all loaded up and began the ride back home. Jeremiah came and sat with me in the back and Katie sat up front with her uncle. Jeremiah didn't say anything, but he couldn't seem to stop looking at me and smiling.

"Your uncle Templeton ever show up around here?" I heard Katie's uncle ask as we jostled along.

Immediately I perked up my ears to listen!

"Oh yes—he's been around a lot . . . I meant to tell

you!" answered Katie. "There's so much to tell. He's been living at Rosewood. He even helped us pick the cotton."

"My brother Templeton . . . picking cotton!" exclaimed Katie's uncle.

"He's really changed, Uncle Ward."

"Then where is he? Why ain't he around? How'd he let you get in this fix with that Burchard fellow?"

"That's what I've got to tell you," said Katie. "He's in trouble."

"What kind of trouble?"

"He's in jail."

"Jail!"

"We got a letter from him more than a week ago. We'd been worried sick about him because we hadn't heard from him for a long time. He left before Uncle Burchard came claiming that Rosewood should belong to him. So Uncle Templeton doesn't know anything about it."

"Why'd he leave?"

"He said he had some things to take care of, people he needed to make things right with. I'm not sure what he meant."

Katie's uncle nodded. I couldn't see his face from behind him where I was sitting. But I had the feeling he understood even if Katie didn't.

"You ever hear of a con artist?" he asked.

"No, sir."

"Well, that's probably just as well, and there ain't no need my trying to explain it to you. Let's just say your uncle made a few enemies along the way, just like I did myself."

"There were some men who came looking for you and your gold," said Katie.

"What kind of men?"

"One was called Hal, I think, and another named Jeb."

Mr. Daniels didn't say anything for a minute but got real thoughtful. "That's them all right," he said. "I figured I hadn't heard the last of them. They cause any trouble?"

"Yes, sir. They had guns and came twice. The first time Mayme and I scared them off by shooting some of my daddy's guns. The second time Uncle Templeton was here. He shot one of them and got shot himself. We thought he was going to die."

"Hmm . . . well, they were a bad lot, all right. Which one of them did Templeton shoot?"

"I don't know."

"And what became of him?"

"He's dead, Uncle Ward. Uncle Templeton killed him. He did it to save me. The man was about to shoot me."

"Whew . . . sounds like it was bad . . . real bad," he said, shaking his head. "Me and Templeton both got mixed up in a few things we shouldn't have. Where's he in jail at?"

"I don't know, Uncle Ward. He didn't say. The letter didn't say either."

"Well, you can show it to me when we get back and

I'll see what I can make of it."

They kept talking, but gradually their voices got so quiet I couldn't hear them above the sound of the horses and the clattering of the wagon wheels. I wondered if Katie was telling him about me, and that even though I was colored, I was his niece.

When we got back to the house forty minutes or an hour later, Henry was waiting for us. There was no sign of Burchard Clairborne, though one of his wagons and a lot of the stuff he'd brought out earlier was still there.

Josepha climbed down and went straight into the kitchen and started fixing us all something to eat and drink. It was mighty strange coming back still another time after I'd thought I was leaving Rosewood for good. It seemed like I was always leaving and then coming back.

"You'll stay awhile, won't you, Uncle Ward?" said Katie as they walked inside. "You're not just going to leave again, are you?"

"I've come too far not to stay and rest up a spell."

"Then what will you do?"

"I don't know, Kathleen. I reckon everything is changed now. I gotta think on it some."

"Do you want to see Mama's grave?"

Mr. Daniels nodded. The two of them walked away from the house while Emma and I and William followed Josepha inside.

Half an hour later we were all sitting around the table in the kitchen eating lunch. This was sure not what we'd been expecting to be doing this afternoon after the day had begun with us all saying good-bye to each other!

"You got that letter from Templeton, Kathleen?" Mr. Daniels asked.

Katie had to think a minute, then remembered she'd put it in her suitcase, which was still sitting where she'd left it outside the door. She brought it in and opened it up, then handed the letter to her uncle. He read it thoughtfully, nodding a couple times.

"Yeah, I reckon I got a pretty good idea where he is," he said after a bit.

"Then let's go get him . . . let's get him out of jail!" said Katie excitedly.

Mr. Daniels laughed. "It ain't quite that easy, Kathleen," he said.

"Why not, Uncle Ward?"

"We don't know what the charges against him are," he said, "—though I've got a pretty good idea."

"We've got to try to help him."

"Maybe you're right. I don't reckon we can just let him rot in jail."

"Yes, Uncle Ward! We've got to help him! Can we, Uncle Ward? Will you take me to find him?"

"I'll think on that a spell too," he laughed. "I can see you must have grown mighty fond of your uncle Templeton."

He paused and glanced at me, then back to Katie.

"But tell me," he said, "what was Templeton talking about 'your uncle and papa'? Who's this Mary Ann he's talking about?"

The whole room went silent. I felt the heat rising on the back of my neck. I glanced at Katie and could tell that she didn't want to say anything I didn't want her to say.

"That's me, Mr. Daniels," I said after a few seconds. "Mayme's what folks always called me, but Mary Ann is my real name."

"But why was he writing to you like that, along with Kathleen?"

I hesitated and looked at Katie. "Because . . . I'm his daughter," I said finally.

He stared back at me with a blank expression for a few seconds.

"Templeton is your *father?*" he said.

"Yes, sir."

"Is your mama Lemuela?"

I nodded. "You know about my mama?" I said.

"Sure. She was just like part of our family before Rosalind was married. Now that I think of it, you look just like her."

He shook his head. "Well, if that don't beat all! So when you called this your family back there, you weren't kidding . . . this really is your *family?*"

"Mayme and I felt like sisters even before we found out we were cousins," said Katie. "That's what made it so hard about Uncle Burchard saying none of them could stay, and why I was going to leave this morning too. I couldn't bear to be here without them. And that's why we've just got to get Uncle Templeton out of jail! He's part of the family, just like you are now too, Uncle Ward."

He laughed again. It was hard not to get caught up in Katie's enthusiasm once she got determined about something!

"Well, I'll read his letter again after lunch," said Mr. Daniels, "and I'll think on it a spell. Then maybe we'll talk about my going up there and finding out what's going on."

"Oh, thank you . . . thank you, Uncle Ward!" exclaimed Katie. "But don't you mean you'll think about *us* going and finding out what's going on? I've got to go too!"

"You?"

Katie nodded eagerly.

"What if it's dangerous, Kathleen?"

"I don't care. He's my uncle. I've got to go."

"Well, then, I reckon I'll have to think on it even harder."

"But we'll try, won't we, Uncle Ward? You'll help me try to find him?"

"I reckon so, Kathleen . . . I reckon so."

"Oh, thank you . . . thank you, Uncle Ward! When can we leave to go find him?"

"I don't know, in a day or two maybe. And you're still intent on going along?"

"Yes, Uncle Ward," said Katie. "If Uncle Templeton's in jail, I've got to try to help him!"

173

32

I wasn't so sure about Katie and her uncle leaving the rest of us alone so soon after what her uncle Burchard had done, knowing that he might still be around. And I wanted to go too! But one of us had to stay at Rosewood, and we all knew that having Katie plead the cause for her uncle would do more good with a white sheriff than anything I could do. One look at me, with me saying he was my daddy, and he'd probably keep him in jail longer! So we asked Henry to come out and stay at Rosewood while they were gone just so that nothing bad would happen with Mr. Clairborne. We also made sure that no townspeople knew they were leaving, especially Mrs. Hammond.

Katie and her uncle Ward planned to take the train up to Baltimore, which was near the town where Mr. Daniels figured they were keeping my papa. Katie took twenty dollars of her money, which Mr. Daniels said would be enough to get them there and back.

They left two days later, rode into Charlotte, spent the night in a hotel, and then got on the next morning's train north to Richmond and from there to Baltimore, where they spent the next night. Then Mr. Daniels rented two horses and they rode out to the little town of Ellicott City, where he hoped they would find his brother. If they didn't, he said, then they were sunk because he had no other idea where he might be. But it was a town where he knew my papa had spent quite a bit of time and was the only place he'd seen him after coming back from California. After riding all that way together on the train, Katie said they got to know each other pretty well. Her uncle Ward was a lot like her uncle Templeton, she said. They were so much alike, she couldn't understand why they hadn't been better friends through the years and had drifted apart like they had.

They got to Ellicott City a little after noon on the third day after leaving Rosewood. It wasn't a very big town, Katie said, about the size of Greens Crossing, though it had a sheriff's office and jail, which Greens Crossing didn't.

"Well, there it is," said Mr. Daniels, pointing ahead as they rode through the main street of the town.

Katie looked ahead of them and saw a small wooden building with the word SHERIFF painted above the door. They rode to it, stopped, tied their horses in front, then went inside.

A young man was seated behind a wooden desk. Katie said he didn't look much older than her. He looked up and nodded.

"Afternoon," he said, smiling at Katie.

"Are you the sheriff?" she asked.

"No, miss . . . I'm just the deputy. What can I do for you?"

"Do you have someone in jail here whose name is Templeton Daniels?"

"That we do, miss," said the deputy, glancing at the

paper in Katie's hand where she was holding the letter. "He's our only prisoner."

"We would like to see him."

"On what kind of business, miss?"

"We're kin. He's my uncle, and this is his brother."

"I see . . . well, I'll have to talk to the sheriff and make sure it's all right."

"When will he be back?"

"Can't say, miss. But if you two will be good enough to step outside so I can lock the door—he always makes me lock the door if I have to leave the office—I'll run over to the saloon and ask him about it."

A minute later Katie and Mr. Daniels were standing on the boardwalk while the young deputy ran across the street. He came out two minutes later with a man at his side. They walked across the street.

"I'm Sheriff Heyes," said the older man. "My deputy here says you want to see Daniels."

"That's right," said Mr. Daniels. "I reckon we want to talk to you too, to find out what kind of trouble he's in. He wrote our niece here a letter, but it don't say much."

"What did he tell you?" asked the sheriff.

"I have the letter right here," said Katie, pulling out the letter. "He said that he had come back to try to pay back some money a man thought he owed him but that he got put in jail before he could and that you wouldn't let him out until he paid it, which he couldn't do as long as he was in jail."

"Well, I reckon that's partially right," said the sheriff. "He swindled one of the biggest ranchers in these parts out of a good piece of dough, and the man's pretty upset about it." He eyed Mr. Daniels carefully. "Don't I know you too?" he asked.

"I was around a time or two with my brother years ago."

"Yeah, I thought so."

"But how can he pay it back if you keep him in jail?" said Katie, bringing the conversation back to the subject of my papa.

"Maybe he can't. But I got the law to think about too."

"There wouldn't be any harm in us seeing him, though . . . would there?"

"No, I don't reckon so. He's not dangerous, and the two of you sure don't look dangerous.—Go ahead, Rob, you can let them see him."

"Thank you, Sheriff!" said Katie.

The sheriff nodded and almost returned her smile, then walked back toward the saloon.

They followed the deputy back to the office and inside. He took out another key and unlocked another door, then nodded for them to follow. He led them through a narrow corridor with empty cells on each side.

"You got visitors, Daniels!" he called out as they went.

Katie was walking behind the deputy. He stopped and pulled out a set of keys and unlocked a metal door to his right, then moved back. Katie stepped into the doorway. There was her uncle Templeton standing there.

"Kathleen!" he exclaimed.

"Hello, Uncle Templeton."

"What in thunder . . . what are you doing here! How did you find me?"

"I had some help figuring out where you were." Katie smiled. "Look who I've got with me," she said, looking behind her.

My papa saw a figure step out of the shadows of the hallway and follow Katie into the cell.

"Ward! What the—"

"Hello, Templeton," said Mr. Daniels, a little sheepishly, Katie thought.

"I figured you for dead . . . I hadn't heard from you in so long. But—"

He glanced over at Katie.

"—How in the world did you two . . . what are you doing here—*together?*"

"It's a long story," said Mr. Daniels.

"There's so much to tell you, Uncle Templeton," Katie burst in. "My other uncle I told you about—Uncle Burchard, my father's brother—he's been trying to take Rosewood away the whole time you were gone. We didn't know what had happened or where you were and we were so afraid. Mrs. Hammond didn't bring us the letter right away, and we didn't know what to do. Finally we all decided to leave Rosewood. Then right at the last minute—after Mayme and Emma and Josepha had all left and were heading up north to find some people Josepha knew—"

"Mary Ann's gone!" my papa interrupted.

"She's not gone anymore," replied Katie. "But she had left, and I was getting ready to leave too. We didn't know what else to do, because you were gone and we didn't know where you were. Then suddenly Uncle Ward came from out of nowhere. And guess what he had with him!"

"I doubt if I could guess in a hundred years . . . he wasn't carrying another sack of gold, was he?" asked my papa, glancing toward his brother.

"No, something even better! Tell him, Uncle Ward!" said Katie excitedly, turning to Mr. Daniels.

"You go ahead and tell him, Kathleen," he said. "I think he'd like hearing it from you."

"He had the *deed,* Uncle Templeton!" said Katie. "The deed to Rosewood. Mama'd given it to him a long time ago and he'd kept it all this time. Once the lawyer looked at it, there wasn't anything more my uncle Burchard could do but leave."

"Rosalind gave *you* the deed?" asked my papa. "What about Richard? He never took much shine to either of us. Can't figure he'd let her do that."

"For some reason, Richard had put the place in Rosalind's name," said Mr. Daniels. "So it was legally hers. When I gave her my gold to keep, after I got back from California, she gave me the deed."

"Why?"

"I don't know—she thought it was the right thing to do."

"Sounds like Rosalind, all right."

"I think Richard was afraid this Burchard fellow'd try

to pull something. Might have been his way of trying to protect the place."

Templeton rubbed his chin thoughtfully.

"I, uh . . . I take it you got my letter?" he said.

Mr. Daniels nodded.

"I don't have much to offer," said my papa, "but there's no sense you two just standing there. You want to come in—I guess you can sit on the bed there."

Katie and her uncle Ward walked inside the cell and sat down while my papa continued to stand. The deputy had been standing in the hallway and now pulled the cell door closed but stayed nearby listening.

"What's it all about anyway, Templeton?" asked Mr. Daniels.

"It's an old beef," answered my papa. "It'll never hold up in court. Roscoe's a greedy man and all I did was take advantage of that—he's the rancher who brought the charge against me. Trouble is, the sheriff here's his brother-in-law. So there's nothing I can do as long as I'm here."

He glanced toward the deputy in the hall, like he wished maybe he hadn't said what he did.

"But couldn't we help, Uncle Templeton?" said Katie. "What if I gave him my money?"

"Gave it to who?"

"Whoever that man is who's making you stay here."

"I don't know . . . might help some, though I doubt you've got enough, Kathleen. And there are some other folks that are waiting for a chance to take it out of my hide too."

180

"If she ain't got enough, I'll chip in," said Mr. Daniels.

"You got money?" asked his brother.

"Not much. But I got a little stashed away left over from the gold. Probably not more'n a hundred dollars. But there's Rosalind's deed too. That's likely worth twice what anybody's got against you."

"Yes, yes!" said Katie, suddenly realizing the significance of what her uncle Ward had said. "We could get a loan again, just like Mama did—a loan against Rosewood."

"You can't be doing that, Kathleen. Not now that you finally got them other two loans paid off and your uncle Burchard off your back."

"But what good is Rosewood, Uncle Templeton, if you're in jail? You and Mayme and Uncle Ward are the only family I've got and—"

Katie started to cry. "I just want us to be together," she tried to go on. "That's all we need—being together. I don't care if we even lose Rosewood, just so we can be together . . . and be a *family*."

BROTHERS

33

The cell was quiet a minute. The only sound was Katie's crying. I don't know what the deputy was thinking.

"I reckon she's right," said Mr. Daniels after a minute.

"Whatever I got is yours too, the hundred dollars, even the deed Rosalind gave me . . . whatever it takes to get you out of here."

Katie said my papa just stood there and stared down at the floor.

Katie gradually stopped crying. When Templeton Daniels spoke again, Katie said his voice sounded soft and husky, like he might have been fighting back a few tears of his own.

"Kathleen," he said, "Ward and I need to have a little talk, between ourselves, brother to brother. You don't mind waiting outside for a spell, do you?"

"No," she said, wiping her eyes. She stood up and walked out of the cell. The deputy made sure the cell was locked, then took Katie back out to the sheriff's office and offered her a chair. Katie noticed that the deputy hadn't closed the door behind them, maybe to keep one ear open and make sure the brothers weren't planning an escape or something. In any case, Katie didn't mean to eavesdrop, but from where she sat, she could hear most of the conversation from the cell down the hall.

"Pretty big shock seeing you walk in here," said my papa after a quiet spell. "I haven't laid eyes on you in, what's it been . . . five, maybe six years. You're looking good, though—just a little gray around the ears. Otherwise you ain't hardly aged a day."

"You look about the same too," said Mr. Daniels. "Not quite so much sparkle in your eye."

"Sitting in jail will do that to you.—What do you

think about that girl of Rosalind's?"

"She's something, all right. Grew up mighty fast."

"Probably not any faster than anyone grows up. You and I just weren't paying attention like we should have."

"I reckon you're right there."

"And that girl of yours . . . Mayme—she seems like a nice kid."

"Mary Ann . . ." said my papa, a little astonished. "You saw her?"

"Yep. What happened anyway?"

"One of Richard and Rosalind's slave girls . . . back when I was visiting Rosewood . . . years ago. You remember Lemuela, who grew up with Rosalind."

"Sure I do."

"A wonderful girl, Ward . . . not the kind of thing you might think—I could have married her, if I'd had the guts. But I was a coward, and Richard ran me off when he found out, then sold Mary Ann's mother to a neighboring plantation. I never knew she was carrying Mary Ann and never saw her again."

"How'd the kid end up at Rosewood?" asked Mr. Daniels.

"Accident of fate, I guess you'd call it. Her family was massacred by the same bunch that killed Richard and Rosalind and the boys. Mary Ann just wandered about and wound up at Rosewood. She and Kathleen didn't know they were cousins till I figured it out later. They were just a white girl and a colored girl doing their best to survive.—But I still haven't got an answer

183

to the question of what *you're* doing here? How did you and Kathleen hook up?"

"I read about the two of them in the Richmond newspaper," answered Ward Daniels.

"What!"

"That's right. Somebody's written a story about this white girl and a black girl whose families had both been killed and who had been secretly running a plantation for two years without anyone knowing there were only kids there. As soon as I saw the name Clairborne, I knew who it was. I had no idea you knew anything about it. I just figured I oughta get down to Rosewood and see what was happening. But when I showed up, it seemed like all heck was breaking loose. That was only four or five days ago . . . and here I am."

Again it was quiet for a while.

"Terrible shame about Rosalind," said Mr. Daniels. "She was a good woman, a good sister."

"That she was." My father nodded. "A better sister than either of us was brothers . . . at least speaking for myself."

"No, you're right. We could have done better by her, that's for sure. I was nothing but a drifter looking for an easy way to get rich. She had to run the place alone for several years after Richard and the boys went off to the war."

"I was a drifter too. You looked for it in gold, I looked for it in cards and schemes. But look where it landed me."

"Yeah, well, I ain't done much better. But maybe we

still got the chance to make it right with Rosalind, if you know what I mean."

My papa nodded. "Yep . . . taking care of Kathleen, I suppose that falls to us now."

"It's the least we can do, especially not being any better brothers than we were, like you say," said Mr. Daniels. "But first we got to get you out of here."

"Did you . . . you really mean what you said . . . that you'd put up your last hundred, and even Rosalind's deed, to spring me?"

" 'Course I meant it."

"Why would you do that . . . for me?"

"You're my brother."

"The two of us haven't exactly been on brotherly terms since we left home."

"I reckon maybe you're right. I suppose we may have had our differences. We've both been rovers in our own way. But maybe it's time that changed. I figure we got people that need us now." He paused briefly, then added, "And maybe we need each other too."

Again my papa said nothing.

In the sheriff's office, the deputy shifted about in his chair, obviously uncomfortable just sitting there, unintentionally listening to the personal talk drifting in from down the hall. He looked over at Katie. "So where are you from?" he asked.

"North Carolina," answered Katie. "From Shenandoah County."

"I thought so. You sound Southern."

"Is it so noticeable?" asked Katie, glancing away from embarrassment.

"Yes, but it's nice. I like the sound of it."

"I've never been to the North before," said Katie. "People do talk different here. I never realized it before. Have you ever been to the South?"

"No. I was in the Union army for a while," said the deputy. "But I'd only just joined when the war ended and so I never got into the South. I was only seventeen then."

"You're lucky," said Katie. "One of my brothers was killed in the war, and my daddy and other two brothers hated it. They said it was terrible."

"But the others made it back?"

"Yes, but they were killed by marauders just after the war."

"Oh . . . I'm sorry, miss."

"That's why my two uncles—the men in there—are helping me with the plantation. They're the only family I've got left . . . except for my cousin, who's my age. So you see why it's so important for me to get my uncle out of here and back home?"

The deputy nodded but looked down at his hands. Katie knew there was little he could do.

Back in the cell, it had been quiet a minute.

"I suppose you're right," my papa finally said. "It's about time for us to settle down. Maybe Kathleen's right, and we got a family now. That's what I was thinking back at Rosewood a few months back. I actually learned how to pick cotton! I was trying to make things right—that's why I came back up here, trying to fix some things. But I lost hope after getting thrown in here."

"Well, we're going to get you out, one way or another," said Mr. Daniels. "In case you hadn't noticed, that niece of ours is a mighty determined girl. She's not going to take no for an answer."

A Determined Katie Takes Charge
34

Katie and her uncle Ward left the sheriff's office a few minutes later and walked across the street to the saloon.

"You wait here," said Mr. Daniels. "I'll go inside and talk to the sheriff."

When the two men came out a couple minutes later they were in the midst of conversation.

"So, Sheriff," Mr. Daniels was saying, "how much of this beef against my brother is just the money? How much would we have to put in your hand to clear him?"

The sheriff thought a minute. "I ain't sure exactly, or even if that'd be enough to spring him. Might help, though Roscoe's still mighty angry about getting swindled."

"All of us together at home have almost two hundred dollars, Sheriff," said Katie excitedly as they walked up the steps. "Please, I'll give you everything I've got in the world if you'll let my uncle go! Please, Sheriff!—Uncle Ward," she said, turning to Mr. Daniels, "can we go back to Rosewood to get it? Let's leave right now. We can have the money back here in two or three days!"

They paused at the door. Mr. Daniels thought a minute.

"I reckon we could at that," he said, "but I figured I oughta talk to this Roscoe fellow to see what we could work out."

"The judge is due any day too," added the sheriff as they walked inside where the young deputy was waiting. "You might want to be here for that, to speak on behalf of your brother."

"Then I'll go back to Rosewood myself," said Katie. "I'll bring the money back while you're doing all that. The judge is sure to let him go if we have the money!"

"You figure you could go back . . . alone?" said Mr. Daniels.

"Yes, Uncle Ward, what's wrong with that?"

"It's a long way, that's all."

"Not that long. You said on the way here that it was only three hundred seventy-five miles."

"That's far enough by train—took us two days."

"Two short days, Uncle Ward."

"Yeah, well . . . I reckon I ought to talk to Templeton about it," said Mr. Daniels.

They stepped into the corridor where the cells were located.

"I heard," said my papa as they approached. "No,

Kathleen, you can't go back all that way on the train alone. Wouldn't be safe."

"I ran the plantation alone," said Katie. "At least Mayme and I did. And I'm older now. I'm seventeen, Uncle Templeton."

"That's what I'm worried about," he said. "A pretty girl like you traveling all that way on the train . . . alone. No, I don't like the thought of it. Ward, you go with her."

"He's got to see that man you sold the property to, Uncle Templeton, and talk to the judge," said Katie. "The sheriff said the judge might come any day, and Uncle Ward has to be here. So I'm going by myself so I can get back here with the money to give them. I don't care if you don't like it—I'm going back to Rosewood."

Her two uncles looked at each other and shrugged. Neither of them had raised any children, though Templeton Daniels was my father. And neither of them had had too much experience at being uncles either. If this was what it was like, having Katie tell them what she was going to do whether they liked it or not, they weren't quite sure what to make of it.

"And what you figure to do then, Kathleen?" asked Mr. Daniels.

"What do you mean?"

"About the money?"

"I'll bring it back with me," said Katie, "so the man you took it from can have it and so the sheriff will let you out of jail."

By now the sheriff had been around the three of them enough to realize that there was nothing sinister about the two Daniels brothers. In fact, it seemed as if he was starting to like Katie and wasn't quite so inclined to be angry at my papa as before. The hint of a smile broke out on his lips as he watched her trying to persuade her two uncles, and watching how helpless they were to keep her from doing what she wanted.

"That's a spunky young lady you've got on your hands," he said, grinning at Katie.

My papa just shook his head and rubbed his chin. "You carrying that much money around doesn't sound any better than you going all that way alone," he said after a bit.

"It's dangerous out there, Kathleen," added her uncle Ward. "There's still bad men about. Don't forget what happened to your family."

The reminder of that quieted things down in a hurry. The next voice to speak up was not one any of them had expected to hear.

"If you don't mind my barging in, Sheriff," said the deputy who had been standing behind the sheriff listening to the whole conversation, "that is, if you think you'd be able to handle things without me, I can't see there'd be any harm in my taking the train south and accompanying Miss Clairborne to make sure she's safe and to get the money back here like she wants."

Katie didn't know what to say. Her two uncles glanced at each other, not quite knowing what to make of the deputy's suggestion.

"Hmm . . . I imagine there's no problem with you being away a couple days," said the sheriff. "Yeah, I reckon that might work."

"Now just wait a minute, Sheriff . . ." said my papa, his protective side coming to the surface again. He paused and glanced at Katie, then further into the corridor at the deputy, then back at the sheriff.

"—Kathleen . . . Deputy," he said, "you mind if we have a few words in private with the sheriff?"

A look of confusion came over Katie's face. But before she could say anything, the deputy began leading her back out into the office.

"Look, Sheriff," said my papa, "Kathleen's all we got left of our sister's family, and we're all she's got too. I don't know if you ever heard of Bilsby's Marauders right after the war, but they killed her whole family—that's our sister and her husband and Kathleen's brothers—and she's only alive because her ma hid her in the cellar."

"Yeah, I heard of Bilsby's bunch," said the sheriff. "Hey, is she the girl I read about in the paper?"

"Yeah. So you see why we're a little overprotective of the girl, you might say. So what I want to ask is what kind of young man is that deputy of yours? Can he be trusted?"

"I see what you're concerned about," replied the sheriff. "She's a fine-looking young lady all right. And she loves the two of you, that much is plain to anyone. You two are a couple of lucky men. As far as Rob goes, I'm surprised you have to ask. You spent enough time in these parts, Daniels—you ought to know the name Reverend Paxton."

"Sorry, Sheriff," said my papa, shaking his head. "I don't know the man. I don't suppose I've spent as much time in church as maybe I should have. But now that you mention it, I think the name has a familiar ring to it."

"It ought to. He's one of the most respected ministers in Baltimore. He preaches here in Ellicott City once a month."

"But what's he got to do with it?" asked Mr. Daniels.

"Just this," said the sheriff. "Rob's his son."

"A preacher's kid toting a gun and a badge! That's a new one."

"Well, I don't suppose every son turns out to be the spitting image of his father. One thing's for sure, though—Rob's about as fine and upstanding a young man as you'd care to find anywhere. He wouldn't touch your niece, unless it was to protect her. I personally guarantee that she'd be as safe with him as with either of you. He can handle that gun he's wearing."

My papa and Katie's uncle Ward were quiet a minute, thinking it through.

"Don't reckon there'd be any harm in it, Templeton," said Mr. Daniels. "If she'd be safe and all."

"How long it take you two to get up here?"

"Couple days. We rode into Charlotte and stayed in a hotel there, and also spent a night in Baltimore."

"Could they make it in one day?"

"I ain't sure."

"I don't like the idea of the two of them in a hotel together, even in separate rooms. Doesn't seem right. But if they could make it all the way back in one day . . ."

"I reckon they might be able to," said Mr. Daniels.

"Depending on the train schedule," put in the sheriff. "They'd have to get an early start."

"And they'd have to get to Charlotte early enough to ride back to Rosewood. It's a long ride."

"What did you do with the horses, Ward?" asked my papa.

"Put 'em up at a livery near the station. Kathleen knows where."

"I suppose they might make it in a day, then."

"I'll talk to Rob," said the sheriff.

SURPRISE AT ROSEWOOD

35

When we heard horses riding in after dark on the fifth day since Katie and Mr. Daniels had left Rosewood, of course we hoped it would be them. But we were sure unprepared for what we saw.

I was the first one out of the house. There was Katie all right, but she was reining in alongside a young man I'd never seen.

I could tell from Katie's face that she was exhausted. I looked back and forth between the two. I think the young man with her was as surprised to see me as I was him. I didn't know what he was expecting, or if he thought I was still a slave or something, or if they didn't have as many coloreds where he came from. I later learned that Katie had told him all about us, but he was obviously surprised to see the affection between us. Whatever Katie had told him on the train, this wasn't how he'd been told white and black folks treated each other in the South!

She climbed wearily down off her horse and practically fell into my arms.

"Hi, Mayme," she said.

"Hi, Katie," I said. "You look tired."

"I'm *so* tired. We've come all the way from Baltimore today. All I want to do is sleep!"

We stood apart and I glanced toward the stranger.

"Mayme, this is Rob Paxton.—Rob, this is my cousin that I told you so much about, Mayme Daniels."

"Pleased to meet you, miss," he said, shaking my hand after he got down off his horse.

"Thank you," I said.

"Rob's the deputy sheriff," said Katie.

"*Daniels* . . ." he began. "I seem to know—right, that's the name of the man in jail."

"My uncle's Mayme's father," said Katie. "—Mayme," she said, turning again to me, "Mr. Paxton will be spending the night with us. He came down with me and we—"

Suddenly it dawned on me what Katie had said.

"But what about Papa?" I blurted out. "Did you find him?"

"Yes," said Katie. "He's safe, and Uncle Ward stayed with him to make sure nothing will happen while I'm gone. We're trying to get him out. I'll tell you all about it. In the meantime, can you have Josepha fix up the sofa in the parlor . . . and is there anything to eat?"

"Yes. I'll get started right away!" I said, turning toward the house.

"Mayme," said Katie behind me, "are Henry and Jeremiah still here?"

"Yes," I said. "They just went to bed a little while ago. They're in the barn . . . oh, here comes Jeremiah," I added. Hearing the horses, Jeremiah was just now coming from the barn to see if everything was all right.

Katie turned. "Hi, Jeremiah," she said, "would you mind taking care of our horses?"

"Sho' thing, Miz Katie."

I hurried toward the house as Katie introduced Jeremiah to the deputy. I was greeted with a dozen curious questions from Emma and Josepha, who had been watching. But I doubt their curiosity was anything like Mr. Paxton's at riding into a great big Southern plantation full of black people. In all Katie's descriptions of Rosewood and all about the rest of us, and in telling him what she and I had done together, she had never thought to mention to him that we were all colored!

When he walked into the kitchen with Katie a few minutes later, and we saw the gun on his hip, Emma's eyes got real big, and I think she was scared for a minute or two. He and Katie sat down at the table, and as they began to eat, everybody began to get used to each other. Pretty soon Henry and Jeremiah came in too.

"Da horses is put up, Miz Kathleen," said Henry. "We put yo bags on da porch. Anyfing mo we kin do fo' you?"

"No, Henry," said Katie. "Would you like to sit down?—Thank you so much for being here while I was gone."

"Don' menshun it, Miz Kathleen."

"This is Deputy Paxton, Henry.—Rob, this is our good friend Henry, Jeremiah's father."

"Pleezed ter make yer 'quaintance, Mr. Paxton," said Henry.

"We're going to have to leave again, Henry," said Katie. "I hope you won't mind staying another few days?"

"Not at all, Miz Kathleen."

"Has my uncle Burchard been around?"

"He jus' came wiff two men da day after yo lef' an' took anudder ob his wagons away, but dat's all. Ain't seen hide er hair ob him since dat."

"Did he say anything?"

"No, Miz Kathleen, he jus' scowled at me an' den went about his bizness."

Katie seemed relieved. As they ate, Katie explained to us what had happened. Before long the kitchen was filled with talk and questions and laughter.

When they were through, Katie and the deputy went back outside to get their things. As they left the kitchen I heard him whisper to her.

"You didn't tell me they were all black," he said.

"Didn't I?" said Katie. "I guess I didn't think about it."

"How could you not think about it?"

"I don't know. I don't think about them as black."

"And that's really . . . your *cousin?* When . . . telling me about her . . . thought she was white. How does she come—"

But then the door closed and I didn't hear anything else. He didn't sound upset at finding out Katie lived with black people, just surprised. According to the Northern newspapers, this wasn't the way it was on Southern plantations!

HAPPY BEDTIME

36

B y the time Katie had eaten and cleaned up and everybody was heading off to bed, and our new guest was in the parlor and Henry and Jeremiah were back outside in the barn, some of Katie's energy was coming back. We decided to sleep in the same room together like we used to.

I was full of questions! I could tell by the gleam in Katie's eyes that she wasn't ready to go to sleep yet either. A good meal and being home seemed to revive her a bit.

"We stayed with Rob's family in Baltimore last night, Mayme," Katie told me as soon as the door closed behind us and we were alone in her room. "It was a big house—even bigger than this. They were so nice to me! Mr. Paxton's a famous minister."

"But what's *he* like?" I said as we snuggled under the blankets after the lantern was down. "The one you came with called Rob. He's handsome."

"I know," giggled Katie. "When I saw him when Uncle Ward and I walked into the sheriff's office, at first I couldn't keep my eyes off him. He was about the handsomest young man I had ever seen!"

"And you called him by his given name!"

"He wanted me to."

"How old is he?" I asked.

"I don't know," said Katie. "What do you think, Mayme?"

"He's older than us."

"He'd have to be if he is a deputy."

"He must be twenty-one or twenty-two."

"That's a lot older," said Katie in a disappointed tone.

"Not so much," I said. "Girls marry men that much older than them all the time."

"Marry!" exclaimed Katie, laughing. "Who's talking about getting married?"

"Nobody," I laughed. "I was just saying it, that's all."

"I hardly know him!"

"I bet you got to know him pretty well riding all that way alone on the train."

"That was nice," said Katie dreamily. I could tell she was getting sleepy again. "He was so kind and polite. I've never talked to a boy like that, Mayme—do you think I should call him a boy or a man?"

"I don't know—he sure looks like a man to me, wearing that gun and all. How can he be a minister's son?"

"He told me all about it. Oh, Mayme, we talked and talked about everything. He told me all about his family and I told him about what had happened to mine and about you and me—"

"But you didn't tell him I was colored?" I laughed.

"I forgot. When I think about you, Mayme, I don't think about the color of your skin. I don't think about color at all. You're just . . . Mayme. But I still want to know if he's a boy or a man. What are *we,* Mayme . . . are we girls or women?"

"I reckon we're a little of both," I said.

"How can that be?"

"Because it takes a while to grow out of being a girl to grow into being a woman. So we have to be a little of both for a while."

"You're so smart."

It was quiet a minute.

"I don't feel like a woman, Mayme," said Katie. "I feel like a girl."

"You don't look like one, Katie."

"Right now I feel like a little girl with my mama here beside me to take care of me."

"We're *friends,* Katie—I'm sure not your mama! Besides, *you* take care of things around here, not me. You're the mistress of Rosewood. Emma treats you like you're *her* mama."

"She does, doesn't she?" said Katie. "She's a dear. I guess Josepha's like all of our mamas . . . well, not mine—I'm too white, but you know what I mean. But I still feel like a little girl."

"You almost look like a grown woman. You are so beautiful, Katie."

"Mayme, stop it!"

"But you are. And shapely too. I bet he's down there right now in the parlor, Mr. Paxton I mean, thinking about you too, because of how pretty you are."

"Mayme!"

We lay in contented quiet a few minutes. I could hear Katie's breathing getting deeper and deeper. I thought she was asleep and was surprised when she spoke again.

"What about Jeremiah?" she said in a soft voice. "Did you and he talk or do anything when I was gone?"

"We talked a couple of times," I said. "But mostly he went into town every day to tend the livery so Henry could stay out here."

"Are you . . . I mean—do you think you and he will get married, Mayme?" Katie asked. The question was so blunt it surprised me.

"I . . . I don't know," I answered. "Sometimes I think so."

Again it was quiet.

"I think he loves you," Katie went on. "I can see it when he looks at you."

I felt my cheeks and neck flush with heat. I guess

down inside I knew Katie was right. I'd seen that look on Jeremiah's face too.

"Do you love him, Mayme?" she asked.

"I don't know," I answered. "Sometimes I think I do, then sometimes I don't know. When we're alone and he takes my hand, that's when I'm sure I love him. But then when I think about getting married, I get afraid and I don't know. Sometimes I get so confused I don't know if I even know what love means. I don't know if I would know what love felt like if I *was* in love. Do you know what I mean?"

"I think so," said Katie. Her voice was so soft I could barely hear it. "But I've never been in love, so I don't know. I'm just a girl, Mayme, remember? I'm too young to be in love. . . ."

"I don't think you're too young anymore, Katie," I said.

But I could tell by the change in her breathing that she had fallen asleep.

WARD PLEADS TEMPLETON'S CASE
37

The next morning it almost felt like normal again. Katie's uncle Burchard was gone and that was a relief. Well, normal except for Deputy Paxton and Henry and Jeremiah all being there!

As soon as breakfast was over, Katie got Emma and Josepha and me together and sat us down to talk to us.

"I'm sorry to have to do this," she began, looking around at us almost like she was nervous, "but Uncle Templeton is in jail because he swindled a man out of some money."

"How'd he do dat, Miz Katie?" asked Emma.

"I'm not sure exactly. I think he sold a man some land for more than it was worth."

"Way I hear it, folks is always doin' dat, effen dey kin git away wiff it," said Josepha.

"I don't know," said Katie. "I think he might have lied about it too. He went back there to try to come clean about it. Whatever he did, it was against the law because they put him in jail for it. And if we're going to get him out, we have to try to pay the man back as much of the money as we can."

Katie hesitated. "I know it doesn't seem right of me to ask," she went on, "but . . . that money I gave you the day Uncle Burchard and Mr. Sneed—"

Josepha didn't even wait for her to finish.

"Laws, chil'," she said, getting up out of her chair, "I jes' been waitin' ter gib it back! I ain't got no use fer no money like dat." She walked toward the pantry. "Speshully since it ain't mine nohow. Made me as jumpy as a flea on a houn' dog just thinkin' 'bout dat money. I jes' been hidin' it here. . . ."

She paused and we heard her rummaging through some boxes and cans. She came out a minute later holding the money Katie had given her.

"—Can't think ob anythin' better fer it den effen it'd help Mr. Templeton git back here where he belongs."

She set the fifty-five dollars down on the table in front of Katie.

"Thank you, Josepha," said Katie with a smile.

Emma and I jumped up and ran to our rooms. Two minutes later each of our fifty-five dollars sat in two piles on the table with Josepha's.

"Thank you . . . thank you all," said Katie. "I wish I hadn't had to ask. But I don't know how else we're going to get him free."

"It's yo money, not ours, Miz Kathleen," said Josepha.

"But I gave it to you."

"Ain't no mo use talkin' 'bout it, Miz Kathleen. You gib it to us, an' now we gib it back an' dat's dat, an' you take it an' git dat uncle er yers back."

"When does you hab ter go back dere, Miz Katie?" asked Emma.

"As soon as we can, Emma. We've got to take this money, and all that I've got left too, to the sheriff."

"You goin' today, Miz Katie?"

"Probably early tomorrow morning, Emma. We have to ride into Charlotte in time to catch a train at ten o'clock. We'll have to leave here at daybreak."

Meanwhile, back up north, Uncle Ward had gone to see the man called Roscoe. He told us all about it later. The minute he said his name, an unfriendly look came over the rancher's face.

"*Daniels,*" he repeated. "You any kin to that varmint who's sitting in jail in town for swindling me?"

"He's my brother."

"Then, get out! I got no business with the likes of you."

"Hold on just a minute, Roscoe," said Mr. Daniels. "I'm here to try to help."

"Help . . . how? What do you mean?"

"My brother wants to make it right with you. I came to see if we could work something out."

"Look, mister, he swindled me. He sold me a piece of worthless land, claimed there was gold on it. Phonied the reports, showed me bits of rock with gold in it. The likes of him come from California and think we're a bunch of bumblers and that gold will turn a man's head. And maybe it does. But we take a man's word as meaning something around here. Ain't no way I can see to make right what that brother of yours done."

"What if we was to buy that piece of land back from you?"

The rancher eyed him skeptically. "You'd do that?" he said.

"I don't know—that's what we figured on trying to do. But my brother's broke. The money's all gone."

"I thought as much. Get out. He can rot in jail for all I care!"

"Now, just hold on a minute, Roscoe. How much you figure that land's worth? Really worth, I mean, for your cattle or whatever you want to use it for."

"A mite hilly for cattle."

"Well, for anything else, then."

"You mean a fair price?"

"Right."

"I don't know, probably a couple hundred . . . maybe two-fifty."

"What did you pay Templeton for it?"

"A thousand."

"So you figure he swindled you out of eight hundred?"

"Something like that."

"What if we was to give you two hundred, maybe three—cash money?"

"Ain't nowhere close to eight? I'd still be out five hundred."

"Right now you're out eight hundred, ain't that it?"

Roscoe nodded.

"Couldn't you use three hundred dollars?"

"Sure, who couldn't?"

"It's more'n you're going to get with Templeton sitting in jail. And what if we was to promise to pay back the whole thousand when we could and take the land back?"

"You think I'd take *his* promise as worth anything?"

"He's changed, I tell you. He's determined to make up for the wrong he's done."

"What'd he do, get religion or something—trying to atone for his sins?"

"Something like that. But we didn't get religion, I reckon you'd say we got family. What's that to you anyway? We got our reasons. So I'm asking if the up-front cash money might tell you that we mean what we say?"

Roscoe thought a minute. "I reckon you got a point there," he said.

"Then when it's all done and we've paid you back the thousand, if you still want the land, you can buy it back at a price you think is fair. You set the price."

The rancher thought again.

"I reckon that's a pretty fair offer all right, though I still got no guarantee I'd ever see the two of you again if I drop the charges?"

"Maybe you wouldn't," said Mr. Daniels. "You're right, you'd have no guarantee. Maybe you'd have to trust us at our word. But you'd have the cash in your hand regardless, which is more than you got now."

"Yep, I reckon that's right. So what you want me to do?"

"My brother wants to talk to you. He told me to ask you to come see him in town."

MAKING AMENDS

38

The man Roscoe walked down the corridor toward my papa's jail cell, already feeling a lot less angry than earlier because of the visit Katie's uncle Ward had paid him. But he still eyed my papa a little warily as the sheriff opened the cell door.

"Thanks for coming, Roscoe," said my papa, standing up and offering his hand.

"Your brother said you wanted to see me, though I

was pretty riled at you."

"You had a right to be."

"I didn't particularly want to come."

"I wouldn't have blamed you if you hadn't," said my papa. "Ward tell you what we had in mind?"

"He said something about your buying back the land you took me for. I figured I oughta come see if that's on the level."

"It's on the level, all right. We'll buy it back."

"He also said you're broke."

"Well, that's true," sighed my father. "But I got a family now who loves me enough to put up all they got as a good-faith start on getting you your money. That's my brother and my niece. They figure they can raise about three hundred."

"Yeah, that's what he said."

"It's not even half of it, I know. But I'm hoping you'll take my word for the rest. There's no reason you should. My word's not meant anything to you up till now and I know that. So you'll have to make your own decision."

Roscoe nodded but said nothing.

"I want you to know," my papa went on, "whatever you decide, that I'm sorry for what I did."

He looked him in the eye.

"I'm giving you my apology and I mean it," he said. "I doubt you can forgive me for it, but I hope someday you can. And I hope you'll see that I mean what I say when I say I want to make it right with you. I did you wrong and I want to make it right, no matter how long it takes."

Mr. Roscoe took in my papa's short speech thought-fully. It wasn't like anything he had expected, or had ever heard before either. Hearing a man apologize and say he was sorry and talk about forgiveness and making things right wasn't something he'd encountered too often in his life. The truth was, he'd *never* encountered it!

The jail cell got real quiet.

"All right, then, Daniels," said the rancher finally. "I'll think some on what you said. I reckon you made me about as fair an offer as a man could who's sitting in jail and got no money. So I'll think on it."

When Katie and Deputy Paxton got back to Ellicott City, after spending another night in Baltimore with Reverend Paxton's family, there had been no change. Her uncle Templeton was still in jail. Her uncle Ward was staying at a boardinghouse in town. They had heard no more from Mr. Roscoe, and the judge had arrived and was supposed to see my papa the next morning and decide what to do.

As soon as Katie heard that, she turned to Mr. Daniels.

"Uncle Ward," she said, "let's go see Mr. Roscoe right away. We've got to talk to him so Uncle Templeton can get out of jail before that judge does something bad."

"I don't know, Kathleen. It might be too late. The judge is already in town."

"Then we have to go today . . . right now. Please, Uncle Ward. I want to see Mr. Roscoe."

Mr. Roscoe wasn't altogether surprised to see Templeton Daniels' brother again, though the sight of the pretty young woman at his side startled him some.

"This is our niece I was telling you about," said Mr. Daniels.

"Hello, Mr. Roscoe," said Katie. "I'm Kathleen Clairborne. I came to give you my money so that you'll let my uncle Templeton out of jail."

Still standing at the door, she took a wad of bills that totaled two hundred and ten dollars from her dress pocket and handed it to him. Beside her, her uncle could hardly keep from showing his astonishment. But before he could say anything, Katie had given the rancher the money.

He took it, seemingly a little reluctantly, shuffled back and forth on his feet, then invited them in.

"Please, Mr. Roscoe," said Katie, following him into the house. "It's all I've got in the world, every dollar. And if we can harvest our cotton, you can have more later this year and the year after that. But I need both my uncles' help to do it. Cotton is a lot of work, and my father and brothers are dead and we don't have any more slaves."

"Yeah . . . well, Miss Clairborne," said the rancher, "I talked to your uncle yesterday, so I'm thinking things over. To tell you the truth, I didn't get much sleep last night from thinking about it."

"And like I told you, Mr. Roscoe," Katie's uncle Ward now said, "I think I can scrape together another hundred for you. I'll have to go down to Richmond. Likely take me a few days to get it together. But what I got's yours."

Roscoe nodded thoughtfully.

"Well, like I told you before, that's a fair offer. I'll think on it some more."

"But you'll hurry, won't you, Mr. Roscoe?" said Katie insistently. "The judge is supposed to see him tomorrow."

"I'll try, Miss Clairborne," he said. "I'll try."

"We'll even give you the deed to our house if we have to," said Katie. "Won't we, Uncle Ward?"

"Well, it's something we can talk about anyway," said Mr. Daniels, "if it comes to that. But that'd take more time than Templeton's got."

As they rode the four miles back to Ellicott City, Katie couldn't understand Mr. Roscoe's hesitation.

"Why did he take my money and not let Uncle Templeton out of jail?" she asked.

"It ain't all his decision, Kathleen," said her uncle Ward. "That's why there's a sheriff and a judge."

"But he took my two hundred dollars. He's got to do something."

"He doesn't have to. As far as he's concerned, Templeton took him for a thousand dollars. He might figure he's entitled to that two hundred but that Templeton still ought to do jail time anyway. And the judge'll likely agree with him."

"Then I shouldn't have given him my money until he agreed!"

210

"I was thinking you were a mite hasty, Kathleen. But before I could say anything, there you were shoving your two hundred into Roscoe's hand. That's why I wasn't too anxious to start shoving the deed at him too. We still don't know what he's going to do."

"Oh, Uncle Ward, then I was stupid!"

"Too late to worry about that now, Kathleen. We'll just have to wait and see what comes of it."

IN FRONT OF THE JUDGE

39

When they got back to Ellicott City, they were in for a surprise.

The first they knew about it was when they walked into the sheriff's office. There sat Deputy Paxton. He jumped out of his chair the instant they walked through the door.

"You two are finally back!" he said. "Since there was only one case, the judge moved Mr. Daniels up to today."

"Today!" exclaimed Katie.

"They're over in the courthouse right now."

The three of them rushed from the sheriff's office. The deputy led the way along the boardwalk, then turned into another street with Katie running along beside him.

"Hurry, Uncle Ward!" she called behind her. "We've got to get there before it's too late."

The deputy led them into a building with a few offices in it, and down a corridor to a large room which was used for a courthouse on the few occasions when one was needed.

He opened the door and they rushed inside, Katie's uncle Ward puffing from the run. There sat the judge in a black robe with my papa standing in front of him.

The judge stopped and looked up.

"What is this?" he said.

"They're Daniels' kin," said the sheriff, "—brother and niece."

"All right, then, sit down," he said. "I'll let you stay if you don't make a disturbance."

There were six or eight chairs in the room and they sat down.

"As I was saying," the judge said, "according to the complaint filed by Mr. Roscoe, you not only falsified legal documents about the parcel of land in question, it says here that you have had a pattern of such behavior, and that this is not the first of such schemes. What do you have to say for yourself?"

"Nothing, Your Honor," said my papa. "I'm afraid it's true, though nothing else so serious as this."

"So you admit it?"

"Yes, sir."

"Well, then, that makes it easier. Though it's commendable of you to own up to it, I don't see that that helps you much. You're still guilty, and I still have to pass a sentence on you."

"I understand."

"Do you have anything else to say in your defense?"

"Only that I intend to try to make amends by buying that land back."

"But you have no money?"

"No, sir."

"I don't see how that changes my duty, then. Good intentions are cheap, Mr. Daniels."

"Yes, sir."

"But please, sir . . . Judge!" said Katie all of a sudden, standing up. "We're going to help him pay it."

The judge glanced about the room.

"Who are you?" he asked.

"Kathleen Clairborne, sir. He's my uncle."

"Well, young lady, as I said, good intentions are cheap."

"But we really are going to help him pay the money back."

"Promises are just as cheap as intentions. I can allow no more such outbursts. Please sit down."

"But don't you want to hear what I have to say?"

"No, I don't, young lady."

Katie sat down, more irritated than contrite.

The judge looked back down at the papers in front of him and was about to start talking again.

Just then the door opened. Everyone turned around as the judge glanced toward the sound.

"Who are you?" he asked again, becoming more than a little annoyed at these continued interruptions.

"I'm Roscoe," said the rancher.

"The man who filed the complaint?" asked the judge.

"That's right."

"I take it you've got something to contribute to the proceedings?"

"Yes, sir," said Roscoe.

"All right . . . step forward."

Mr. Roscoe walked toward him, glanced toward my papa as he stopped and stood beside him, then looked up at the judge.

"What I've got to say is simple enough, Your Honor," he said. "I'd like the charges dropped."

A gasp of delight from Katie sounded, and a whispered comment or two from the others.

"Why dropped?" said the judge.

"Because Daniels is trying to make amends, Judge. He's offered to buy the land back from me."

"But he has no money. He's admitted that."

"Yes, sir. But I think his offer is on the up and up."

"You believe him?"

"I'm willing to trust him."

"After he swindled you?"

"Yes, sir. This young lady even offered me the deed to her place. People don't do that unless they're serious."

The judge thought a minute. "I don't know," he said. "I'm still inclined to give him some jail time . . . but if you'll sign off on dropping the charges—" He glanced at Roscoe.

The rancher nodded his agreement. "I'll sign it," he said.

"—well, then, I don't suppose we ought to waste the

taxpayers' money. Charges dismissed."

He rapped the top of the desk with a wooden hammer, although the sound could hardly be heard above a shriek of happiness from Katie and her uncle Ward's whoops as he hurried up to congratulate his brother.

The judge didn't seem to share everyone else's enthusiasm.

"Next time you haul me out here, Sheriff," he said, "make sure I don't waste my time with a case that's going to be dropped. This was an unnecessary trip for me to make."

As he left his room in his long black robe, everyone else gathered around my papa and Mr. Roscoe.

"Oh, thank you, Mr. Roscoe!" exclaimed Katie, jumping up from her chair and running over to give the rancher a hug. "We'll pay you back all of the money, just as soon as we can!"

Flustered at Katie's show of emotion, the rancher hemmed and hawed a little as Katie stepped back. Both Katie's uncle Ward and my papa now offered their hands.

"I want to thank you too," said my papa. "And she's right, Roscoe. I meant what I told you."

"And I'll get you that other hundred within a week," added Katie's uncle Ward.

"Well, I want to talk to the two of you about the money," said Roscoe. "I been thinking a lot about it, and I reckon that if the two of you believe in Daniels enough to give every cent you've got—"

He glanced at Katie and her uncle Ward.

"—and if he's given me an apology and a shake of his hand to back it up, then maybe I oughta practice what I preach and take him at his word. I reckon trust has gotta start somewhere. And there's one other thing too—" he said, then paused again.

It was silent as they all waited.

"The three of you've shown that you're willing to accept responsibility for what happened," he went on after a minute. "You're willing to buy back the land and give me back every penny. But that's got me thinking, and I've got to look at my own side of it too. You can't con a man who doesn't want something that maybe he ain't altogether entitled to. If I hadn't been so greedy, Daniels, you'd have never been able to swindle me. People who get conned are usually trying to get something for nothing. The gold did go to my head," he said, turning to Katie's uncle Ward, "just like I told you. That was my own fault. I should have known there couldn't be gold on that land. You only made me believe what I wanted to believe. I got no one to blame but myself. I gotta take my own share of the responsibility for what happened."

He paused again.

"So what I'm proposing is this," he said. "Let's us split the difference for what happened right down the middle. You give me five hundred and I'll keep the land, and we'll call it square."

"That's a generous offer, Roscoe," said my papa.

"No more than what's fair. You all showed that you want to do right by me. Well, I figure that's my way of showing I want to do right too. The young lady here's given me two hundred ten dollars. I hate to take the last of her money, but with the two of you to take care of her, I reckon she'll be all right. I'm willing to wait for the rest till you harvest your cotton, whenever that may be. Keep your other hundred, Daniels," he said to Katie's uncle Ward. "And you keep your deed, Miss Clairborne. I'll trust you for the rest."

He and my papa shook hands again and I think for the first time they really meant it.

They all left the courtroom and walked through the building and outside, the sheriff following behind them. My papa said he felt humbled and thankful. He'd never had to depend on people like this before in his life. He'd always figured he could talk his way out of anything that happened. It was humbling, in a good sort of way, to realize how much others cared about him and how much he had to be thankful for.

"So, Sheriff," he said, slowing and turning behind him, "what's to be done now?"

"Nothing more to be done," replied the sheriff. "The two of you've worked out your differences as far as I can see. The judge is heading back to Baltimore. You're free to go."

Katie and Deputy Paxton had fallen behind and were slowly walking together back in the direction of the sheriff's office.

"What are you going to do now?" asked the deputy.

"I imagine we'll go home," said Katie. "I'll have to talk to my uncles. I want to thank you for your help."

"Don't mention it. I enjoyed making the trip with you."

"Me too. Be sure to give your family my regards."

"I will. And if you need a place to stay in Baltimore on your way back, I know my mother would be delighted to put you up again."

"But I'll be with my uncles."

"I know. I meant them too."

"All three of us?"

"Of course. You saw how big our house is."

"That's right, I did!" laughed Katie.

"My mother loves to have guests. Hospitality is her middle name."

"It sounds like she should have been a Southerner!"

RETURN TO ROSEWOOD

40

It was maddeningly distracting trying to do anything during those days Katie was gone. I could think of nothing else but wondering when they would get back and when or if I would see my papa again. Emma kept busy with William, and Josepha always managed to find plenty to do in the kitchen and pantry and the rest of the house. It seemed like she had twice as much to do as Katie and I ever had. And Henry too seemed to keep busy in the barn and with the animals, and checking and fixing equipment and hoeing the weeds out of the rows of cotton growing in the fields. The milking and washing and cooking used to take up all my day, and now Josepha was doing so much of it. Even though she needed some help, there still wasn't as much for me to do as before.

Sometimes I didn't know what to do with myself. I helped Henry with the hoeing some. But also I took a few long walks and I prayed more than I think I'd ever prayed before. I couldn't stand the thought of my papa having to be in jail, no matter what he'd done.

How many times I must have prayed, "God, bring him back . . . please bring my papa home!" Sometimes I couldn't pray anything else.

So when I was walking back toward the house one day from being at Katie's secret place in the woods, my heart started pounding when I saw three horses, still saddled, standing in the yard.

I started running toward them. Before I was halfway there, a tall figure, still wearing his hat from the ride, walked out of the kitchen door.

It was him!

"Papa . . . Papa!" I cried, running all the faster toward the house.

He turned toward me, hurried down the three steps of the porch, and ran toward me. Vaguely I saw two or three other people following him outside, but right then I was only looking at him.

He stopped before I did and opened his arms and I ran straight into them. He clasped me close, and I just stood there happy and content and crying against his chest.

Finally I felt him relax and I stepped back. He looked down at me, smiled, and wiped at the tears falling down my cheeks with one of his fingers. It was almost like he had never seen tears before, though I knew that wasn't true. But maybe these were the first tears since my mama's that had been shed just for him. Then he stooped down and kissed me on the forehead and hugged me again.

"It is good to see you again, Mary Ann," he said. "I missed you."

"Oh, Papa, I'm so glad you're home!" I said. "We were so worried before we got your letter, and then I've been anxious about what would happen to you ever since Katie left again."

"Well, it all seems to have worked out," he said.

"Did Katie tell you what happened with her uncle Burchard and us leaving and everything?"

"She told me every detail," he said, chuckling a little. It was so wonderful to hear him laugh again! I don't know what my papa would have been without his laugh and sense of humor. I could tell that he was tired and that his time away had changed him. Even with his laugh, he seemed quieter and more somber. But seeing his eyes sparkle and hearing his laughter made everything suddenly all right again.

"But what happened?" I asked. "How did you get out of jail?"

"Kathleen charmed a few people," laughed my papa, "and gave almost every dollar she had to her name. And we've got to pay the man more money later. But he agreed to drop the charges. We just have to harvest this cotton of ours."

"We can do it, Papa. We did it before to pay off the bank—or part of it, at least. This year we'll harvest the cotton to pay *your* bills."

"In the meantime, we've got no money!" he laughed. "We may not have much to eat between now and then."

"I don't care," I said. "We're all back together, that's the only thing we need."

"As long as we don't starve in the process."

"We won't. There's plenty to eat at Rosewood. Don't you worry—Katie and I know what to do."

"I'm sure you do.—But it looks like there's someone else who's as glad to see you as I am!"

I turned and saw Katie coming toward us.

"Katie!" I said, feeling myself starting to cry all over again.

"Hi, Mayme," she said. "I think we're finally home for good."

We hugged each other, a long quiet hug without words. Sometimes those are the best kind, when the hug itself says all there is to say.

"You remember my uncle Ward," said Katie as we stepped back and she glanced behind her.

"Yes. Hello, Mr. Daniels," I said to my papa's brother, who had walked out from the house with Katie.

"Howdy, Miss Mary Ann," he said.

"And he's your uncle too, isn't he, not just mine?" Katie added.

I didn't know what to say. Neither did Mr. Daniels.

He seemed a little embarrassed by what Katie had said. Maybe he wasn't quite ready to have a colored girl think of him as kin, though now that I was calling myself *Mayme Daniels,* like Papa had said he wanted me to if I thought it would be right in respect of Mr. Jukes, we did share the same family name.

THE TWO UNCLES

41

It took a little time for all of us to get used to each other again. My papa was his same cheerful self, and it was obvious he was glad to be back at the place he now considered home. But with his brother with us now too—the *other* Mr. Daniels, who none of us other than Papa really knew much, except for Katie, who'd traveled all that way north with him on the train—sometimes we didn't know what he was thinking.

We couldn't help wondering what would happen, and whether *he* might decide to start making a lot of changes too. The fact that he was the legal owner of Rosewood added to the uncertainty. I don't think Katie was nervous about it. But she wasn't black. Things happened to blacks that didn't to whites. And if I was secretly a little anxious about what Mr. Ward—that's what we called him—might eventually do and whether he might want to send us away like Katie's uncle Burchard, then I knew Emma and Josepha probably wondered too. I don't know whether the fact that I was his niece too, like Katie, made any difference to him. We never talked about it again after Katie'd said what she did, and at first I was afraid to call him *Uncle* Ward like she did and didn't know what to call for him for a spell. Something like that seemed a liberty without the person giving you permission first. But the fact was, one of Katie's uncles owned Rosewood now, not Katie.

The day after they got back, he and my papa got shaved and cleaned up and into clean clothes and looked real nice. With clean-shaven faces they looked more like brothers than ever, except for my papa's little thin mustache. And then slowly over the next few days, we began to pick up where we'd left off several months ago before Papa'd left and Katie's uncle Burchard started coming around. And after Henry and Jeremiah went home, I took over the milking again.

At first Mr. Ward acted kind of like a guest. We all gradually went about our business like always. There was plenty to do, and now with even more mouths to feed—and two hungry men—and clothes to wash, we kept busy enough. Henry and Jeremiah came out from town oftener than before too, and when we were all together, even without Aleta, there were nine of us and that's a lot of food. We had to start making bread almost every day and were more careful about saving all the milk for cheese. We would have to butcher another hog or cow pretty soon too. It was almost starting to be like a real plantation with enough people around that it took some doing and some planning to keep food on the table. It sure was changed from Katie's and my first days together when we just milked the cows to keep their bags empty and dumped out the milk we didn't drink.

We'd started something all right, and it was becoming a bustling, active place!

And things changed inside the house too. There were five bedrooms and it seemed only right that the two Daniels brothers ought to each have one to themselves. Emma and William needed one too. I could have shared a room with Josepha, but Katie wanted to share her room with me, so I moved my things back into her room like we'd done in the beginning. It might have seemed pretty uncommon for blacks and whites all to be sharing bedrooms on the same floor under the same roof. But that's how Rosewood was, and Mr. Ward didn't seem to pay any more attention to anyone's color than my papa did. And every time Josepha or I suggested it, Katie wouldn't hear of anyone going to the slave cabins. It was just a great big family full of all kinds of people—a little colored boy, two grown-up white men, a huge colored woman who didn't know any other way of life than cooking and taking care of people and loved it all the better the more people she had to feed, and me and Katie and Emma . . . cousins and uncles and babies and half-whites and half-blacks. I couldn't imagine a more complicated and unlikely gathering of folks that called themselves a "family" anywhere.

Since my papa had already been with us before, he

knew how life at Rosewood was. He'd settled himself into a kind of daily working routine back then and now fell back into it within just a few days. He asked Henry to stay around as much as he could to show him whatever he might need to know from when he'd been gone. It was obvious he considered Rosewood home. But it was different with Mr. Ward. After the first few days, he seemed a little bewildered and restless about it all, like he didn't know what to do with himself or how he fit into life at Rosewood. Everyone else got up every day and just went about their chores. But he didn't know what to do. It had been a long time since he'd lived a regular life as part of a household.

One day I saw him out standing by the grave markers. He'd taken his hat off and was just standing there quiet and respectful.

I suppose it was something we all had to face and deal with in our own way eventually—the death. We'd all lost family and were now trying to figure out how to live and act with the new family God was giving us. We'd thought we'd lost everything and then had discovered that we still had some family after all. I had a wonderful cousin and father. Katie had me and two uncles.

But it all took some getting used to. Change always does, and sometimes change isn't easy. Now I reckon it was Mr. Ward's turn to have to face some of these things and the changes that were coming to his life. It wasn't that he and his sister had been that close. It was still hard to think of her as my own *Aunt Rosalind*. It seemed presuming of me to think like that, even though it was true. She was still *Katie's mama* in my mind. But what I was getting around to saying is that death is a fearsome thing even if you aren't close to someone. It makes you wish you had been closer. Death can't help but bring a few regrets along with it, and I had the feeling as I watched him standing there that those kinds of regrets were going through Mr. Ward's mind right then, who was my uncle just like Katie's mama was my aunt. It was sure hard to get used to!

I heard a step behind me. I turned to see my papa walking forward. He smiled, paused with me for a minute, put his arm around me and pulled me toward him for a second, then continued on toward the graves.

He stopped beside his brother and now put the same arm around Mr. Ward's shoulder. I couldn't hear what they said, but my papa told me later.

"Makes you think of all the things you wish you'd said and done, doesn't it?" my papa said after they had been standing beside each other a minute or two looking at their sister's grave in silence.

Mr. Ward nodded.

"Time is always too short. You never realize it till someone's gone," my papa said. "It was real hard for me at first, knowing how little I'd been there for her and that now it was too late to do anything about it. But then I realized, like we were saying when I was sitting in jail up north, that I still had a chance to do right by her by watching over Kathleen."

It was quiet again. Then finally Mr. Ward turned away

from the graves. He glanced at his brother, blinking a little harder than usual. My papa understood. He knew what Mr. Ward was thinking. He'd felt the same uncomfortable warmth in his eyes a few times since he'd been here too. But there were some things that were best left unspoken between men. Like tears.

Slowly they began walking away and I turned back toward the house so it wouldn't seem like I was staring at them, even though that's just what I had been doing.

"It's different for you, Templeton," said Mr. Ward as they walked out on one of the paths toward the fields. "You was always closer to Rosalind. At least you came around every once in a while."

"Not too often," said my papa. "Only when I needed something from her, I'm afraid. I'm ashamed to admit it, but I even stole money from her a time or two."

"Yeah, that may be, but at least you saw her, and saw Kathleen when she was growing up."

"Don't be too hard on yourself, Ward. We both did a lot of things we regret. Now we're trying to make up for it however we can. Don't forget, it was your gold that saved this place from the bank."

"I reckon. But what am I going to do now? When I came back I didn't count on all this. Suddenly everything's changed."

"I know what you mean. That's just how I felt when I showed up. It knocked me so hard in the head that I left again. Especially finding out about Mary Ann. It threw my life upside down for a while. But eventually I realized that this was my home now."

"That might be so for you. You got not just a niece, but a daughter. A fine girl too, that Mary Ann. Her mama must have been quite a woman when she grew up."

My papa nodded. Now it was his turn to fight back the inner tears of memory.

"But it's different for me," said Mr. Ward. "Kathleen and all the rest of them—they know you better. You can tell they look up to you."

"Just because I've been here longer."

"It's more than that, Templeton. You fit here. You like the work, you know what to do. I've watched you with those cows, milking and cleaning out those stalls—if I didn't know any better I'd think you liked the stinking smell of that manure!"

"You get used to it," laughed my papa. "It's not so bad."

"That's just what I mean. This life agrees with you. I've never seen you look better or more content with yourself. You talk to that fellow Henry like you've been running a plantation all your life."

My papa laughed again. "I had to learn," he said.

"Yeah, but it seems to come natural to you. I'm just a drifter, Templeton."

"You could have said the same for me a year ago."

"I don't know if I could change like that."

"Nobody's asking you to."

"Then what am I going to do? You and Kathleen got a plantation to run. You got a daughter to look after. But me . . ."

228

His voice trailed off. By now they had come to the field where the stalks of cotton were growing up to their knees.

"Look around, man," said my papa. "What do you see?"

"I don't know . . . I'm no farmer. What is it?"

"It's cotton, Ward. Acres and acres of cotton. *King cotton!* Built the South into what it was before the war. Made more men more money than all the gold in California. We planted it, Ward—the girls and I and Henry and his kid. I planted some of that cotton myself and I'm proud of it. And do you know whose it is?"

"I don't know . . . what do you mean?"

"Whose cotton is it?"

"I don't know . . . Kathleen's, I reckon. What are you driving at?"

"No, it's *yours!* You're the owner of Rosewood now. It's your name on that deed of Rosalind's."

"That don't mean nothing."

"Of course it does. Rosewood belongs to you."

Mr. Ward took in his words like he'd never actually considered the fact before. They almost seemed to stun him.

"I'm no plantation man, Templeton," he said after they had walked along a little farther. "I could never be."

"That's what I thought. But I helped plant this field of cotton. And it's a good feeling now watching it grow and knowing I had a hand in planting it, and knowing when harvest comes that I'll pick my share of it and pay

229

off Roscoe with my own hard work, with maybe enough left over to buy those girls of ours each a new dress."

"You sound like a plantation owner all right! You sound downright excited about some green plants growing in the ground."

"I suppose I am, Ward. Because it's honest labor, and you can make money and make a good life for yourself that way too, just like men have been doing for centuries. Sure I panned for a little gold, though I never broke my back at it like you. But other than that, when did I ever do two days' honest hard work in a row in my life? Maybe that's why I like it. I go to sleep at night thinking that maybe I accomplished something worthwhile that day."

"Yeah, you've changed all right, Templeton."

"Maybe this land's finally got into me. I suppose those two girls have got into me too," he added. "I helped a little with it last year. But it was different. It still didn't feel like it was mine, like the work really *mattered*. Now it does. Maybe family's like that, Ward. It gets into you. That's what it's made me realize, that maybe I'm finally ready to settle down and think of the land and the work I can put into it as the kind of life I want to live."

"I don't know," said Mr. Ward, rubbing his chin like he did, even though there were no more whiskers on it.

"So if I've learned a thing or two," my papa went on, "I'm offering my services to you as your foreman."

Mr. Ward turned and looked at him, then began to laugh.

"I'm serious," said my papa. "You're the *owner* of Rosewood . . . I'll be your *foreman*."

"I don't know. I'll think on it. I still ain't sure I'm cut out for this life."

"Too late. Your name's on the deed."

"I'll sign it over to you or Kathleen," said Mr. Ward, "just like Rosalind did to me. No reason I couldn't if she did."

"I'm not so sure Kathleen would want you to. I think she'd say the same thing that I'm saying. She'd want you to stay."

Mr. Ward thought a while more. Then they both turned back toward the house. As they went he brushed his hand through the green stalks, seemingly looking at them in a new way, like he was thinking about everything his brother had said.

My papa saw the look in his eye and recognized it, in the same way he had known what he was thinking while standing at their sister's grave.

"All right, then," said Mr. Ward after a couple more minutes, glancing at my papa with just the hint of a grin, "I'll let you be my foreman for a spell . . . a week or two . . . till I see if I can get the feel of this place . . . at least just till I decide what to do with that deed."

42

The summer came on. It got hot and dry and the cotton grew.

By the middle of August Henry was starting to come out and check on it every few days.

One day in the middle of the morning I saw Mr. Ward standing at the kitchen window looking out. I went and stood beside him. There was Henry in the distance walking through one of the fields.

"Why is Henry always looking over the cotton?" he asked.

"He's looking to see when it's ready to pick. Then we've got to start harvesting."

"How will he know?"

"Come on," I said. "I'll show you."

We went out into the cotton field.

"We've got to start the harvest as soon as we can, the minute it's ready," I said. "You've got to get it in when it's dry. Two years ago a huge storm came and ruined half the crop before we were done and we didn't get enough to pay off the whole loan at the bank. That's why Katie looked so hard for your gold that she finally found where her mama had hidden it."

We walked about a little further and I picked a few bolls and showed him the growing cotton and what to look for.

"When it's ready, how do you harvest it?" he asked.

"Like this," I said, showing him how to pluck it with your fingers. "It's slow, hot work," I said. "That's why plantation owners had so many slaves. But we all work together. You should see Katie. You'd be real proud of her. She's real good at it. Henry's the best. He can pick so fast you can hardly see his fingers. Are you going to help, Mr. Ward?"

"I suppose I'll have to do what my foreman tells me," he answered with a smile.

He seemed more interested than usual and stood a long time looking at the field and just walking around among the rows. As we started back to the house, there was my papa walking out to join us.

"What are you two up to?" he asked, with his familiar grin.

"I was showing Mr. Ward the cotton," I said.

"And are you now an expert, Brother Ward?" he said.

"Not quite yet!" laughed Mr. Ward. "That will take a little longer, I'm afraid."

He continued on toward the house, and my papa and I walked off together in the other direction toward the river.

"What's going to happen?" I said after a while. "What will happen to me and the others?"

"What do you mean?" he asked.

"Mr. Ward . . . I mean, will he want us to leave?"

"Don't you mean your *uncle* Ward?"

"I reckon, though I still have a hard time thinking of him that way. But do you think, after he learns how to

233

do everything, he'll want to run Rosewood by himself without the rest of us—like Burchard Clairborne was going to do?"

"No, of course not. What would make you think that?"

"I don't know. It's hard to know what he's thinking."

"I suppose that's true. He can be quiet at times. Sometimes men are like that, and you can't go reading more into it than is there. He's got a lot on his mind. But he especially wouldn't make you leave whatever happened. You're his kin, just like Kathleen is. He knows that you're my girl. No . . . Ward may be a little quiet, but he would never do anything like that."

We reached the edge of the river and stood watching it for a while in silence.

"Two years ago, when it flooded," I said, "the river came all the way over the bank and spread out almost all the way to the house."

"That must have been something to see!"

"It was scary."

We turned and began walking back toward the house.

"Uncle Ward doesn't seem to take to the work like you do," I said as we went.

"Give him time, Mary Ann," said my papa.

"What about Emma and Josepha?" I asked.

"He won't do a thing without talking to me—I'm his foreman, remember! We're a family, Mary Ann, and Emma and Josepha are part of it too. I won't let anything happen to anyone."

"Thank you, Papa," I said.

43

B eing a mama was hard work. All you had to do was
watch Emma for a day to know that. She'd been a
slave but had never really known hard work as I had.
But she was sure ahead of me in learning to be a mama.
Every day she was learning new things about it. Having
a baby who was getting on to two years old to look
after—running around and getting into things all day
long—wasn't easy.

I walked into the parlor one Sunday morning. Katie
and I liked to gather everyone in the parlor on Sundays
and read out of the Bible and sing a few hymns. Emma
sure could sing! But I could tell she was tired.

After our singing on that day, Katie read for a while,
and the sound of her voice gradually put Emma and
William, and even Josepha, to sleep. The rest of us left
after a bit as quietly as we could to go do our own kind
of resting. Katie went out for a walk. Papa and Uncle
Ward went out to the barn to saddle the horses, and I
heard them ride off a little while later. I went upstairs to
our room to practice my reading.

After a while I heard sounds on the stairs. I got up and
went to the landing. There was William slowly
crawling up the steps talking to himself the way little
children do, though most of it was just babble. Well, I
guess I don't really know how children talk to them-

selves other than from listening to my brothers and sisters when they were little. William could walk and even run, but the steps were too high for his little legs, and he couldn't quite walk up and down them yet. I sat down on the top step and waited for him to reach me. When he got to the top and saw me, a big grin came to his face and he hurried toward me and crawled into my lap. I gave him a hug.

"You're going to be a history-making baby, did you know that?" I said. "You are living between the history of the slaves and the free coloreds. There's no telling what life will be like for you when you grow up. I guess now maybe we're all living in that history. But you'll get to be part of more of it than I will. You haven't ever been a slave. You won't ever know what it was like. And that's something not too many colored folks can say. So you're a lucky little fellow."

William stared up at me with his big dark eyes surrounded by white. He probably couldn't understand a thing I was saying, yet somehow it almost seemed like he could. But I think he thought I was telling him a story.

"If you'd have been born even just five years ago," I went on, "you might have had a completely different life by now. Your mama might have been sold away. You might never have even known who your daddy was—well, maybe that's not going to be different for you. But you sure wouldn't have had your mama with you every day all day long like you do."

By now William was losing interest and was starting

to squiggle out of my lap. I guess my story had gotten a little too long!

But saying what I had to him got me thinking, and I found myself thinking about it for the rest of the day. Later that afternoon I was shelling peas in the kitchen. Josepha was at the breadboard kneading a new loaf of bread. I had a huge basket of peas and wasn't even near half done. I'd been thinking about my mama and brothers and sisters and how my mama had lived up north with the Daniels family but had by a long way around ended up at the McSimmons plantation. My mind was wandering with the pea shelling, and I found myself wondering how Josepha had wound up there.

"Josepha," I said.

"Yes, chil'."

"Where were you born?"

She turned around to face me, her hands covered with flour. Then she began to chuckle.

"Now what in tarnashun does where I wuz bo'n hab ter do wiff dem peas or dese here biscuits an' bread?"

"Nothing, I suppose," I said. "I just wondered. It seems like a lot of us don't know much about where we came from."

"Dat's right," said Josepha. "Speshully ef you got sol' a few times an' separated from yo elders."

"Do you know anything about your parents?"

"Nuffin' at all. I always reckoned dat I just sorter happened," Josepha said with another chuckle. "By da time I was old enuff ter 'member, I wuz jus' one er a parcel ob colored slave girls gittin' sol' ter Master McSimmons in sum big city. I don' eben know which one. We wuz all young an' too scared ter pay much attention t' nuthin 'cept stayin' alive. I wound up in da kitchen an' sum er dem wound up in da fields. Dat's all I know."

She turned around and looked at me again. But she wasn't chuckling now. "You's be a right lucky girl, Mayme, chil'," she said. "I know you's been through a lot an' has seen yo share er killin'. But you foun' out who you is an' who yo daddy is. You got er family, an' dat's mighty nice."

I could tell she was happy for me.

"You've got a family now too, Josepha."

"I know dat, chil', an' I's got you to thank fo' it too."

Papa and Uncle Ward had come back from their ride. While Papa was getting in a little Sunday afternoon snooze, right about the same time Josepha and I were talking in the kitchen, Uncle Ward came upon Emma and William out by the laundry tub, where Emma'd been washing him up and giving him a bath. She was so involved she didn't hear him approach and went on chattering and babbling with William like she did. He stood and just listened for a minute or two, hardly able to understand a word. Gradually she became aware that William was looking at someone behind her. She turned and the instant she saw him went silent. She kept on with bathing William but now not saying a word.

"How come you always clam up when I'm around, Emma?" said Uncle Ward, walking over to her.

She didn't answer.

238

"You act like you're afraid of me or something. You're not afraid of me, are you, Emma?"

"I learned my lesson, dat's all," she said.

"What lesson?"

"I learned dat it's bes' fer a colored ter keep her mouf shut aroun' white men. Hit's jes' bes' ter avoid dem."

"Why's that?"

"'Cuz you neber know what a white man's gwine do."

"You mean you don't trust white men?"

"Dat's sumfin' like it."

"What about Templeton? You seem to get along all right with him."

"Mr. Templeton's different. He's got a colored girl who's his daughter. Dat makes him different, an' I's used ter him." She thought a moment about what she had said. "But now I's thinkin' 'bout it," she added, "maybe he weren't no different after all back den."

"But I'm not different, is that it?"

Emma didn't reply.

"Why, Emma," Uncle Ward went on after a minute, "I'm surprised at you—you're not too proud to talk to me just because my skin is white, are you?"

"I din't say nuthin' like dat, Mr. Ward."

"You said you avoided white men."

"On account ob what dey might do ter me."

"When have I ever given you cause to make you think I'd hurt you?"

"Neber, Mr. Ward. I reckon you an' Mr. Templeton's 'bout as kind as white men could be."

"But you still don't want to talk when I'm around?

That don't seem right. If we're all a family around here, seems like you gotta do your part in accepting me just like I accept you. Ain't that right?"

"I reckon so."

"We gotta be family to each other whatever the color of our skin. I don't have any family but this. Do you, Emma?"

"No, I ain't."

"So we all gotta be family to each other.—So why don't you put William down a minute and come here, Emma."

Emma looked at him a little skeptically, then slowly set William down and stood up.

"Come on, let's shake hands, Emma, and be friends," said Uncle Ward.

Slowly Emma approached with a wary look on her face as Uncle Ward held out his hand to her. It was obvious that she was nervous, but she had always been taught to do what any white man said.

She allowed Ward to shake her hand, then pulled hers away quickly.

"That wasn't so bad, was it?" he asked.

"I reckon not."

"I'll never let anyone hurt you, Emma. You can trust me and your uncle Templeton to take care of you just like we do the others. From now on I want you to call me and Templeton Uncle Ward and Uncle Templeton, just like Kathleen and Mary Ann do."

Emma looked down at the ground. "I's try . . ." she said.

ANOTHER HARVEST

44

T he summer was a hot one. By the middle of August most of the plantations in Shenandoah County were starting to pick.

A morning came when I woke up real early. It was almost like I could feel the fields calling to me, and I knew I had to get up and go out. There's something about the approach of a harvest that gets into you like that. You know how much work it's going to be, but the anticipation can't help but fill you with excitement. Even though it comes every year, there's a feeling of challenge, almost adventure.

I got up and tried to dress quietly and sneak outside without waking Katie up. But I couldn't.

"Where are you going?" she whispered behind me.

"I'm sorry. I didn't mean to wake you," I said. "I was just going to check on the cotton."

"I was already awake," said Katie, sitting up in her bed. "I'll go with you."

A few minutes later we tiptoed downstairs and outside. The sun was just coming up. It must have been around five-thirty, and it was cool and still. There wasn't a breath of wind, and the delicious smell of a multitude of growing things hovered in the air. It was so nice, just like a perfect summer morning. But you could tell that by noon it was going to be sweltering and that the sweat would be dripping from you.

We walked out into the fields together. It was a good feeling, so much different than when we'd done this the first time. Then Katie had been so inexperienced and hardly knew what a cotton boll was. Now she and I were seventeen, and I'd be eighteen in another week. We weren't exactly grown-up yet, but we were a *little* grown-up. And we knew what we needed to do. This would be our third harvest.

Maybe what we felt as we walked out to the fields that morning was confidence or something like that. We walked beside each other like two young *women*, not like two little girls. Growth is one of those things you can't see up close. You have to stand back to see how something or someone has changed as time has passed. And on that morning, I saw how different Katie and I were from the day we'd met, devastated and alone. We had run a plantation, and now we were going out to check to see if it was time to start another harvest. Our own harvest. A black girl and a white girl making a big decision like that . . . all by *ourselves*. What an amazing thing it was. God had been so good to us!

We didn't stop until we were standing in the middle of one of the fields of green, with tiny explosive little bursts of white all around us. We each picked at several plants, plucking the tiny round fluffy balls, holding them in our hands, examining them, like each one held a little unseen mystery inside, as I reckon they did. I suppose all growing things have a mystery inside them—the mystery of life.

We looked at each other, holding some cotton in our hands. We didn't say anything but just nodded.

We both knew the day had come. I could see in her eyes that Katie was excited too.

As we turned back toward the house, we saw a figure coming toward us. We paused as he approached.

"Good morning, ladies!" he said. "Up early, I see."

He opened his arms and took us in them. The three of us stood a few seconds in each other's arms, then stepped back.

"What are you doing up so early, Papa?" I said.

"I woke up with the sun," he answered. "It's the farmer's blood in me, I guess. What about you two?"

"We were checking on the cotton, Uncle Templeton," said Katie.

He glanced behind us toward the field we had just come from, like he was looking to see something he couldn't quite make out with his earthly vision, almost like he was peering into what that expanse of growing cotton might *mean*.

Leaving us where we were, he slowly began walking toward it. We turned and followed him with our eyes as he walked into the long rows. He stooped down and tried to pluck at a few of the bolls.

After a few minutes he came back toward us, holding several clumps of white in his hand.

"And what did you conclude?" he said.

Katie and I looked at each other, then back at him.

"I think it's ready, Uncle Templeton," said Katie,

then glanced at me with just a hint of question in her eyes.

I nodded. "It's time," I said.

By the middle of that morning we had the two wagons out of the barn and the baling boxes and satchels ready and loaded into the first wagon. Then Josepha began carting out jugs of water and milk and baskets of bread and dried meat and cheese.

Sometime about eleven we all climbed into the wagon. Henry clicked the reins, and we were off. Everyone was excited and talking and we bounced along, Henry flicking the reins occasionally to keep the horse slowly plodding along. We tried to explain to Uncle Ward what to do as we walked and rode out to get started. Even little William was babbling away like he couldn't wait to get to picking along with us. I couldn't even imagine what it was going to be like for him to grow up never having been a slave!

Josepha had packed up water and more food than twice this many people would need, especially since the house wasn't that far away and we could just walk back for lunch. I think one of Josepha's goals in life was to try to make everyone else as fat as she was, so she tried to feed anyone who'd eat as much as she could get down them.

Henry reined in beside the closest field. "Here we be!" he said.

We all piled out. While Henry unhitched the horse, Katie and Emma and I took satchels and slung them over our shoulders. My papa and Uncle Ward watched. Even after all we'd been talking about, Uncle Ward seemed a little bewildered about the proceedings.

Papa got two more satchels out of the wagon and handed one to his brother. Unconsciously everyone glanced at Uncle Ward.

"Hey, don't look at me!" he laughed. "I may be the owner of this place, at least that's what some people keep telling me, but I know less about this than William!"

"We pik kottin!" chimed in William, and we all laughed.

"Well, your niece is the expert," said my papa. "She taught me what to do. We'll let her give you a demonstration."

Uncle Ward glanced toward Katie.

"No, I mean Mary Ann," said my papa, "—your other niece."

"Ah yes . . . right," said Uncle Ward, smiling at me and waiting.

"Henry's better at it than I am," I said, "but I suppose I can show you as well as anyone. I've picked enough of it, that's for sure."

I walked over to the edge of a row.

"We each pick a row," I said. "You just work your way down it to the other end of the field. You get your fingers around the little clump of cotton and just pluck it out . . . like this . . . and put it in your satchel. The main thing is not to get too many leaves or bits of stalk in the bags with the cotton. If Mr. Watson at the mill in town—that's who Jeremiah works for when he's not at the livery—sees too many leaves, he won't give us as good a price. But you can't go too slow either or it'll take too long. So you gotta try to pick fast but clean."

I stopped and looked around at everyone.

"Then, let's get started," said the foreman enthusiastically. "Let the harvest begin!"

We all spread out along the edge of the field and started at the beginning of our rows. Since we weren't in such a big hurry this time—unless rain clouds suddenly appeared on the horizon!—I worked alongside Katie so we could talk. Josepha got tired pretty quickly and couldn't work as long as the rest of us. But while she did I was amazed at her speed. It was obvious she'd picked lots of cotton in her life too before she became a house slave. She could almost keep up with Henry! The two of them worked alongside each other and chattered away in colored talk so fast sometimes that even I could hardly understand what they were saying.

Gradually Henry and Josepha moved out toward the middle of the field ahead of us in the two rows alongside each other. A little way back Katie and I came along in our two rows. Then farther back my papa and Uncle Ward went a lot slower but seemed to be enjoying themselves. Every once in a while I heard a great laugh from my papa, and it made my heart warm every time I heard it. Without knowing it, he had brought a whole new energy and optimism to Rosewood. He was so cheerful and pleasant to everyone, and excited about Rosewood's possibilities, that his spirit infected us all in a good way.

Farther back, Emma walked along with little William, trying to show him what to do and talking to him like mothers do. They didn't get much picked, but it was sure cute to watch.

Seeing Emma with William, seeing how she'd grown and changed from being a mother, and watching William gradually grow up himself, had made me start thinking for the first time in my life about what it would be like to actually have a baby of my own. Not that I was in any rush to get married. But it didn't seem so fearsome a thought to me as it once had.

We only worked a couple of hours, then took a break for lunch, sweating and beginning to get tired but still enthusiastic. The talk around the table in the kitchen was more animated than anytime since we'd all been together, full of questions and stories, even Uncle Ward talking more than usual. A little while after lunch, Jeremiah came out to help.

We only worked another two or so hours in the afternoon. On the first day it's best not to try to do too much. A harvest takes a long time. We didn't have near as much land planted as some plantations, or as Rosewood once did. But we didn't have that many people either. The cotton would take us two or three weeks to get in. So we knew it was best to start gradually and get used to it. Your muscles get sore, and it gets mighty tedious soon enough. After a while the daily rhythm of the harvest takes over and the days begin to flow one into the other and the cotton begins to pile up.

That's how it was. Slowly we made progress, and Papa and Uncle Ward gradually got faster, and after a week we had one wagon piled high with hundred-pound bales, and we'd finished the first field and were starting on the second.

We took a day off the next week for my eighteenth birthday. Josepha made me a great big cake and we sang and Katie played the piano. We taught the two men some old slave revival songs, and now with more people we could dance better too. We moved the furniture in the parlor to one side and Katie taught everyone the minuet and then played the music for it on the piano while Henry and Josepha, Jeremiah and I, and Papa and Emma all tried to do it.

It was so much fun! Then we switched people so that Uncle Ward could try it, and by then we knew the music well enough that Emma and Josepha and I could sing it as we danced so that Katie didn't have to play. With her dancing along with us, we had four couples dancing in the parlor.

We didn't go to bed that night until hours after dark. We gradually got tired and sleepy, but no one wanted to leave the parlor and go upstairs to bed. The whole room got quiet for a spell, and I found myself starting to hum another one of the old songs that had always been so special to me. Before long, Katie and I were softly singing together:

"Day is dying in the west, angels watching over me,
my Lord.
Sleep my child and take your rest, angels watching
over me.
All night, all day, angels watching over me, my
Lord.
All night, all day, angels watching over me."

Again it got quiet after we'd sung it through a couple times.

"That was right pretty singing, Kathleen," said Uncle Ward. "You two ladies sound mighty fine singing together, don't they, Templeton?"

"They sure do."

Then my papa looked at me. "From everything that's happened," he said, "it sounds like you two have had angels watching over you, all right."

Katie and I looked at each other and smiled.

"We sure have, Uncle Templeton," said Katie, glancing at her two uncles. "And two of them are right here in this room with us."

That brought a chuckle out of both of them. Then Katie spoke to me again.

"Tell them one of your black-uncle stories, Mayme," she said. "I'm so sleepy, I'm in the mood to fall asleep with you telling a story."

I thought a minute, then started in with one I didn't think I'd told Katie before.

"Well, de animals en de creeturs ob da fores, dey wuz gittin on mighty well wid wunner nudder," I began, "so well dat Brer Rabbit en Brer Fox en Brer Possum got tar sorter bunchin' der perwishuns ter gedder in de same shanty. Atter w'ile de roof sorter 'gun ter leak, en one day Brer Rabbit en Brer Fox en Brer Possum, 'semble fer ter see ef dey can't kinder patch er up. Dey had a big day's work in front un um, en dey fotch der dinner wid up. . . ."

I glanced over at Katie and Emma, and already I could see their eyelids drooping as I went on. I knew I'd better make it a short story! When I finished, by then we were finally ready to go to bed. Slowly we got up and all trudged upstairs.

A little while later, after the lanterns were all put out, I lay peacefully in my bed thinking. I could tell from her breathing that Katie was almost asleep.

The house was completely quiet. I breathed in a long sigh of satisfaction, and lay there in the silence a long time before I felt my own eyes getting heavy. I was so thankful to God for everything He had done for us, and especially for bringing the two men to be part of our lives.

It was just about the best way of turning eighteen I could imagine in all the world.

And maybe Katie was right. Maybe they were angels!

45

T he weather held.

No storm came this time to interrupt the harvest. We took the first load into town, both the Daniels brothers sitting on the board seats holding the reins, Katie sitting beside Uncle Ward in one wagon, me beside my papa in the other.

I could tell he was proud as we entered town and clattered slowly along the street toward Mr. Watson's mill. We may not have had the biggest cotton crop in Shenandoah County, or the prettiest bales. But it was *our* crop and we were proud of it!

Mrs. Hammond, as usual, heard us coming and came out of her shop to look. Everybody knew, of course, about me and Katie and about Katie's two uncles on her mother's side who had come and were now operating Rosewood. No one that he'd had dealings with in town had particularly liked Burchard Clairborne anyway, so that helped "the Daniels brothers," as people called them, be accepted by most people. Whether all that would change if they knew that the white man and colored girl riding alongside each other in the first of Rosewood's wagons that morning, and seeming so friendly with each other, were father and daughter, who could say. Even not knowing it, Mrs. Hammond had the same disapproving scowl on her face that she always did.

"Morning, Mrs. Hammond!" called out my papa as we passed, nodding with a smile and tipping his hat. "Fine day, isn't it?"

I could almost hear her mutter as she turned back into her shop, *Well I never! That ugly colored girl is going to get uppity, Mr. Daniels, if you let her take liberties and ride beside you like that!*

But I didn't care what she thought. I was about as happy as I could be.

My papa continued to greet other townspeople as we went. He'd already made a lot of friends in Greens Crossing because he was so friendly and personable. He'd even been to see Mr. Sneed in Oakwood a couple of times about legal things. That didn't make Katie none too happy, but he just said you catch more flies with honey than vinegar, and that it never hurt to be on the good side of folks like that. And maybe it's good he did too, because that's how we eventually found out a little more about some of Mr. Sneed's conversations with Katie's uncle Burchard.

As we continued on through town, there were two or three spinsters and a widow or two that watched my papa with even more interest than everyone else. Because he was handsome too.

We reached Mr. Watson's mill. Papa bounded down and went inside. I searched high and low, hoping to catch sight of Jeremiah, but didn't see him. A few minutes later Papa came out chatting and laughing with Mr. Watson.

". . . wondered why their bales were so light," Mr.

Watson was saying. "But I've got to hand it to those girls, they picked a lot of cotton."

"Well, our bales may not be very tight or very heavy either, Mr. Watson," Papa said. "But our cotton is as good as anyone's. And there is a lot more where this came from."

By then Uncle Ward had walked up.

"I don't think you've met my brother, Ward Daniels, Mr. Watson. Ward—say hello to Mr. Watson."

"Pleased to meet you, Mr. Daniels," said the mill owner. "So you're Kathleen's other uncle I've been hearing about."

"I guess I'm the guilty party, all right."

"Well. We're glad to have you as part of our community.—I'll get some of my men and we'll get this cotton of yours unloaded."

By that same afternoon we were back from town and out in the fields again. We kept on working and the cotton bales continued to pile up. The total on the Rosewood page of Mr. Watson's ledger mounted also as we took in a new load every time we had the wagons full.

Most of the big plantations around had their crops in by the first week of September. But we were still picking.

There was only one interruption to our harvest, though that was not one that slowed our work down.

During one of our trips to town we stopped at Mrs. Hammond's store. Papa and I waited outside while Katie and Uncle Ward went in to get some coffee beans.

After Mrs. Hammond had given them the coffee and

they'd paid for it, she handed Katie an envelope.

"You've got a letter, Kathleen," she said. "It's addressed to you."

Katie took it, more than a little curious. It was the first time she had ever seen an envelope with her own name handwritten on the front: *Miss Kathleen Clairborne.*

"Who's it from, Kathleen?" asked Uncle Ward as they walked outside.

"I don't know," replied Katie.

By the time she walked outside she knew who it was from.

"What is it?" I asked when I saw her pulling out two sheets from the envelope and starting to read even while she was walking back to the wagon.

"It's . . . it's a letter from Rob Paxton. You remember . . . from up north."

"The deputy?" said my papa, glancing at me.

I nodded.

Katie climbed back on the wagon beside Uncle Ward without saying another word, her face buried in the letter. I jumped up and sat down beside her.

"What does he say?" I asked finally as we got underway, my curiosity getting the better of me.

"Here, you can read it when I'm finished," she said, handing me the first page.

I started to take it, but then hesitated. "Uh, no . . . that's okay," I said. Even though I was curious, it didn't seem right to read someone else's letter.

"Then I'll just tell you what it says. It's not, you know, personal or anything." Her eyes scanning the letter, Katie said, "His parents send greetings and want us to know we are welcome to stay with them whenever we are next in Baltimore . . . which isn't likely to happen anytime soon. And Rob writes, *'Please give* my *warmest regards to your uncles and cousin Mayme—as well as to the other kind folks I met at Rosewood.'*"

Katie read to herself for a few moments. "Let's see, then he goes on to tell about everything he's been doing and about his family in Baltimore and things around Ellicott City. Oh!" Katie chuckled. "Listen to this: *'I arrested a man twice my size a few days ago and ended up with a black eye as big as a flapjack. I'm glad this didn't happen before you came here, or your uncles might have thought better of allowing me to escort you home. Too bad you're not here to see my shiner.'*"

Uncle Ward winked at her. "I think someone's taken a *shine* to you."

Katie's cheeks turned pink, but she said nothing.

When we got home a couple hours later and by then I was again riding beside Papa, Katie was unusually quiet, and stayed that way for the rest of the day.

That night, after I'd gone to bed, she was still sitting at her writing desk with a small candle beside her and her pen in hand, writing page after page in reply.

46

K atie and I were in the barn early one morning milking the cows. Most of the time my papa helped, but on this day Katie and I were milking alone like we used to. We were so accustomed to the routine of getting up early, building a fire in the cook stove, and then heading out to the barn to take care of the cows, and we usually kept to that same pattern. As often as not, Josepha was already stirring in the kitchen. That was her special domain. But when we got up real early and the whole house was still asleep, sometimes it seemed as though we were still moving in a dream too.

We were gradually tiring out from the picking day after day. And so on this particular day, when morning came, we were practically asleep on our feet and went through the motions of the milking without saying a word. Then we opened the gate and let the cows out and slowly led them along the road toward the pasture.

Katie began to lag behind and soon the cows clomping slowly along began to pass her. After another minute or two I heard her starting to laugh. I glanced back and there she was surrounded by cows, doing her best to keep walking in the midst of them.

"What are you doing back there?" I said.

Katie struggled her way forward, slapping a few of the cows on their sides and rumps to get by, until she had caught up with me again.

"The funniest thing just happened," she said. "I had a dream as we were walking."

"A dream—are you still asleep?"

"I feel like it."

"So do I!" I laughed. "I'm *so* tired."

"But you know what I mean, don't you?" said Katie. "It's a sort of awake-dream that happens when everything around you automatically becomes part of a dream."

"What was yours?"

"As we were walking along, suddenly I found myself dreaming that I was in Mrs. Hammond's store. But she didn't want me there."

"That sounds like her all right! Then what happened?"

"She tried to make me leave," said Katie. "But there were other customers in the store and she didn't want them to see her being rude to me. So she silently inched over toward me and tried to bump me toward the door and outside."

"*Bump* you out?" I laughed.

"She pushed and shoved at me with her hips so that nobody would notice she was trying to knock me out the door. Then suddenly I woke up and realized I was surrounded by the cows bumping at me as we walked along."

"Now, that's a funny dream!" I laughed.

"How did I get back there in the middle of the cows?" she asked.

"You just gradually fell back," I said. "I wasn't really paying much attention. I was nearly asleep myself."

"That must have been when I started thinking about Mrs. Hammond."

We were nearly to the pasture. We led the cows into the field, closed the gate behind them, and walked back to the house. By then we were good and awake, though still tired. Josepha and my papa had come down and were in the kitchen talking, Papa sitting at the table and Josepha bustling away at the counter. The smell of brewing coffee filled the room. Within an hour or two another day in the fields would begin.

Ten hours later the picking was nearly done for the day. Josepha and Emma had gone back to the house a little while before.

"Why don't you and Katie go on in and get started cleaning up," said my papa. "It's about time to call it a day. We'll be right behind you."

When Katie and I got to the house, there were Josepha and Emma sitting on the porch with William, who was playing with Rusty's ears.

"That's one patient old dog," I said wearily as Katie and I sat down on the steps. We were too tired to clean up just yet. For a while it was silent as we all just sat there, except for William babbling away to Rusty. One wagon sat in the yard all loaded up and ready to be taken in to the mill the next morning. Beyond it we found ourselves gazing in the distance at the field we'd just come from, by now about half picked.

"That's some sight, isn't it?" said Katie with a quiet smile.

"What are you looking at?" I asked, trying to follow her eyes.

"The men," she said.

"What about them?"

"That's our field, Mayme," said Katie. "Don't you remember the first year when it was just you and me out there picking our cotton?"

"And me," Emma piped up.

"Of course," laughed Katie. "I meant you too. And Aleta. Then Henry came and started helping. And then last year both Henry and Jeremiah helped, and even Uncle Templeton worked as much as he could after his injury. But now look at it. Here we are sitting on the porch, and there are *four* men out there picking our cotton together."

"Dey's good men, all right," said Josepha. "I seen lots er men in my time, an' dere be plenty ob bad men in dis ol' worl'. So we's mighty lucky ladies ter hab four strong men like dat who's good men besides."

"*Our* men," said Katie. "Don't you like the sound of that? Just seeing them like that, and knowing we're not alone anymore, makes me feel safe somehow."

"Dat Henry, he's 'bout one ob da finest colored men I've eber knowed, jes' like his son is too," Josepha went on. "And dem two uncles er yers, Miz Katie, dey're da kindest white men tard me I eber knowed.

Dey don' eben seem ter act like dey knows we's colored at all."

We didn't know it as we sat there, but out in the fields the men were thinking about us too. They had just reached the end of the row they had been working on, then paused and stood up straight to stretch and straighten their backs.

"Anyone ready to call it a day?" asked Uncle Ward.

"I's been ready fo' a couple er rows," said Henry with a chuckle.

"If I'd known that, I'd have sent the girls in an hour ago!" laughed Templeton.

"I din't want ter be da one ter say't," Henry added. "I ain't so shure I like da noshun er a couple er green pickers workin' harder'n me an' showin' me up!"

"Now I know you're making sport of us!" laughed Uncle Ward as Henry went on chuckling.

"No'suh, Mr. Ward," he said. "I may er made jes' a little joke, but you an' Mr. Templeton's jes' 'bout da fastes' white men I eben seen wiff da cotton. Dat's why we's gettin' hit in so fas'. We's goin' twice as fas' as las' year."

"All I knows is dat ef we's all ready, why we be standin' roun' talkin'?" Jeremiah now said. "Why don' we get outer dis field an' see what da women hab waitin' fo' us?"

The four men turned, full satchels slung over their shoulders, and began making their way, side by side, toward the house.

"I'm afraid I have some bad news for you, Jeremiah,"

said Templeton when they were about halfway back to the house.

"What dat?"

"I don't think the women have *anything* waiting for us! Look at them," he added with a laugh, "—they're all just sitting there on the porch staring at us."

"'Peers dat's what dey's doin, all right," said Henry.

"But I'm hungry!" moaned Jeremiah.

"Den maybe we dun worked 'em too hard," said his father.

"I doubt that," said Ward. "It's all I can do to keep up with Mary Ann and Kathleen."

"Don' fo'git dat Josepha," Henry replied. "She may not be able ter las' so long, but w'en she's a'pickin', I can't hardly eben see dose fingers er hers!"

"They're all good workers, and that's a fact," said Templeton. "More than that—they're good women and young ladies. I'd say we're a bunch of fortunate men, all right."

As they walked past the barn and came toward us, we could see them laughing and chatting.

"What are you four talking about?" I said.

"Oh, nothing much," replied my papa with a smile. "What about you? Looks like you got no farther than the porch. And we're hungry!"

"We just sat down and got distracted and started talking."

"What about?"

"Nothing in particular—just the cotton."

"Yeah, that's what we were talking about too."

THE LOOSE COW

47

O ne day in the middle of the cotton harvesting, Uncle Ward left the field and went back toward the barn to use the outhouse. Emma was outside hanging some wash up on the line while William was napping inside. Emma was singing an old field song when Ward came into the yard. But when she saw him, she stopped singing. She knew he wanted her to trust him, to be comfortable around him, but a lifetime of fearing white men didn't disappear so easy.

When he came back out, he glanced again toward the house where Emma was still hanging clothes. Right at that moment a black-and-white cow ambled across the yard between the house and the barn almost between them. The cows had been taken out to graze in one of the grass fields hours earlier, and yet there was one of them wandering along not fifty feet from the back door of the house!

"What the . . ." began Uncle Ward. He glanced about quickly, wondering if others had got loose too or if it was just the one.

"Emma!" he called. "Get over there and block the road."

Surprised, Emma called out to the cow, "Where you come from? Dis ain't where you belong." She set down the clothes basket and started walking in the direction Uncle Ward was pointing.

But the cow was already a little spooked to find itself out in the middle of the road where it'd never been before. And now seeing a white man and a black girl moving toward it from opposite directions, it gave a little *moo* of fear and began to move faster.

"Emma, quick!" cried Uncle Ward.

Emma dashed in the same direction it was moving to try to block the road. But though cows are generally pretty lazy and don't do much but stand around and eat, when they put their minds to it, they can move mighty fast, and this one decided to put its mind to it. Almost the instant Emma took off from the clothesline to block the road, the ornery thing bolted straight in the direction of town and shot past her.

"Hey, git back here, you dumb thing!" she shouted, sprinting after it.

But the cow was already past her and there was nothing she could do. If she kept running, it would too. She slowed and Uncle Ward ran up behind her.

"We gotta get that stupid outfit back into the field," he said, "before any more get out and get spooked and start running off in every direction."

"What you want me ter do, Mr. Ward?" asked Emma.

Uncle Ward thought a few seconds, watching the cow and glancing about the surrounding fields.

"You think you can circle around over there?" he said, pointing across the horse pasture. "You gotta go all the way to the end of the pasture, then toward the river, and come back around to the road on the other side of it."

"I kin do it, Mr. Ward."

"But you gotta go slow so it doesn't see you and make another run for it. Try to get back onto the road just this side of the bridge. We don't want that dumb thing falling in the river."

"Den what I do w'en I gits dere?"

"Then you just start walking back this way. I'll be off on the other side, and when she sees you, we'll hope she'll turn around and go back where she came from."

"I's do it, Mr. Ward," said Emma, and hurried off toward the pasture, climbed the fence, and half ran, half walked perpendicular to the road until she was way on the other side of it, past the horses, then started circling toward the bridge like he'd said.

Ten minutes later, Emma had succeeded in getting to the bridge ahead of the cow, who had by this time stopped along the road and was nibbling here and there on grass between the road and the fences on both sides. Uncle Ward had gone into the field opposite the pasture and had slowly made his way past the cow too. Now they had to try to head her back the way she had come. So far they didn't see any other cows getting out of the grazing field.

From where he was about a hundred and fifty yards away from her, Uncle Ward motioned to Emma to start walking along the road back in the direction of the house. She did, and in two or three minutes she was close enough that the cow looked up and saw her. It gave another *moo* that sounded like it was protesting the idea of being disturbed, then turned around and started walking back toward the house just like they wanted.

But whatever had gotten into its crazy head, this cow wasn't being altogether cooperative on this day. It had only gone a little way when it glanced to its right and saw Uncle Ward in the field there inching his way along sort of beside it. And there was Emma in the road coming along behind it. In front of it was the road to the house, wide open without a soul in the way, and you'd think any ordinary cow would just keep walking along it. But then it glanced to the left into the horse pasture Emma'd come through to get to the bridge. And even though there was a fence in the way, that cow got it into its head to try out the grass there. Suddenly it lurched into a run, turned off the road, and ran straight for the fence. It tried to jump over but didn't clear the fence. Its hooves hit the top rails and knocked the boards every which way. Then it ran clumsily off into the horse pasture.

"After her, Emma!" cried Uncle Ward. "Cut her off before she stampedes the horses!"

Emma was off in a flash, climbed the fence, then picked up her dress to her knees and tore off across the pasture in a wide arc to get behind the cow. I wish I could have seen that! Emma had long skinny legs and she could run mighty fast when she put her mind to it, like she was doing now. Uncle Ward said she was yelling at the cow as she went, though he couldn't understand a thing she was saying.

She got to the far end of the pasture and curved around. The few horses, seeing the commotion, had begun to get a little frisky themselves. But they were still far enough away so that it didn't do too much harm.

At the far end of the pasture there was a small pond, which now, near the end of a hot, dry summer, was pretty much a big, muddy puddle. The cow, obviously thirsty from all the running, was trying to get a drink from the little water left in it.

"Come on, girl," Emma said softly. "We git you back home, you's kin have all the water you wants."

The cow, still nuzzling the mud in search of water, clumped farther into the puddle, sinking deep into the sticky soil.

"Don' you git stuck in dere," Emma warned, carefully stepping closer. The cow looked up at Emma but didn't move. She waved Ward over, calling in a hoarse whisper, "I think de fool thing's stuck in dis mud."

Ward groaned and walked over, assessing the situation with the cow, now ankle-deep in the mud.

Ward moved toward its back. "I'll give her a push and you stand on that side so she doesn't take off for the river again once we get her out."

Ward stepped gingerly in the mud, which rose nearly to the top of his boots. His feet made a sucking sound each time he pulled them from the mud to take another step closer to the cow. The cow swung its head around to look at who was approaching but didn't attempt to move.

"Stupid outfit," Ward muttered. He put both hands on her rear flank and pushed.

But the cow didn't budge. Emma stood at the edge of the pond bed, arms outstretched, ready to shoo the cow in the opposite direction. Ward pushed again, this time leaning his whole body into the effort.

"Come on, girl, git," he scolded, then lifted one hand and swatted the cow on its rump.

Suddenly the cow bolted, picking up its hooves and lurching toward Emma. Ward, who had been leaning all his weight against the cow, fell face first into the mud. Emma, shrieking and trying to jump out of the path of the charging cow, lost her footing and fell on her hands and knees. The cow's hooves splattered mud on her face and neck as it kicked its way loose of the pond.

Ward lifted himself from the mud, "You okay, Emma?"

Emma swiped at her eyes with the back of her hand, spreading even more mud on her face. "I been worse." Looking down at her hands, she said, "I been cleaner too."

She looked up at Ward then and asked nervously, "You's all right, Mr. Ward? Sorry I cudn't stop dat fool thing."

Ward struggled to his feet. "Not your fault, Emma. If I didn't know better I'd say that cow wasn't stuck at all—just wanted to teach us a lesson."

Emma looked at Ward's mud-covered face and bit back a smile. "I think she did."

Ward reached out a hand to Emma. She looked up at him, then put her hand in his.

"Look at us, Emma," Ward said as he helped her to her feet. "Our hands are the same color."

Emma smiled shyly. "You oughta see yo face. I don' know *what* color you is."

He chuckled. "Maybe that's the way it should be."

She looked at him soberly then and nodded. "I reckon you's right . . . Uncle Ward."

By now the mud-splattered Holstein was both confused and frightened, and seemed determined to keep going the wrong way. Emma ran after it again, and Uncle Ward tried to position himself to help Emma get the cow back in the direction they wanted it to go. But even tiring like it was, the cow was too fast for them. By the time they had urged it back toward the road and the hole in the fence it had just made, all three of them were about worn out.

"Watch the road, Emma!" called out Uncle Ward. "I'll stay here to keep her from running back into the pasture. You get back on the road to keep it from making for the bridge!"

Emma broke off the chase and ran parallel to the road a ways, then climbed back over the fence onto the road, and started back toward them. She was now back where she had been ten minutes earlier.

"All right, I'm going to walk her gently through the break in the fence," called Uncle Ward. "You just stay where you are.—Hey, you!" he called to the cow. "Okay . . . get back through and onto the road."

Slowly he walked forward with his arms outstretched, and slowly the cow began to amble toward the broken part of the fence. But then it gave another moo that sounded a little more rebellious than just protesting, and suddenly bucked a few awkward times and took off running, straight through the hole and onto the road. It was just what they'd wanted.

But instead of turning toward the house, it kept going straight across the road, crashed through the fence on the opposite side, and ran off out of sight across the field.

"That blamed fool outfit!" yelled Uncle Ward, and they both dashed after it again.

A few minutes later is when the rest of us finally found out what was going on and why Uncle Ward hadn't come back. Suddenly we heard the sound of thudding feet and a frantic moo and a great big clumsy cow came wildly running through the cotton field right in the middle of us, crashing down plants and sending us scurrying to get out of the way. And there were Emma and Uncle Ward huffing along behind it.

"What's going on, Ward!" said Papa, half laughing as he watched the cow running away from us toward the house.

Then he started laughing all the harder when he saw Uncle Ward covered head to foot in mud.

"That blamed cow got loose somehow," said Uncle Ward as they stopped. "It just walked through the barnyard and then bolted for the bridge when we tried to head it off. Emma and I have been chasing it, trying to get it back into the field."

"Without much success by the looks of it!"

"You're right there."

"How'd it get loose?"

"Don't know."

"Any other out?"

"Not that we've seen."

"Well, then, we'd better get that one back in. With all of us we ought to be able to shoo it in the right direction."

We all set down our things, and Papa and Uncle Ward planned how to do it and where to put us all so that the cow wouldn't have any direction to go except the way we wanted her to. Then we all took our positions and began slowly moving toward the grazing field, spreading out as we went, and keeping the cow in sight in front of us. Within ten minutes she was back inside and grazing contentedly with the rest.

A part of the fence had broken down, which was how she got through. They had Katie and me stand guard while they went back to fetch some boards and nails and wire to repair it with.

As they went, I saw Uncle Ward throw his arm around Emma's shoulder. "Well, I guess we got that ol' outfit back in, didn't we, Emma?"

"Dat we did," she said back. "But I don't reckon we wuz eber gwine git it dere alone."

He laughed. "You might be right there," he said. "But maybe we tired her out enough so that everyone else could finish the job."

"Dat may be, Uncle Ward," she said, and as she spoke I saw Emma glance up at him with a grin. "Maybe you's right 'bout dat after all."

CELEBRATION

48

It was near the middle of September when we finished the last field of cotton. Just the faintest hint was in the air of the weather thinking about starting to turn. We were all exhausted but ecstatic. Our hands were dry and cracked. But there's no feeling quite so good as having the harvest in. The two brothers and Katie were so brown from the sun that from a distance a stranger might have thought we were *all* coloreds—except for Katie's light hair, that is!

We took the last load into town, Katie and I and Papa and Uncle Ward, just like we had the first time. When Mr. Watson came out and handed Papa a check, he and Uncle Ward looked at it in as much astonishment as Katie and I had felt after our first harvest.

"That's over a thousand dollars, Templeton!" said Uncle Ward. "Tarnation . . . I didn't know there was that kind of money in cotton. This is a dang sight *better* than gold!"

The four of us walked down to the bank together, the two brothers still incredulous at how much money our harvest had raised. I hesitated when we got to the front door. I was always conscious that the color of my skin was different from the others, and that people looked at me different, especially when I was with them. If I'd have been alone, they might have turned up their noses a little but that's all. But whenever people saw blacks and whites together and being friendly with each other, they didn't like it. If a white was yelling at a black or treating him rudely, nobody minded. But when someone like Katie or my papa treated a colored person with respect or worse, familiarity, for some reason they hated that. It made them despise the white person and hate the colored person all the more.

Katie knew instantly what I was feeling.

"Come on, Mayme," she whispered to me. "You're part of this family too."

When we all walked into the bank together, I don't think I've ever felt so proud. There we were, the four of us. We didn't have anything to be ashamed of now. Rosewood was a plantation we could be proud of.

"Mr. Taylor," said my papa, shaking hands with the bank manager, "I want you to meet my brother. This is Ward Daniels.—Ward . . . Mr. Taylor, the manager of the bank."

"Yes, I . . . uh, saw you a few months ago," said Mr. Taylor, "during the proceedings with, uh . . . Mr. Clairborne."

The two men shook hands.

"Our harvest is in," my father went on, "and we want to deposit this into Rosewood's account—all except for a hundred dollars of it. Ward and I have some plans for that."

I glanced at my papa, wondering what he meant. Then I saw Katie whisper something in his ear.

"Make that a hundred twenty," said my papa. "Deposit all but one-twenty."

The banker took Mr. Watson's check, handed it to one of his assistants, said a few words, then turned back to us.

"I have been meaning to talk to you, Mr. Daniels," he said. "As it presently stands, the Rosewood account is still in Rosalind Clairborne's name. I need to have you sign new papers in order to effect a change of ownership on the account. Whose names shall I place on the documents, yours and your brother's?"

"All four of ours, Mr. Taylor," answered my papa. "Templeton Daniels, Ward Daniels, Kathleen Clairborne, and Mary Ann Daniels—all to be equal owners of the account. You draw up the necessary papers, and we will all sign them."

"Yes, sir, I shall attend to it. But I am a little confused," he added in a puzzled tone. "Who is Mary Ann Daniels?"

Just then his assistant returned with the hundred twenty dollars. He handed it to Mr. Taylor, Mr. Taylor handed it to my father, who handed one of the twenty-dollar bills to Katie, who then handed it to me.

I looked back at her in question.

"It's for you, Mayme," she said quietly, "for your account, just like I gave you last year and the year before. Go on . . ." she added, nodding toward Mr. Taylor.

I turned to the bank manager.

"Mr. Taylor," I said, "I would like to deposit this in my account."

"Uh, yes, miss . . . of course.—That's Jukes, is it not?"

"Yes, sir. But if you don't mind, I would like you to change the name on my account."

"Of course . . . but what kind of change?"

"Change the name to Mary Ann Daniels."

The banker glanced toward the two Daniels brothers, then back at me. He was more stoic than Mrs. Hammond, so you couldn't so easily tell what he was thinking. Whatever it was, he kept his thoughts to himself.

"And one more thing, Mr. Taylor," said my papa. "Would you draw up a draft for three hundred dollars and wire it to a Clinton Roscoe in Ellicott City, Maryland, and withdraw the amount from the account."

"I shall see to it, Mr. Daniels."

When we left the bank a few minutes later, I felt rich. I had sixty dollars of my very own in the bank, more money than I ever thought I would lay eyes on in my life. And instead of *owing* the bank money, Rosewood's account would have almost six hundred dollars in it after my papa's debt was all paid.

"What's the hundred dollars for, Uncle Templeton?" asked Katie as we returned to the wagons.

"You'll just have to wait and see, young lady!" he replied.

We all found out soon enough what they had planned to use the money for.

That same evening at supper, Papa announced that they wanted to take us all into Charlotte again to celebrate the successful harvest.

"Just like last year," he said. "I told Ward about it and he suggested we do it again. We'll make one of the wagons as comfortable as we can, and we'll all go together. That includes you too, Josepha. And we'll see if Henry and Jeremiah can join us. Maybe we can find one of the neighbor boys to come over and tend the animals."

"Lan' sakes," said Josepha, hardly able to imagine it. "I ain't neber slep' in no hotel afore. Does dey really let black folks stay in hotels?"

"Not all hotels do, Josepha," said my papa. "But we know a nice hotel where we went last year where they'll let anyone stay."

"But won't it cost too much," said Katie, "—that many people?" She'd been under the debt of her mama's loans for so long she could hardly imagine Rosewood having enough money to spend frivolously on ourselves like that.

"What is money for if you can't enjoy life?" said my papa. "We're a family, so we'll all enjoy it together. We all picked the cotton together, so we'll all celebrate together. We'll make it a yearly Rosewood tradition."

Making Plans

49

We spent four days in Charlotte and had such a good time. I don't know what people thought when they saw us, whites and blacks together in the hotel and eating in restaurants and laughing and talking. And all of us women got new dresses. I think it is safe to say that we turned a few heads in Charlotte!

One thing we didn't do when we were there was go visit Katie's uncle Burchard, who lived just outside the city. I think Katie was still a little afraid of him, though my papa said there was nothing more he could do.

A few days after we returned to Rosewood and things settled down and we were trying to get back to normal, Katie said she needed to talk to her two uncles. She wanted me there too.

We sat down in the parlor one afternoon and Katie closed the door. She didn't want Emma or Josepha to hear. She was acting so serious that at first I was worried. It wasn't like her not to share with me what she was thinking, so I didn't know what to make of it. But as soon as she began to talk, it was obvious she'd been doing a lot of thinking about our future. She had been a little amazed too, about how much money the harvest had brought in, but realized how much more could be done if we applied ourselves all the harder.

"We've got to start making plans for next year," she began when we were all seated.

"Already!" exclaimed my papa. "We just finished *this* year's harvest."

"If you don't make plans in advance, there's never a next year's crop," said Katie. "The weather's still good, and now's the best time to plough and prepare the land for planting."

"When do we plant?" asked Uncle Ward.

"Just as next winter begins to turn," answered Katie. "In late February or March. Different crops have different growing seasons. But you have to have the fields ready to plant before that. And I've been thinking that we ought to get *more* land ready for next year."

"How much land do we have?"

"Oh, lots more, Uncle Ward. But some of the fields have just gone to grass and weeds. My mama couldn't keep it up during the war after the slaves left, and I was too young to be much help. There's lots more land. If we get it cleared, then we can replough it too and use it for more cotton or other crops, like wheat and everything else my mama and daddy used to grow." By now Katie was talking more and more excitedly. "You have to plant different things, so that if one crop isn't good in a certain year, you'll have something else that is."

My papa and Uncle Ward looked at each other almost dumbfounded.

"Who will do all that?" my papa finally asked.

"You've got to learn everything, Uncle Templeton . . . Uncle Ward. Henry can show you how to plough. I could too, though I'm not strong enough to hold a plough very well. But I've seen it done a lot."

"Hold on, Kathleen!" laughed my papa. "That sounds like a pretty major operation you're talking about."

"No more than what Rosewood used to be."

"But we don't have enough people to do all that . . . do we?"

"We can hire more, Uncle Templeton. There are other blacks who used to be slaves who need work that we can hire to work the fields with us. And we need to get the vegetable garden even bigger too, though we girls and Josepha can do that. And then there are repairs that haven't been made for a long time, fences and the barn and corral. And if we're going to do all these things, we might need some new equipment. We also need to salt and smoke enough meat for winter. With so many of us now, we've got to be putting lots more food away than we did when it was just Mayme and Emma and me."

"But we don't know anything about any of that, Kathleen."

"Mayme and I will show you. And Josepha—if it's got anything to do with food, she will know what to do. We should probably butcher a cow pretty soon, don't you think, Mayme?"

"We've still got about a month's worth of dried beef," I said.

"That's not too much."

"Who does the butchering?" asked Uncle Ward.

"Last time Henry helped us," said Katie.

The two brothers looked at each other and kind of

shook their heads in bewilderment, wondering the same thing they'd wondered so many times before, if they'd gotten themselves into more than they had counted on. Their young niece was reminding them more and more of her mother!

"And that brings up one other thing I need to talk to you about," Katie went on. "I don't know how much you know about how the war changed everything here in the South. After the slaves were set free, nobody owned slaves anymore. A lot of them stayed at the plantations where they were, but then the owners of the plantations had to start paying them. That's how it was with Josepha before she came here. She was getting paid five cents a day. Henry was already a freedman and so he was getting paid at the livery even before that. But what I'm trying to say is that we need to pay Emma and Josepha, and Henry and Jeremiah too, for all the work they did helping us with the cotton. I don't think Emma or Josepha expect it because they are living here and have plenty to eat, and I don't know if Henry expects it either. Henry just helps us because he's a friend and we've been alone. I've been trying to pay them all a little whenever I could, but now that Rosewood is starting to make money again, it's only right that we pay them."

"That makes sense, all right," said my papa. "There's no reason the money from the cotton shouldn't be shared with everyone. How much should we pay them?"

"I don't know," said Katie. "After every harvest I've

been giving Mayme twenty dollars. But I don't know what we should give the others. What do you think, Mayme?"

"I don't know," I said. "It always seems like you are giving me too much. But colored folks don't have much experience with money. It still seems strange to have any money to call your own at all. I'm still trying to get used to it. All I know is that Josepha told me she was getting five cents a day at the McSimmons place. And if I know Master McSimmons, he wouldn't pay any more than he had to."

"Well, then, why don't we pay her, say, three dollars a month," suggested my papa, "—that's fair, isn't it, along with room and board?"

Katie and I looked at each other and nodded. It seemed like a lot of money to me. But maybe it was fair.

"What about Emma?" said Uncle Ward. "She doesn't do much work."

"I don't think she needs to be paid," said Katie, "as long as we're taking care of her and William. At least not every month . . . though maybe something from the harvest money. We just need to make sure she's got everything she needs. She's got no one else but us."

"What about you?" asked my papa. "Do *you* get paid?"

Katie laughed. "We're kin, Uncle Templeton. I know your name's on Mama's deed, Uncle Ward," she said, turning to Uncle Ward, "but it's kind of like Rosewood belongs to all of us, isn't it, since we're all part of the

Daniels family? You don't have to pay family."

"You said you've been paying Mary Ann."

"Not for her work, just because she's my friend . . . I wanted to do it for her. I wanted her to have a bank account with her very own name on it."

"So what you're saying, Kathleen, is that we need to pay Henry and Jeremiah some of the harvest money, and also Josepha and Emma, and then start giving Josepha a wage too?"

Katie nodded.

"Well, then . . . if you paid Mayme twenty dollars and she's family, would it sound fair to pay Henry forty dollars because he picked more cotton than any of us, and then pay Jeremiah and Josepha both twenty dollars each, and Emma ten. What does that sound like?"

"I think that sounds fair, Papa," I said. "I know they will all appreciate it."

"Do you have a bank account, Kathleen?" asked my papa. "One with *your* name on it?"

"No. I just used my mama's."

"All right, then, here's what we'll do—the Rosewood account will belong to all of us. But we'll open a new account just for you too. It will have Kathleen Clairborne's name on it, no one else's. Then we'll put sixty dollars in it for you, just like is in Mary Ann's."

"Thank you, Uncle Templeton," said Katie.

"Good, then it's settled. Why don't you talk to them all, Kathleen, and I'll get the money from the bank next time I'm in town."

"I think it would mean more coming from you, Uncle

Templeton," said Katie. "I think you ought to give them the money. And I think you should talk to Josepha and tell her that you and Uncle Ward want to start paying her a monthly wage for all her hard work."

"All right, if you think that's best, we'll talk to her. I'll talk to Henry too."

We were all quiet for a minute.

"Now that we're getting all these financial dealings settled, and all these plans made," said Uncle Ward, "I got one more item of business to bring before this here family committee . . . if you all don't mind."

"Go on ahead, Ward," said my papa. "We're listening, aren't we, ladies?"

We all turned toward Uncle Ward and waited.

"Well, it's like this," he began. "You know that when I came here I didn't know what I was getting into. I never took much stock in my name on that deed of Rosalind's, though I'm sure glad I kept it all those years. Otherwise we'd all be picking Burchard Clairborne's cotton instead of Kathleen's. But to tell you the truth, I'm still a mite uncomfortable when I think about that deed. And I been thinking that if anything should happen to me—I ain't no spring chicken, you know—there's no telling what that Burchard fellow might try to do. I know you all been mighty kind telling me you wanted me to stay on here and that I was the rightful owner and all. But you gotta admit that having my name just handwritten on the back of it don't sound too altogether the way it oughta be."

"What are you driving at, Ward?" asked my papa.

"I been thinking that maybe we oughta go see that Sneed fellow, and have him draw up a brand-new deed, like he done for Richard's brother, and make it all legal so nothing could ever happen, and put *all* our names on it—all four of us. It's just what Kathleen said a little bit ago. It's like all four of us kind of own Rosewood together, now that Richard and Rosalind are dead and there's no one else. If that's true, I don't like only my name being on it."

We sat a minute in silence thinking about what he'd said. My brain was spinning at the notion! He couldn't mean *me* too!

Finally my papa spoke up.

"I see what you're saying, Ward," he said, nodding thoughtfully. "Makes a lot of sense. Not that I want to take anything from you, but what you say makes a lot of sense."

"I'd feel a darn sight better about it myself," said Uncle Ward. "You'd be doing me a favor and lifting a big load off my mind."

"I don't like Mr. Sneed," said Katie.

"He's a lawyer," said my papa. "That's all that matters. He can draw up legal documents whether we like him or not. But we could go see another lawyer in Charlotte or anywhere else if you want."

"I don't care, Uncle Templeton. I just don't like him, that's all. But you can talk to him if you want."

Finally it was my turn to say something.

"But . . . you can't really mean . . . me too?" I said.

"I'm colored. You can't put *my* name on a deed."

"You're my daughter, Mary Ann," said my papa. "You may not be quite as related to Rosalind as we three. But you've still got half Daniels blood in your veins, and that makes you kin."

"She could have a smaller share, Templeton," said Uncle Ward, "if she wanted."

"No," said Katie. "I won't let you add my name to the deed unless Mayme's share is equal to mine."

"My sentiments precisely!" added my papa.

"Fine by me," said Uncle Ward. "So it'll be just like I said at first—all four of us, equal partners."

"But we're women, Uncle Templeton," said Katie. "And we're not old enough to own things, are we?"

"Mary Ann's eighteen. You'll be eighteen next year. And I don't care if you are women or how old you are or what color anyone is—we'll tell him whose names go on it and that's that."

He glanced around at the rest of us with such a look of finality and authority that there wasn't much else for anyone to say.

"Good, it's settled, then!" said my papa. "Ward, what do you say that you and I go see Sneed tomorrow and set it in motion."

And that's how a former slave girl—me!—who left her home without anything to her name and not a penny in her pocket, got to be a one-fourth owner of a big plantation in Shenandoah County, North Carolina, called Rosewood, where she lived with her white cousin, her uncle, and her papa.

Just as we were getting through, a gentle knock sounded on the parlor door. Katie got up to answer it. There stood Emma.

"I'm sorry ter disturb y'all, Miz Katie," she said, "but Jeremiah's outside. He's ax'ed ef he kin call on Miz Mayme."

"We're all through here, aren't we?" said my papa. "—Kathleen, was there anything else we needed to talk about?"

"No, Uncle Templeton . . . I'm done."

"Then, go on, Mary Ann," he said, throwing me a wink and smile. "You go ahead and visit your young man!"

A FAMILY . . . TOGETHER

50

That same night, after everyone had gone to bed, my papa wandered into Uncle Ward's room. He hadn't been planning to have a long conversation, so he didn't close the door behind him. He sat down on the chair at the desk while Uncle Ward was sitting on the edge of the bed, and they began talking about all there was to do and everything Katie had said when we'd been talking earlier.

"I don't think this place needs a foreman as long as Kathleen's around!" laughed Uncle Ward. "It's a good thing we're getting that deed changed. Truth be known, Templeton, you and I shouldn't be on it at all. Kathleen's the one who's running this place, not you or me—she and Mary Ann, I ought to say, 'cause what Kathleen doesn't know, Mary Ann does. They know about the money and crops and livestock and everything."

I heard my papa chuckle lightly.

They didn't know it, but as they had been talking, the door to our room was a little ajar, and we could hear every word. We couldn't help glowing inside from what they said about us. There's nothing quite like hearing praise when the person saying it doesn't know you're listening.

"When we were talking up in Ellicott City," I heard Uncle Ward say, "—remember, we were saying how we needed to take care of Kathleen now, for Rosalind's sake?"

My papa said something I couldn't make out.

"We were a couple of fools, Templeton!"

There was some more chuckling.

"She didn't need nobody to take care of her—it's them who are taking care of *us!*"

I almost started laughing out loud when I heard that.

"Yeah, those two are really something!" my papa said. "We're a couple of pretty lucky guys, to have two girls like that."

As we lay listening in our bed, I felt Katie's hand take mine. We lay there a long time in silence after my papa and Uncle Ward stopped talking and went to bed. I knew she had overheard them talking like I had and felt the same happiness inside.

As we lay there, hand in hand in the darkness, both of us felt totally at peace for the first time in years. Yes, more changes would come to Rosewood. Our troubles weren't over—nor our joys. If someone had asked us right then, we'd have never been able to guess the many roads and adventures that still lay ahead of us.

But for now, we were together. And for right then, it was enough.

Finally Katie spoke up.

"We did it, Mayme," she finally said softly in the darkness. "We actually did it. We got Rosewood going again!"

"I guess we did at that," I said. "I would never have believed we could . . . but I guess we did."

Center Point Publishing
600 Brooks Road ● PO Box 1
Thorndike ME 04986-0001 USA

(207) 568-3717

US & Canada:
1 800 929-9108